Realms Of The Fae 4
An Unexpected Betrayal

Realms Of The Fae 4
An Unexpected Betrayal

Avril Sabine

Cracked Acorn Productions
Australia

Realms Of The Fae 4: An Unexpected Betrayal

Published by

Cracked Acorn Productions

PO Box 1365

Gympie, Queensland 4570

Australia

978-1-925617-49-8 (Kindle)

978-1-925617-50-4 (EPUB)

978-1-925617-51-1 (Print)

Genre: Young Adult Urban Fantasy

Copyright 2018 © Avril Sabine

Cover design by Caitlyn Petersen

For those who I can always count on.

Trinity has a tendency to rescue things. Taking home three stone statues that were going to be demolished, might cause her to be the one in need of rescuing. Troll enchantments and being hunted by Fae are the least of her problems. A supposedly unattainable dream might end up being her downfall.

*

This story was written by an Australian author using Australian spelling.

Name Pronunciation

Like many names there is more than one way to pronounce the following ones. These are the pronunciations used in this story.

Arwyn (ar-win)

Braeden (bray-den)

Cai (rhymes with tie)

Darak (dar-ack)

Kinnon (kin-en)

Naida (nay-da)

Tarrant (tar-ent)

Chapter One

Trinity wandered along the overgrown garden path, the broken pavers barely visible through the weeds and leaf litter. The path wound around a large tree trunk, the many branches having been removed the previous day and left in a pile to one side. Once she was past the tree she came to an abrupt stop, her gaze drawn to three stone statues that hadn't been there yesterday afternoon.

Her steps were slow as she moved closer to them, stopping when she stood in front of the one in the middle. He had to be at least six foot, possibly a little taller. The statues on either side of him were a similar size. Tall and slim, wiry muscles showing beneath the clothes they wore. "How did you get here?" Her voice was soft as she placed a hand on his stone chest. It was cold beneath her hand, warming quicker than she would have expected at this hour of the morning.

She drew her hand away, circling him. His long hair was tied at the nape of his neck and his clothes had a medieval look to them. There was a sword at his side, a slight point to his ears and his glare was fierce. Even without colour, and being made of stone, it was clear the warrior was angry.

"Who put you here? And what are you?" Images from different movies ran through her mind. "Are you meant to be an elf?" She examined the other two statues, finding them to be similar in appearance to the first one. "Warrior brothers?" She stopped in front of the middle one again, staring up into his face. Whoever had created him was extremely talented. He looked alive. Like he'd speak any second now.

"I didn't think it'd take you long to find them, Trin."

She spun to face her father. "Where did they come from?"

Rod's skin was several shades darker than her own due to the amount of time he spent outdoors. His once dark brown hair, the same shade as hers that was scraped back into a ponytail, was now salt and pepper coloured, but his deep blue eyes remained the same colour as hers. He had a square jaw, currently covered in dark stubble, while she had her mother's high cheekbones and narrower chin. He shrugged.

"Someone probably saw the dozer and thought it was a good way to get rid of their rubbish."

She waved a hand towards the statues. "These are not rubbish." They were too beautiful to be discarded in a garden scheduled for dozing.

Rod shrugged again. "Who knows what they were thinking. People are incomprehensible most of the time. Why do you think I like working on gardens? Most times it's just me, the dirt and the plants."

She grinned. He didn't dislike people as much as he frequently said he did. "What about the times you go to the pub after work? Where are the plants and dirt then?"

Rod held out a hand, palm up. "The dirt is permanently ground into the pores of my skin which is stained from the sap of plants. I take the plants and dirt with me wherever I go."

She laughed softly, nodding her head in the direction of the statues. "What are you going to do with them?"

"What can I do other than doze them? Everything in this garden is to be dozed."

"No." Surely he didn't mean that.

"You're not keeping them, Trin."

"You can't destroy them." She faced the middle statue, pressing her hand against his chest, over his heart. "Look at them." Again the stone began to warm beneath her palm. "I want them." She looked over her shoulder at her father. "All of them."

He slowly shook his head. "Where would you put them? Our backyard isn't much bigger than a postage stamp."

"At least two of them would fit. The yard isn't that small. Or I could put them down the side, near the sliding door into my bedroom." Reluctantly lowering her hand, she took a step towards her father. "Come on, Dad. Please. It'd be a crime to destroy them."

"I'm going to stop letting you visit me at work. You bring home too much junk."

She grinned. "Visiting? Does that mean I don't have to work with you these holidays after all?"

"Nice try," Rod said. "How about you get some work done instead of trying to bring home more rubbish."

"Like you don't bring anything home?"

"Plants are different."

"They're also the reason why we have very little room in our backyard." She paused a moment. "Can I have them?" When it looked like he'd speak, she spoke again. "Please." She drew the word out.

Rod sighed heavily. "Only if you can find a way to get them home. If they're not gone by the time the dozer reaches this part of the garden they'll get cleared out along with everything else." He pointed a finger at her in warning.

She threw herself at her father, hugging him tightly. "You're the best."

Rod returned her hug, muttering, "Only when you get your own way."

"Of course." Grinning, she let him go. "Do you know where Troy is?"

"Now don't go hassling him. I don't pay him so he can run around after you."

Her grin didn't falter. "Where is he?"

Rod sighed again, gesturing towards the house. "Out the front."

"Thanks, Dad." With a last glance at the statues, she ran towards the street, avoiding fallen branches and broken pavers as she skirted the house. She spotted Troy leaning against his ute, drinking coffee from his travel mug and talking on the phone. She perched on the tray of the ute while she waited for him to finish talking to a supplier about a delivery of plants that hadn't arrived.

At twenty-four, he was seven years older than her. He'd been working for her father since he'd finished school at seventeen and was like a brother. A permanent fixture in her life for the past seven years.

She'd once asked him why he didn't do an easier job. Being a landscaper could be strenuous at times. He'd tugged on the plait she'd worn at that stage and told her that was half the reason. Being paid to stay fit. The other half was being outdoors. With his broad shoulders, sun bleached hair and green eyes he certainly looked fit.

She was about to ask him how much longer he'd be, when he said goodbye and slid his phone into a pocket of his well-worn jeans. She remained on the tray of the ute. "Morning."

Troy looked her up and down as he had another mouthful of coffee. "What do you want?"

She hopped off the back of the ute. "Who says I want anything?" She couldn't hold back a grin.

"Think I don't know that look by now? You do know I have work to do." He glanced upwards. "The sky might be clear right now, but an electrical storm has been forecast for Brisbane this arve."

She barely suppressed a shudder at the thought of thunder and lightning. It didn't matter how many times she tried to tell herself that she wasn't a little kid anymore, and shouldn't be frightened of them, she still felt an overwhelming fear each time there was an electrical storm. She'd been terrified of them long before a tree had been struck, only metres from her, when she was six. A memory she'd never been able to forget.

"Will you stop looking at me with those big blue eyes? Remind me to thank my parents for not giving me any siblings."

"I need you to rescue something for me. Well, actually three things."

Troy sighed heavily, putting his empty mug in the front of the ute. "You're not going to let up until I say yes, are you?"

She grinned, his sigh having reminded her of her father's sighs. "Nope. You might as well save yourself the hassle and give in now."

"All right. Show me what you want 'rescued'. You do know when normal people talk about rescuing things they're usually referring to people or animals."

"How boring of them." She led the way around the house. "Not to mention how limiting." She stepped over a rotting branch. "No wonder I've never aspired to be normal."

"Like that wasn't obvious," Troy muttered. "Any–" He broke off as they rounded the tree, coming to an abrupt stop in front of the statues. "Where did they come from?"

Trinity shrugged. "No one knows. But I'm keeping them. Dad said I can have them if I can get them out of here. You're going to help me rescue them."

Troy slowly walked around the statues. "You know that might actually be the correct word to use for a change. The details on these statues are amazing. Look at the bow at the back of this one. Where are you going to put them? I don't suppose you want to part with one. How about the one with the bow?"

She chuckled. "I should have known. They are gorgeous, aren't they?"

Troy stopped in front of the one on the left, running a hand over the statue's shoulder and down his arm. "Stunning. Why can't I meet someone like him in real life?"

Trinity moved closer to the warrior in the middle. "I thought that for all of one second. But look at them. I bet they'd be arrogant, overbearing and complete chauvinists."

"Probably only be interested in women too," Troy said.

She ran a finger over the warrior's lips and down to his chin. "More than likely. But they are elves or something. Look at their pointy ears. Aren't elves meant to be more open minded?" Her finger continued downwards, stopping in the middle of his chest.

"Fae. They're Fae warriors," Troy said.

"That sounds more interesting than elves." She pressed her hand against the statue's chest, feeling the stone warm beneath her palm. "Is stone meant to warm so quickly?"

"What do you mean?"

"Rest a hand on your warrior."

Troy did as she said. "I like the sound of that a little too much."

"The sound of what?"

"My warrior."

She laughed softly. "You're not keeping him. They're mine."

"But you do want me to help you rescue them."

"They belong together. Look at them."

Troy frowned. "Stone doesn't warm that quickly. And the day isn't advanced enough that the sun would be making much of a difference."

The sound of the dozer starting had Trinity spinning to face the direction of the house. "We have to move them now. Before Dad reaches here with the dozer."

Troy wrapped his arms around the statue, moving it slightly. "I'm not going to be able to move them far like this." He stepped back. "I'll get the furniture trolley and some packing blankets. We don't want to damage them."

"I'll wait here." Trinity grinned. "I'll lie down in front of them if I have to, but Dad isn't destroying them."

Troy stared at the statues a moment longer before he spoke softly. "It'd be a shame to destroy them." He glanced over his shoulder before returning his gaze to Trinity. "Give me a few minutes." He strode towards the street.

Chapter Two

Trinity paced in front of the statues, the sound of the dozer coming closer. Surely her father wouldn't really destroy them if she didn't have them out of the way before he was ready to clean up this area. It wasn't like he'd given her that much time to deal with them. Spotting Troy coming towards her, she hurried forward, taking one of the packing blankets he'd thrown over his shoulder. "I'll get started on wrapping them up." She ran to the statues.

"Why does yours get wrapped first? Why not mine?" Troy asked.

"I was the one who found them."

Troy came to a stop next to her, tossing a packing blanket over each of the other statues. "I'm the one who'll be doing most of the work."

She tucked the end of the blanket into a fold and stepped back. "I'll wrap yours next while you take mine out to the ute." She started wrapping the next statue, glancing frequently towards Troy as he put the statue on the trolley and strapped it into place. As he headed for the street, she began to wrap the last statue.

They had all three statues on the tray of the ute, the furniture trolley next to them, held into place with ratchet straps, before the dozer reached where they'd been. Trinity sent her father a text message as she climbed into the front of the ute, letting him know Troy was giving her and the statues a lift home. She grinned when she read his reply.

"What did he say?" Troy slid into the driver's seat, starting the engine once he'd closed the door.

She chuckled before reading out the comment. "Not only are you not helping, but you're stealing my right hand."

Troy pulled out onto the street, laughing. "You'd think he'd be used to it."

"I'll work extra hard once we've got the statues to safety."

"I was serious about what I said."

"What exactly?"

"I'd love that statue."

She wanted to tell him yes, but the thought of separating them seemed wrong.

"I'm guessing your silence means no."

"Maybe. They just seem like they belong together." She shrugged. "Maybe I'll change my mind later."

Troy laughed. "Like that ever happens."

She grinned. It happened. But he was right. Sometimes she could be a little bit stubborn. Looking out the window, she watched the passing scenery, her grin fading. It was the first day of the September school holidays and she'd agreed to help her father these holidays. It didn't look like she was off to a good start. She was meant to be figuring out what she wanted to do when she finished year twelve at the end of the year. University didn't really appeal to her. Neither did landscaping. But she had to do something.

"You okay?"

Her gaze was drawn to Troy. "How did you know you wanted to be a landscaper?"

"Still worried about next year?"

She shrugged.

Troy glanced at her. "There aren't many jobs that allow you to play in the dirt." He glanced at her again, grinning. "Although if we don't get done before the rain starts we'll be playing in the mud."

"What about if you have no idea what you want to

do? Or at least no realistic idea of what you want to do."

"Go with the unrealistic."

"I don't think that's possible. Witches and wizards don't exist."

"You talking bubbling cauldrons or magic wands?"

She made a face. "Certainly not cauldrons. I'd hate to think of some of the things you'd need to put in one."

Troy parked at the front of her house. "You've been watching too many fantasy movies."

"Yeah. And reading too many fantasy books." She got out of the vehicle, helping Troy undo the straps. "But that's the problem. I don't want to do magic tricks, I want to do actual magic. Can you imagine how amazing that must be?"

Troy rolled up the straps, placing them on the tray before removing the trolley. "I think we're going to have to take your fantasy books and movies from you."

She helped him take one of the statues off the back of the ute. The one that they'd loaded last. "That's okay. It still leaves me with my urban fantasy."

"You're a lost cause." He strapped the statue to the trolley and tilted it back. "Where do you want this one?"

"Outside my room." She led the way down the narrow grassed area between the right side of the house and the eight-foot paling fence. "Put him here." She pushed away the leaves that had come from the neighbour's tree, stepping out of the way so Troy could set the statue in front of the fixed panel of her sliding door. While Troy collected the next one, she unwrapped the warrior. "You look as arrogant as your mate." She stared into the stone eyes. "Although you don't look as angry as he is." If she had to pick an emotion, she'd choose shock or surprise. Particularly with the way his lips were slightly parted.

Troy came towards her with the next statue. "Where do you want my warrior?" He grinned. "And I don't want to hear you chatting him up. He's mine."

She laughed, stepping back. "Put him next to this one. I'll open my room so you can bring mine inside."

"Cruel. Bring yours in out of the cold and leave mine and the third warrior outside. I should take these two home with me since you're not going to treat them right." He unwrapped the statue.

"Like it's cold at this time of year." Trinity unlocked the sliding door, slipping her keys back into her pocket before opening the door. "If I had the space I'd bring them all in." She glanced around her room, trying to decide where to put the statue while Troy returned to the ute for him.

Her room wasn't overly large, her queen-sized bed taking up most of the space. At the foot of the bed was a desk pressed up against a built-in wardrobe that took up a corner of the room. There was a skinny bookcase in the other corner, opposite the foot of her bed, with only a small space between it and the desk.

"Where do you want him?" Troy stood at the sliding door.

"Between the desk and the bookcase." She stepped out of the way. "Why would anyone want to get rid of them?" Once the statue with the sword was in place, angled to fit in the gap, she unwrapped him.

Troy shrugged. "Beats me. People are strange and illogical." He headed for the sliding door. "Will you be long? We need to get back to work."

She pressed her hand against the chest of the statue. "I'm glad no one wanted them. Because I do." She touched a finger to his lips. "If I could do magic, I'd bring them to life." She stared into the stone eyes, wondering what colour they might be.

Troy remained in the doorway, grinning, the packing blankets over a shoulder. "What would you do with three men? Weren't you the one who swore off males when you broke up with your last boyfriend?"

"Is it any wonder? I don't know what made him think I'd follow him like a lost puppy and be waiting around for him when he wanted to do something at the last minute."

Troy's grin didn't falter. "He obviously didn't know you." Troy nodded towards the statue. "What's your answer?"

"Fine. If I could bring them to life, you could have your warrior. One would be more than enough for me." She stepped outside, pulling the curtains closed before locking the sliding door. Glancing skywards, she followed Troy to the ute. "Are you sure we're in for a storm this afternoon? The day looks perfect."

Troy strapped the trolley to the tray and put the packing blankets and extra straps in the tool chest bolted to the front of the tray. "Doesn't mean much."

"You want to join us for dinner tonight?" She got in the cab of the ute.

"What are you having?"

"Probably order in pizza. I doubt either of us are going to be interested in cooking after working all day." Particularly since they had less time to get the work done.

Troy started the engine. "Sounds good. I'll bring

the beer." He grinned, glancing over his shoulder before pulling out onto the street. "For Rod and me, not you. So don't go getting any ideas."

"I was thirteen. Are you going to go on about that forever?" Her and Yvette, her best friend, had drunk her father's beer. They'd found the carton in the garage, set aside for Christmas, and had convinced themselves he wouldn't miss it. They'd drunk it hot, making faces at the taste, goading each other until the carton was gone. Both had been sick and their hangover the following day hadn't been helped by Rod and Troy's excessive noise and overly cheerful reminders that they deserved to suffer.

"You're not planning to invite Yvette to dinner, are you?"

"Nah. Although it'd serve you right if I did after bringing that up again." She grinned at Troy. Yvette was convinced Troy would also like females, if he gave them a chance. Starting with her. That he couldn't know if he hadn't tried. For the past six months she'd steadily become more determined. It was probably past time she stopped hinting and told Yvette how little Troy liked the attention.

"She's annoying and clueless. Even you've got more brains than her and you're a year younger."

"Thanks. Your compliments are heart stopping. No wonder all the guys are chasing after you."

"I'll remember that comment next time you want something from me."

She laughed. "Sure you will."

He pulled up out the front of the house they'd been at earlier. "It's only because you're my boss' daughter."

"Keep telling yourself that." She got out of the vehicle, walking around the side of the house with him. She slipped her arm through his. "You do know I appreciate it, don't you?"

"All the times I run around after you?"

"No. How weak and easily you give in." She let go of him, running ahead, her laughter ringing out over the sound of the dozer.

"I will get even with you for that," Troy called out.

She answered him with more laughter, staying well ahead of him even though she knew his threat was empty. She slowed as she came close to the potted plants at the back of the house. That was her first task for the day. Sorting the plants into their groups, ready to be planted once each area was cleared. And if the missing delivery arrived, she'd need to sort it too.

The day went quicker than Trinity had expected. She was kept busy with one job after another, some more strenuous than others. It wasn't until she heard the distant thunder that she realised a storm was approaching. A shiver ran through her and she tensed as she stared at the sky, waiting for the lightning. She jumped when Troy draped an arm around her shoulders.

"Time to knock off. Rod asked me to take you home."

She leaned against him, unable to see any lightning. "I'm fine. We aren't finished." The statues had put them well behind and they hadn't managed to catch up. No matter how hard she'd tried.

"Come on." Troy guided her along the side of the house.

"I haven't finished–"

"It'll be here tomorrow. Time to knock off."

Thunder sounded again and she shuddered. She tried to avoid searching the sky, but she couldn't resist. Not finding lightning didn't help. She knew it'd come eventually. "I'm fine."

"Yeah, right. If we had a bed nearby you'd probably be under it."

She jabbed him in the side, pulling away to glare at him. "I do not cower under my bed." Or at least she didn't anymore.

He grinned, tugging her towards the street. "You

could always make dinner instead of forcing us to eat takeaway."

"I'm not your slave. Cook your own meal. I worked as many hours as you did today."

Reaching the ute, Troy unlocked it, holding the door open. "I'll make a deal with you. How about if I help we have a home cooked meal?"

"Sounds fair." She glanced skywards again. Still no sign of lightning. Either that or she was looking in the wrong direction.

"Hop in. The storm is miles away. We'll be home before it arrives."

She hoped he was right. Getting in the ute, she buckled up, checking out each window, searching for the first sign of lightning. It wasn't until they were nearly home, the stereo loud enough to drown out the sound of thunder, that she saw it. Turning down the music she counted the time between the lightning and thunder.

Troy pulled into the double garage, an empty space beside his vehicle for Rod to park. "Told you we'd be home before the storm arrived."

"Yeah." It didn't help. She could clearly see the tree being struck by lightning, the memory replaying over and over. She barely managed to suppress a shudder.

"You have a shower first." Troy got out of the ute and unlocked the garage door that led into the house.

Chapter Three

Trinity followed at a slower pace. Although Troy had his own place, he spent enough time here he kept several changes of clothes in the spare room which had pretty much become his room over the years. He mostly stayed when him and Rod were up late planning a new job or the three of them had been sitting around talking late and he'd had a few too many drinks with Rod.

Reaching her room, Trinity turned on the light, the room dark with the curtains drawn. But she wasn't about to open them. Not with the storm outside. Music filled the house, loud enough to drown out the sound of thunder and she smiled, grabbing underwear, jeans and a t-shirt. Troy always looked out for her, like now, putting on music so she didn't have to hear the thunder. He'd started out being like an older brother, but over the years, he'd become as much of a friend as a brother, despite the age difference. He'd also promised to take her to her first nightclub when she turned eighteen next year. That was after she'd tried to convince him to sneak her into one a few months back.

They planned to be waiting at the entrance, ready to enter the moment the first of January arrived, less than four months away. She'd been born just after midnight, missing out by minutes to be the first baby born in the hospital that year. Her father regularly accused her of throwing herself into everything like it was a competition, not wanting to miss out on coming first again. A smile formed. He was wrong. She didn't mind not having the terrible baby photo, her father had taken of her, in the paper. Not like the other poor kid who had probably never lived down his photo.

After she showered, she headed for the kitchen where Troy was rummaging in the fridge and cupboards. "The bathroom is all yours." She spoke loud enough to be heard over the music.

"How does a stir-fry sound?"

She nodded. "Sounds good. I'll get started while you wash." She made a face. "I can smell you from here."

"You didn't smell much better earlier. I nearly had

to wind down the window of my ute." He headed towards the bathroom.

"Sure." She spoke before he was out of sight, stepping around the kitchen bench that divided the kitchen from the dining area, the lounge suite past the dining table. The laundry was in a room behind the kitchen so there were no windows to give her a view of the storm. The closest window was on the other side of the open plan area and the curtains were drawn. As were the curtains at the sliding door, near the dining table, that led out to the patio and the outdoor eating area. There was no way she'd be eating out there tonight, even though it was sheltered from the rain.

She tried to push thoughts of storms, lightning and thunder from her mind, focusing on the music that filled the house as she took ingredients from the fridge. When Troy joined her, he silently helped prepare the food, moving easily in the kitchen with her after the amount of meals they'd prepared together over the years. He'd been the one to teach her most of what she knew about cooking. She handed him a hand towel when he turned off the tap after washing his hands.

"Have you thought about cooking for a job?"

She shook her head. "I enjoy it, but not that much."

A lull in the song occurred in time for thunder to be heard. She shuddered.

"It's okay." Troy wrapped his arms around her. "We're safe in here and as soon as Rod is home we'll have dinner."

Rod strode towards the kitchen bench separating the kitchen from the dining area. "Anything I should know?"

"Yeah." She let go of Troy, drawing away from him, catching sight of the glint of humour in her father's eyes. "Troy is softer than a marshmallow."

"Tell me something I don't know." Rod breathed in deeply. "Dinner smells good. Give me a few minutes to shower and I'll join you." He strode towards his bedroom doorway, stopping before he entered. "Grab a beer out for me." He closed the door behind him.

Dinner was on the table before Rod returned and the music remained loud. He glanced at the stereo in the lounge area, but didn't ask for it to be turned down before joining them at the table. They spoke over the music as they ate, the meal filled with laughter and teasing.

When Rod and Troy began to talk landscaping, Trinity rose from the table, having already finished her meal. "I'm going to read for a bit." An old favourite might help keep her mind off the storm outside. It wasn't like she could go to bed. Seven o'clock was far too early to expect to fall asleep.

Troy grinned. "No fantasy or urban fantasy."

She poked her tongue out at him. "I'll read what I want. For that comment, you can do the dishes." She strode to her room, ignoring his protests and her father's question about what they were going on about.

Stepping into her room, she pushed the door closed as she reached for the light switch. A moment before the light went on, she saw the curtain lit up from behind, causing her to shudder at the reminder of the storm she couldn't hear. Light filled the room and she took several steps forward before freezing, staring at where the statue had stood.

Her mouth opened, but no sound came out, the music continuing to play in the background. Closing her mouth, she slowly shook her head, unable to believe what she saw. She closed her eyes, counting to five before she opened them again. A sound escaped. She shouldn't have closed her eyes, he was a lot closer now. "Who are you?" Her words were soft and for a moment she thought he might not have heard them over the music.

"Kinnon." He came a little closer, his hand resting

on the hilt of his sword. His white blond hair was pulled back and tied at the nape of his neck, his tawny gaze was direct and sharp and his legs were encased in leather breeches.

Her heart sped up at the sound of his deep voice, her gaze drawn to the chest she'd rested her palm against that afternoon. "You can't be real." She started to reach for him, stopping before her hand made contact.

He stepped forward. His chest pressed against her palm. "I'm as real as you."

She slowly shook her head. This was impossible. Yet he felt warm and solid beneath her hand. "Statues don't come to life."

"Those under a Troll enchantment do."

"Troll-" She broke off to shake her head again. Obviously he wasn't real. Something had happened. Had she been struck by lightning? A shudder ran through her as the image of the tree being struck played over in her mind. She should have known that'd be the way she'd go. She could almost smell the burning timber.

"What did you do with my brothers? I know you took them with you. I heard you talking about them even after you wrapped the cloth around me."

"You heard me?" Realising her hand remained against his chest she lowered it.

Kinnon grinned. "I'm not a chauvinist."

She noticed he didn't deny being arrogant or overbearing. Her gaze was drawn to his tawny eyes and she watched as the humour in them faded. "Did I die?"

He grabbed her upper arms. "How can I convince you I'm real?"

She backed away, pulling out of his grip at the urgency in his voice, thinking of Rod and Troy at the dining table. "Don't touch me." She had no idea what was going on, but Kinnon was a stranger. An armed one at that.

"I'm not going to hurt you."

She turned reaching for the door handle. His hand closed over hers, his body pressing her against the wall near the door. "I'll scream." His body was warm and solid, the music loud enough a scream wasn't likely to be heard.

"Don't. I'm not going to hurt you. I need your help." His breath brushed across her cheek.

"Please."

He loosened his grip. "I'm not going to hurt you. I want to know that my brothers are unharmed."

She twisted so she could meet his gaze. "Your brothers? The warriors with you?"

"The knights that were with me."

"They're outside." She dreaded the thought of opening the curtains and seeing the lightning, but if it would make him release her, then she was sure she could manage. "If you let me go I can draw back the curtain and show you where they are."

"No. Don't open the curtains." His grip tightened on her. "Promise me you won't open the curtains while I'm in the room."

Before Trinity could answer, there was a knock on her door. "You okay in there?" Troy called out.

"Answer him."

His sharp tone startled her, causing her voice to fail.

"Trinity?" Troy called out louder.

"Tell him to go away. I never said I wouldn't hurt him."

Fear raced through her and she tried to escape. Kinnon was stronger and it was impossible. The door opened and Troy stared at them for a couple of seconds before he tried to drag Kinnon from her. When Kinnon's hand went to his sword, she ran across the room, grabbing hold of the curtain. "Back off or I'll open it." She had no idea why he didn't want it opened, but that didn't matter.

Kinnon backed away from Troy, who stood gaping when he got a good look at him. "I don't want to hurt either of you, but I'm not about to let you activate the enchantment or harm my brothers."

Troy looked from Trinity to Kinnon. "What the hell is happening?"

"That's what I'd like to know." She continued to hold the edge of the curtain. "If you don't tell me why I can't open the curtain, then I'm going to open it."

"Starlight activates the enchantment. It lasts for twelve hours. I need to be out of the light before those twelve hours can expire." Kinnon took a step towards Trinity. "Let go of the curtain."

"The days must be twelve hours long by now." Trinity kept hold of the curtain.

Troy shook his head. "Not for a couple of days." He looked Kinnon up and down. "Is the archer real too?"

Kinnon faced Troy. "All of us are real and none of us belong to either of you." He faced Trinity. "The Trolls are cunning. Starlight is the perfect way of keeping a curse going. The sun is but a star that is close to us. Longer days won't help."

Rod entered the bedroom. "I'm going to turn..." His voice trailed off as he caught sight of Kinnon, his mouth remaining open for a moment. "He looks like one of those statues."

Kinnon again reached for his sword.

"Don't think about it," Trinity warned.

"If you take a message to my mother she'll take care of everything." Kinnon lowered his hand, looking between each of them.

"What is going on?" Rod's voice was unnaturally loud as the last song of the play list ended, bringing silence.

Chapter Four

Thunder sounded and Trinity jerked involuntarily, the curtain opening enough to fill the room with light as lightning streaked across the sky, thunder directly following it, a third lot of lightning and thunder on its heel. Kinnon stood close enough to her that his body was bathed in light, colour draining from him as he turned to stone. She dropped to the floor, clasping her hands together. "I didn't mean to change him. Shouldn't the clouds have stopped the light from getting through?"

Troy tugged the curtain fully closed. "The clouds aren't completely covering the sky. A handful of stars are visible." He crouched beside her. "Are you okay?"

She nodded then shook her head. She had no idea. Thunder sounded again and she shuddered. Staring up at Kinnon, she felt like she should apologise. More thunder rumbled overhead.

"I'll put the music back on." Troy ran from the room.

Rod sat heavily on Trinity's bed. "I've never… this can't be… I need to cut back on work."

A song began and Trinity started to laugh, covering her face with her hands. "I wish it was that simple."

Troy returned to the room and scooped her up off the floor, placing her on the bed and sitting beside her. "Are you okay?"

She clung to him. "I didn't mean to do that. Do you think it hurts being turned to stone? We have to help him."

"I know you didn't mean to do it." Troy hugged her tightly. "You'd never do anything like that. It was the thunder. I should have put the stereo on repeat."

Rod sat beside them, shaking his head. "Never thought I'd have a mental breakdown."

Her father's words caused a half sob, half laugh to escape. She partially pulled away from Troy to wrap an arm around Rod. "You're not having a mental breakdown. Or if you are, we are too."

"Maybe we stirred up something with the dozer today. Something that's not good to inhale," Rod said.

"I've got a feeling it isn't that simple," Troy said.

Rod looked from the statue to Trinity, taking a

deep breath. "Right. I know how to fix this." He rose from the bed.

"What are you going to do?" Trinity followed her father from the room, worried with the tone of voice he used.

"I never should have let you bring them home. I told you only rubbish would have been dumped there." Rod opened the door that led to the garage, turning on the light.

"What are you going to do?" Trinity demanded.

"Rod don't–"

Rod interrupted Troy, who'd followed them. "They're dangerous." He grabbed a sledgehammer from the tools stacked in the corner.

Trinity stepped in front of Rod. "No. You aren't going to kill them."

"They're statues."

Troy stopped beside Trinity. "You know they're not." He held out his hand. "Give me the sledgehammer."

Rod gripped it in two hands. "I'm not about to let anything happen to Trinity."

"Do you think I'd let anything happen to her?" Troy kept his hand held out towards Rod.

"We need to bring the other two statues inside." Trinity took a step closer, placing a hand on the sledgehammer. "Please. Don't kill them. You know they're…" She started to say human. "Real. They're real." In the background the music continued to play.

"If anything happened to you-"

"You think I want you to murder people for me?" Trinity demanded. "Three people."

Rod lowered the sledgehammer. "We're not bringing them inside."

"We are." Her words were firm.

Troy chuckled. "You might as well give up now. She's more stubborn than you."

Rod sighed heavily. "We'll take them somewhere. They can be someone else's problem."

"Since when do you turn your back on someone needing help?" Troy asked.

"They aren't normal. All they'll bring is trouble and danger." Rod returned the sledgehammer to the corner. "We'll take them to the tip tomorrow. Someone else can take them home."

Trinity turned to Troy. "Can you bring them into my room?" There was no way she'd be able to go outside in an electrical storm.

"I'll leave them in the entryway. That way we can wipe them over before we take them to your room." Troy took the furniture trolley with him.

"Is anyone listening to me?" Rod demanded.

Trinity stared at her father. "Do you really think you would have been able to kill them?" She glanced towards the sledgehammer.

He ran a hand over his face. "They carry weapons. You're not having anything to do with them."

"Kinnon and his brothers." She should have asked the names of the other two knights.

"I don't care what they're called or who they are. You're not having anything to do with them."

She started to argue, smiling instead. They knew about enchantments. They might know about magic too. Maybe this wouldn't be so bad after all.

Rod pointed at her. "Get that look off your face."

Her smile remained in place.

"How can you be so calm about this?" Rod demanded.

She hadn't been calm earlier, but it helped that she wasn't the only one experiencing it. They'd all seen the same thing so they couldn't be going insane. "Because you and Troy wouldn't let anything happen to me." Her smile widened into a grin. "Didn't Mum threaten something drastic if anything happened to me while I was living with you?"

"She was the one who decided to have another kid. Don't know what she was thinking at her age," Rod muttered.

"Yeah. Cute certainly doesn't make up for screaming in the early hours of the morning for a feed. She could have waited and had Sebastian after I finished year twelve." She tried not to smile at her last comment.

"Then she'd have been older." Rod's gaze narrowed. "All right. You've had your fun at my expense."

Troy stood in the doorway, his hair plastered against his head, using his shirt he'd bunched up in one hand to wipe the rain from himself. "They're in the entryway."

Trinity grabbed two of the rags, kept under her father's workbench, before heading inside. She stopped when she caught sight of the statues, the trolley behind them. They looked larger in the narrow entryway, which was basically a hallway between the garage and the small hallway leading to the bathroom, her bedroom and the spare room.

Rod nodded towards the statues "What are we going to do with them? The answer better not be keep them."

She had no idea what to do with the statues, but she wasn't about to let her father get rid of them. At least not until she learned about Troll enchantments, if there was such a thing as magic and why an enchantment had been used on them. She tossed one of the rags to Troy with a grin. "You can dry the archer."

Troy caught the rag. "You just earned yourself an extra large Christmas present."

Laughing, Trinity began to dry the second statue. "They can go in my room once they're dry."

"You can't sleep with them in there," Rod protested.

"They won't be alive… or real again until tomorrow morning." Trinity knelt to run the rag over the legs of the statue. She looked upwards. "Sorry about this. But you'll be safest in my room and I don't want puddles on the floor."

"He's a statue," Rod stated.

"He can hear what's happening. And see." She didn't know if he could feel. Trinity rose to her feet, stepping back to survey the statue. "I think he's dry now."

"We can't leave them alone in the house." Rod gestured towards the statues. "You're meant to be helping me these holidays."

Surely he wouldn't make her follow through on that. "But, Dad–"

"I'll take those holidays you keep telling me to take

and keep an eye on things here." Troy put the archer on the furniture trolley, strapping him on.

"Be careful." She clasped her hands together, wanting to grab hold of the statue.

"Not the first time I've moved things on a trolley." Troy pushed it towards Trinity's bedroom, a grin fleetingly appearing. "Or the first time I've moved these guys."

She followed behind. "Leave him against the wall where we put Kinnon earlier." She glanced around the room. There wasn't going to be a lot of space in here once the third statue was brought in. Checking the time, she found it was nearly eight-thirty. She turned to her father. "I need to be here at seven-thirty tomorrow morning." She wasn't sure exactly what time Kinnon had been turned back into stone, but it had to have been close to eight.

"No."

"Troy will be with me."

"I haven't agreed to him taking his holidays."

Troy grinned, sliding the archer off the trolley. "Make up your mind. Either you want me to take them or you don't." He left the room before Rod could answer.

"Please, Dad. Troy will be here. He'll look out for me."

Rod sighed. "Why do you bother asking me? Why not tell me what you're going to do?"

She tried not to grin. It escaped anyway. "I've tried that before and you didn't like it either."

Troy wheeled the last statue into the room, leaving him not far from the doorway. "I'll draw the curtains in the spare room in case the sunlight reaches this far in the morning." He took the trolley with him.

Trinity drew her father back to the entryway, closing her bedroom door as they left, not wanting Kinnon to hear the conversation. "You always tell me to grab hold of opportunities. That too many people let them slip through their fingers, mistaking them for hard work."

"This isn't an opportunity."

Troy joined them. "It certainly looks like one to me. Come on, Rod. How often do people encounter the fantastical?"

"For all we know, more often than we think." Rod gestured towards the hallway doorway. "Do you plan on telling anyone about them? They'd think we were crazy. We probably are for all I know."

"Let us stay home." She met Rod's gaze. "Please, Dad." Thinking he was going to disagree again, she quickly spoke. "You keep telling me I need to figure out what I want to do with my life. I've got a feeling it has something to do with them." She didn't say the word 'magic' even though it rang in her head.

"In what way?" Rod demanded. "You're not talking about dating him, are you?"

Chapter Five

Trinity shook her head. "No, not that." She didn't want to say the word that continued to ring in her head. Even to her it sounded crazy and would sound worse to her father. "Something that isn't ordinary."

Troy slung an arm around Trinity's shoulders. "Do you honestly think I'd let something happen to Trinity?"

Rod sighed once more, rubbing his hand across his face. "Tax forms are easier than dealing with you."

Trinity grinned. "I know." He'd told her that more than once.

He looked from Troy to Trinity. "Ring me every half an hour or I'll be calling the police."

"Hour," Trinity said.

"This isn't a negotiation."

"Every half hour," Troy agreed. "I'll set the alarm

on my phone. We can alternate between phone calls and text messages."

"Fine," Trinity muttered when her father nodded. "Even though it's more than excessive."

"You're never to be alone with any of them. Troy is to be with you all the time. And you're to remain by the sliding door while you talk to them. That way you can pull the curtain open if you need to."

"I'm sure-" Trinity began.

"Not a negotiation." Rod's voice was firm.

Troy squeezed Trinity's shoulders. "It's okay. Phone calls or a text every half hour and we'll stand by the sliding door."

Rod pointed a finger at Troy. "If anything happens to her I'll be taking that sledgehammer to you."

"Nothing will happen."

Trinity opened her mouth to speak, closing it to glare at Troy when he squeezed her shoulders tightly.

"And get to bed. Both of you. No sleeping in tomorrow. You need to be awake and alert before those statues come back to life." Rod paused a moment. "If there was any way of cancelling the job for tomorrow I would. As it is I'm going to have to find people to fill in for both of you." His gaze was drawn to Troy. "How long are you taking off?"

Troy shrugged. "A week? Maybe two. Actually, I have no idea."

"Two weeks. This better be sorted by then." Rod looked towards Trinity. "Before school starts. You're not taking time off school." He strode away, heading for the living room, not giving Trinity a chance to protest.

She stayed beside Troy, his arm remaining around her shoulders. "What if it's not sorted that soon? An enchantment doesn't sound like a simple thing to deal with."

Troy shrugged once more. "I guess we renegotiate."

Her father had sounded pretty adamant about her not taking time off school. "We better get ready for bed. Dad will probably expect us to contact him every half an hour from when he leaves in the morning." Not that she wanted to sleep in. She wanted to be awake and ready when Kinnon came back to life tomorrow morning.

"I'll set the stereo to turn off in a few hours. The storm should be finished by then." Troy headed in the direction Rod had taken.

Trinity returned to her room, opening the door. She stood in the doorway, her gaze drawn to each of the statues, stopping at Kinnon. It was hard to believe he was real. She crawled across her bed, finding it easier than going around with the two statues in the way. Rising to her feet, she stood in front of Kinnon. "I'm sorry." She glanced towards the curtain. "I didn't mean to let the light in." She stared at him a moment longer. "I'll move you further away from the door." There wasn't a lot of space for her and Troy to stand by the curtain edge in case they needed to draw it in the morning. She pushed at the statue, shifting Kinnon a fraction at a time.

"What are you doing?"

She looked over to see Troy in the doorway. "Moving him away from the curtain edge."

Troy walked around the bed, turning sideways to get past the statues. "Let me."

She stepped back. "I'll set an alarm on my phone for when Kinnon should wake." She also set one to wake her before her father left. As she'd pointed out earlier, he'd probably set a half hour timer from the moment he left.

Troy finished moving Kinnon along. "I'll do the same." He walked around the bed, pausing in the doorway. "Goodnight, Trinity."

"Night." She remained where she was a few more minutes, her gaze drawn to Kinnon. Once again she felt like she should apologise. She remained silent. It was no point telling him tonight. She'd tell him in the morning. When he was able to speak.

It didn't take long to get ready for bed and she climbed in, pulling up the sheet and light blanket, leaving her doonah pushed to the end of the bed. Her gaze was once more drawn to each of the statues. A smile slowly formed, a shiver of excitement travelling through her. These school holidays were going to be unique. Turning off the bedside lamp she lay back, closing her eyes, the day replaying through her mind. Sleep was a long time coming.

Her alarm woke her when the room was still dark. It took her a couple of attempts to find the switch on her lamp, blinking rapidly once it was on. Her gaze went immediately to Kinnon and relief rushed through her. It hadn't been a dream. For a few seconds she'd feared he hadn't been real.

"They're real."

She looked towards Troy in the doorway, wearing only a pair of jeans sitting low on his narrow hips, his words similar to her thoughts. "Yeah. They're real." A grin formed, widening at Troy's answering grin. "Want to help me make breakfast?"

Troy nodded. "Give me a few minutes."

"I'll meet you in the kitchen." She flung back the bed linen.

Quickly getting ready for the morning, she dressed in jeans and a t-shirt. She used the bathroom since the Fae knights were able to see even though it looked to be an impossibility while they were turned to stone. Arriving in the kitchen, she helped Troy serve breakfast, Rod joining them at the table. The meal was silent, both of them frequently glancing in the direction of her bedroom, Rod looking like he regretted last night's decision.

He tried to talk Trinity out of letting the statues come back to life before he left for work. Her answer was a hug and a reminder that one of them would call him in half an hour. Grumbling about needing to be practical and turn up to the job, unlike some, he got in his vehicle and drove away.

Trinity remained in the garage with Troy, staring out at the early morning. "It looks so ordinary out there. Almost impossible to believe we have three enchanted statues in my bedroom."

Troy checked the time on his phone. "The morning is going to pass very slowly."

"We could clean up the kitchen. That should help pass some of the time." She closed the roller door, locking it.

"Or make it go slower." Troy walked to the kitchen with her.

It didn't take long to clean up the kitchen and the pair of them prowled the house, frequently returning to Trinity's room even though it wasn't time for Kinnon to come back to life. In the end, Trinity sprawled on her bed, trying to read a book, spending more time staring at each of the statues than the pages.

Troy dropped onto the bed beside Trinity. "Give up the pretence. I bet you haven't read a single word." He nodded towards the book she held open, busy sending a text.

"I've read more than one word." She placed the book on her bedside cabinet. She'd read at least half a dozen.

"Relax and enjoy the view." Troy grinned. "It's not often you have four gorgeous guys in your bedroom."

She hit his shoulder with the back of her hand. "Someone doesn't think highly of themself now, do they?" she asked dryly.

His grin didn't falter. "Not at all."

She leaned against him, resting her head on his shoulder. "Where do you think they're from? We'd have known of their existence before now if Fae were wandering around our world."

"Maybe not."

Her gaze travelled over each statue again, finishing at Kinnon. It wouldn't be long and he'd be able to answer her questions. And she had a tonne she wanted to ask. Starting with where they were from. No, maybe she should ask about magic. She was still trying to figure out what she wanted to know first when her alarm rang, startling her, Troy's going off at the same time.

"Not long now." Troy turned off his alarm.

Trinity turned off hers as she climbed off the bed to stand by the sliding door. "You can ring Dad."

Troy chuckled, touching the screen of his phone. "Worried he'll change his mind?"

"Something like that." It was more likely that she'd argue with him about the need to contact him so frequently.

Troy raised the phone to his ear. "It's all good." He paused a moment. "I'll message you in half an hour." He disconnected the call.

Trinity slowly shook her head. "Excessive." Before she could make another comment, a shiver seemed to go through the statue and Kinnon gained colour, his hand reaching for the hilt of his sword. Trinity grabbed hold of the edge of the curtain. "Stay where you are or I'll let the light in."

"I don't plan to harm you." Kinnon lowered his hand.

"How did you end up as statues?" Troy asked.

"Can you do magic?" Trinity spoke at the same time as Troy. She grinned, glancing at Troy before her gaze returned to Kinnon. "Can you?"

Kinnon looked to Troy. "Deceit." His gaze travelled to Trinity. "Yes."

She nearly took a step towards him, wanting to beg him to teach her magic. Forcing herself to remain by the sliding door, she asked, "Can anyone use magic?"

Kinnon nodded towards the curtain she held. "Can you move away from there? I wouldn't want you to turn me to stone again."

She felt her cheeks heat. "That was an accident."

He inclined his head. "I heard. Which is why I would appreciate you moving away from the curtain so you don't have another such accident."

Troy motioned for Trinity to stay where she was. "Rod only let Trinity remain here if she stayed by the sliding door."

Kinnon looked from one to the other a couple of times before inclining his head. "What can I offer you for your help?"

"Magic," Trinity said.

"No." Troy shook his head at Trinity. "He could ask anything of you."

"All I need is a message delivered to my mother. She'll take care of everything." Kinnon took a step towards Trinity.

"How would I find her?"

"Trinity! Do you really think Rod is going to let you go off somewhere to deliver a message?"

Trinity grinned. "Do you think I'll let that stop me?" She paused a moment. "Magic, Troy. Don't you understand?"

"We need more information." Troy faced Kinnon. "What are the negatives of magic? How dangerous is it to deliver a message to your mother? How will we get there?"

Chapter Six

Trinity wanted to tell Troy it didn't matter, but it obviously did. Getting herself killed trying to gain magic wouldn't be good. "Okay, how dangerous is it?"

Kinnon shrugged. "I don't know what's happened at home since I was last there. I don't even know how much time has passed."

"It's September–"

Kinnon interrupted Trinity. "That doesn't help. Time runs differently between the realms."

At the word 'realms' a shiver of excitement raced through Trinity. "Realms?" She had so many questions she needed to ask.

"Realms of the Fae. Home to all Fae and Demi Fae." Kinnon spoke again when Trinity would have spoken. "Will you help us?" He took another step towards her.

She met his gaze, drawn by the plea in his tawny eyes. She opened her mouth to agree.

Troy spoke before Trinity could. "Don't go agreeing to anything until you've talked to Rod. I told him I'd look out for you."

Kinnon glared at Troy. "I didn't ask for your help."

At the anger in Kinnon's voice, her grip tightened on the curtain. "Don't speak to Troy like that."

The other two statues shivered to life. The archer had his bow and an arrow in his hands in seconds. "Let go of the curtain and step away from it."

Trinity continued to clutch the fabric, her gaze going from Kinnon to the archer. How fast were they? Could she draw open the curtain before he shot her?

Kinnon stepped between Trinity and the archer, his gaze meeting hers rather than facing his brother. "Lower your bow, Darak. They aren't going to harm us."

She continued to grip the edge of the curtain, unable to retreat further. "I want magic, but I don't want to die to gain it." Her voice was soft enough that she doubted Troy would have heard. Her gaze was drawn between Kinnon and Troy, worried about what might happen.

Troy advanced on Darak. "Lower your bow."

Darak faced Troy, his arrow remaining drawn back, now pointed at Troy. "Back away and keep your hands to yourself."

"You can put your hands on me any time you want." The third Fae smiled. Like both his brothers, his white blond hair was drawn back from his narrow face and tied at the nape of his neck. His golden eyes had a hint of mischief.

Darak narrowed hazel eyes as he turned his gaze to his brother, keeping the arrow pointed at Troy. "Don't think about it, Braeden. They're human."

Braeden eyed Troy up and down, a smile slowly forming. "Oh, I've done more than think about it."

"Lower your bow or I will fill my room with sunlight." She wasn't about to get Troy killed. No matter how badly she wanted magic.

"I'm sorry."

Before Trinity had the chance to ask Kinnon what he meant, he'd crossed the space between them, pressing her against the sliding door, untangling her fingers from the curtain, capturing her other hand as well. "Let me go." She spoke through gritted teeth. Behind Kinnon the other three argued, alarms going off to let them know it was time to message Rod.

"We are the victims here." The room filled with a sweet scent as Kinnon drew Trinity away from the curtain. He held out his hand, a fine dust forming. It had a glitter to it like mica in sand. "Help us and this magic will be yours."

She started to reach for it, glaring at Kinnon when the dust sank back into the palm of his hand. "How did you do that?"

The alarms ended. "What do I tell Rod?" Troy demanded.

"That we're okay." Trinity's gaze remained on Kinnon who continued to keep an arm around her.

"Are we?" Troy asked.

She desperately wanted magic. Real magic. Not something along the lines of card tricks. "Yes. We are." She placed her free hand against Kinnon's chest, holding his gaze a moment. "I want magic."

"Deliver a message to my mother and it's yours," Kinnon said.

How many times had people told her over the years that something couldn't be done? And how many times had she proven them wrong? Magic was real. And it could be hers. "Yes."

"No!" Troy called out as the same sweet scent filled the room.

"Our agreement has been sealed," Kinnon said.

"How? And what is that sweet smell?" It was familiar, but she couldn't quite place it.

"With magic and the scent is mock orange."

"I thought I recognised it, but it's sweeter than any I've ever smelt before."

"Trinity, are you crazy?" Troy demanded.

She looked towards him with a smile, relieved Darak no longer had an arrow pointed at him. "Certifiably. But this is what I've wanted for a long time." She tried to step back from Kinnon, but his arm remained firm around her. "You can let me go. I'm not going to turn you to stone." Her gaze was momentarily drawn to Darak. "As long as your brother doesn't threaten us with his bow and arrows."

"Darak will do nothing to harm either of you as long as neither of you do anything to harm us." Kinnon glanced at Darak before returning his attention to Trinity. "When will you take the message to my mother?"

"How long will it take?" Trinity asked.

"Not before you talk to Rod," Troy said.

"Is there anywhere else we can go?" Braeden glanced around the room. "It's not that I don't appreciate no longer being stone, but it is rather cramped in here." He glanced around again. "Surely this antechamber isn't your bedroom."

"They are peasants. Of course it's her bedroom," Darak said.

"We aren't peasants." Trinity glared at Darak, once again trying to pull away from Kinnon. "Will you let go of me?" She momentarily glared at Kinnon before returning to glaring at Darak. "My dad has his own business."

"What type of business?" Darak asked.

She raised her chin at the disbelief she heard in Darak's voice. "Landscaping."

Darak smiled, no humour in it. "A gardener. A peasant."

She tried once more to pull away from Kinnon, her hand curling into a fist. "Let me go."

"You can't fight Darak. You'll only get hurt," Kinnon said softly.

"I'd rather be a peasant than an arrogant arsehole," Troy said.

Darak's smile faded. "You think your words matter to me?"

"No." Troy grinned. "But that goes both ways. You think your words matter to me?"

Trinity slowly let out her breath. This wasn't getting them anywhere. She only needed to put up with them long enough to gain magic. She'd been right about them being arrogant. A pity. "How do I find your mum?" His arm remained around her.

How could she convince him she wouldn't draw the curtain open and he didn't need to keep her from it?

"Trinity–"

She interrupted Troy. "Tell him you tried to talk me out of it, but I wouldn't listen. He can't be angry with you over that."

"If I was to take you to our home, using magic, there'd be no chance for you to prevent me," Kinnon said.

"You're not going without us," Darak warned.

"If you can magic yourself to your home, then why do you need me to take a message to your mum?" Trinity asked.

"I'll have to take you to a location that's always dark and you'll have to find your way from there. I'll explain how to find the various locations where my mother would typically be," Kinnon said.

Trinity supposed she should once more protest Kinnon's arm around her, but she had no way of convincing him she wasn't about to turn him to stone. "Can I take a torch with me?" She was going to need one if he planned to take her somewhere that was always dark.

Troy interrupted Kinnon's answer. "You could take her anywhere. And leave her wherever you want."

"I can give you my word that I'll take her to my home and return her here after she gives my mother a message," Kinnon said.

"Your word means nothing to me," Troy said. "You could say anything."

"Fae can't lie." Braeden moved closer to Troy. "We must always speak the truth the way we see it." He looked Troy up and down, lowering his voice. "I meant everything I said earlier."

"I can bind my words with magic. That way I'll be compelled to abide by the terms," Kinnon offered.

"Don't," Darak said. "What if something goes wrong?"

"I'd find a way to bring Trinity home no matter the situation." Kinnon met his brother's gaze. "Do you doubt me?"

"Nothing will have changed. Tarrant will find another way to get rid of us when he learns this didn't work," Darak said.

"How did he put an enchantment on you?" Troy asked.

"In our drinks," Kinnon said. "There was long enough for him to tell us what he'd done and for us to rise to our feet, but not enough time to prevent the enchantment."

"Did you really expect to be able to do something in less than a minute?" Darak demanded.

"Who's Tarrant?" Trinity looked from Darak to Kinnon. Neither of them answered. Darak continued to glare at Kinnon, who held his brother's gaze.

"Our stepbrother," Braeden said. "Of a fashion."

"Your brother is trying to kill you?" Trinity demanded. No one answered her. Silence filled the room, Darak and Kinnon continuing to glare at each other. She started to demand an answer again, but Braeden interrupted.

"Are we all going?"

"No," Troy said.

At the same time, Trinity said, "Yes."

Troy shook his head. "Rod will expect us to ring or text every half hour. I doubt passing along a message will be that quick that we can do it in between contacting him."

"They can't spend the rest of their lives in my bedroom, hiding from the sun. Or stars." She glanced at each of them. Not that it'd be a terrible view. That wasn't the part that would be difficult. Her gaze remained on Darak, who scowled at her. "I doubt it'd be a very peaceful place with the three of you here." She managed not to mention Darak specifically, but she did keep her gaze on him a moment longer.

"It'd kill us anyway," Braeden said.

Trinity frowned.

Troy spoke before she could. "What would kill you?"

"Iron sickness," Braeden said.

Kinnon brushed his fingers across Trinity's jaw, drawing her attention back to him. "Will you come with me?"

How could she resist the plea in his deep voice and the look in his eyes? She'd never been able to ignore a cry for help. "As soon as I get a torch."

"Do you promise me?"

"No," Troy said.

Trinity smiled. "Yes." Her smile faded when the smell of mock orange again filled the room. "Why can I smell mock orange again?"

"It's the scent of my magic," Kinnon said.

"You bound her promise with your magic?" Troy demanded.

Kinnon inclined his head. "Along with my earlier one to bring her back here once the task has been completed."

Chapter Seven

Trinity drew away from Kinnon, surprised he finally let her put space between them. "What does that mean?" Maybe Troy was right and she shouldn't have agreed.

"That you'll feel compelled to journey to the realms of the Fae with me."

She momentarily closed her eyes. That didn't sound good. Her eyes opened when his fingers brushed across her jaw again. "Will it hurt?"

"Were you planning to go back on your promise?" Kinnon asked softly.

Trinity tried to ignore the argument between Troy and Darak, Braeden playing peacekeeper. "No."

"Then you have nothing to worry about." Kinnon paused a moment. "Where is your torch?"

She glanced between Kinnon and the doorway a couple of times before she spoke. "I won't be long."

She crawled across the bed rather than go around it, the way blocked by Fae knights.

Troy grabbed Trinity's arm as she stepped into the hallway. "What do you think you're doing?"

She broke free of his grip. "Please don't try and stop me." She drew Troy further away from her room, stopping by the door leading into the garage. "Magic. Can you imagine?" Excitement welled up in her and she wanted to squeal and jump up and down. Only the thought that Kinnon and his brothers might hear kept her silent.

"I can imagine a lot of things. Not all of them good. What if this is like wishes?"

"What do you mean?" She glanced towards her room, opening the garage door and stepping inside, closing the door once Troy had joined her. "Troy?"

"All those tales of genies and three wishes. It never ends well."

"They're not genies."

"They're Fae. For all we know, they could be worse."

"This has been my dream since I was little." She saw the worry in his green eyes. "Would you turn your back on your dreams?"

"Mine aren't so unrealistic."

She grinned at his words. "Maybe not."

"Trinity, think about it. We know nothing about them. They're warriors. Knights. They carry weapons. And they aren't human. Who knows what they think. Apart from Darak. He's very clear about how little he thinks of us. What if the others think of humans the same way?"

"I'm not doing this to help him."

Troy eyed her for a moment. "You've made up your mind."

She nodded.

He sighed heavily. "What am I going to tell Rod?"

"Nothing?"

"I can't lie to him."

"You don't have to. Tell him we're both fine. That's all you have to say."

"Make sure you're back here before he's home from work. I don't want to face him alone."

Laughter bubbled up at his words. "I'll try. But he wouldn't really hurt you. Not you."

Troy remained serious. "I don't think you understand what he'd be willing to do to protect you." He rested a hand on her shoulder. "What we'd both be willing to do." His grip momentarily tightened.

Trinity threw her arms around his waist, resting her head on his chest. "I'll be okay. Kinnon will take care of me. He has to. He made a promise to bring me back and bound it with his magic."

"Nothing was said about bringing you back unharmed. Or alive."

His words caused a shiver to run through her and she drew away. "I'll be okay." She couldn't think of anything else to say. She nearly repeated the words a third time, stopping when she realised how afraid that would make her sound. And she was. Travelling to another realm with the help of magic didn't sound safe. But she wanted to have magic. Something she'd always thought was an unrealistic dream.

"When you get that determined look on your face things go crazy."

Trinity couldn't resist smiling again. "But it also means that things happen." She would have magic. How hard could it be to deliver a message?

"Not always good things."

She shrugged, collecting the small LED torch from the shelf it was kept on. "It will be good." She headed for the door, glancing over her shoulder, the urge to return to Kinnon building. "Try not to let Dad know I'm not here. Give me a chance to tell him this afternoon when he gets home from work."

Troy sighed heavily again. "He's going to kill me." He glanced at the corner. "With his sledgehammer."

Trinity opened the door. "No he won't. You're his right hand man. He couldn't manage without you."

He drew her back, meeting her gaze for a moment. "There's only one person he couldn't manage without. So make sure you come back in one piece."

She nodded, smiling reassuringly before she headed back to her bedroom. She paused in the doorway, her gaze travelling across each of the Fae. "What is wrong?" Darak's glare was more intense than before.

Braeden smiled. "How could anything be wrong?" He looked past Trinity. "I get to keep Troy company."

She looked from Kinnon to Darak. "You're both going with me?" She nearly groaned when they nodded. "Let's get this over and done with then." Once again she crossed the bed to reach Kinnon, first grabbing her sneakers from beside her bedroom door and slipping her feet into them once she stood next to him.

He drew her close. "Thank you for this." His arm tightened around her and he held out his hand, opening it to reveal a white flower with large petals and yellow stamens. "It will be dark. You might want to turn your torch on."

She pressed the button on her torch, pointing it

towards the floor. "Where did that come from?" She nodded towards the flower.

"Magic." Kinnon crushed it in his hand, the scent of mock orange filling the room. The world shimmered and reformed around them. Kinnon staggered, breathing in sharply.

Darkness pressed in around them, only the beam of light from the torch breaking it. She wrapped an arm around him. "Are you okay?"

"My magic doesn't feel as powerful. Something's wrong with it."

"Kinnon?"

Trinity shined the torch in the direction the voice had come from, surprised to find a man chained to a rock wall. He was bruised and battered, his clothes hanging on his painfully thin frame.

"Father?" Kinnon let go of Trinity to stride to the man's side.

"That's your father?" She followed Kinnon. "He doesn't look much older than you."

Before anyone could reply, Darak appeared in the cell with them, stumbling, the smell of cloves momentarily filling the air. "What did he do to us? To our magic? I'll-" Darak stared at the man for a second. "Father?" He joined Kinnon. "What are you doing in the dungeon?"

"You brought us to a dungeon?" Trinity cast the light of the torch around the room, confirming it was a dungeon. The walls were made of rough hewn rocks and the timber door had bands of metal with a barred window high in it. There were two sets of chains embedded in the wall across from the door, one set hanging empty, the other set keeping the man imprisoned. "You brought us to a dungeon." Troy's words came back to her. What had she got herself into?

"You have to leave," the man said. "If they catch either of you, they'll kill you."

"How long has it been?" Darak demanded.

"You disappeared nine weeks ago." The man gestured to the wall beside him. "I've been in here only two of those weeks."

Trinity shuddered when she saw what he referred to. A tally had been made on the wall. In blood. "I want to go home." Her voice was soft.

Kinnon was at her side in seconds, having crossed the space between them at an unnaturally fast pace. "Trinity, this is my father. Arwyn."

"He looks too young," Trinity blurted out.

Arwyn chuckled, then winced and clutched at his side. "You judge me by your human standards. I am young as the Fae reckon things, but at seventy-four you humans would think me old."

She gaped, eventually closing her mouth with an audible sound. She turned to Kinnon. "Are you old too?"

Kinnon shook his head. "Eighteen. I'm the youngest. Then there's Braeden at twenty-one and Darak is twenty-two."

Darak took hold of the chains imprisoning Arwyn. "We need to bring back something to cut these chains."

Trinity looked from Kinnon to Arwyn. "The Fae don't have children until they're old?" Her head was reeling with all she'd learned and what was going on around her. She struggled to make sense of it.

"I met Lili twenty-five years ago," Arwyn said.

"Where is our mother?" Kinnon asked.

"They've incarcerated me in here until I tell them what I did with her body."

Trinity stared at Arwyn, barely able to believe his emotionless words. "You killed your wife?" She took a step backwards.

"He would never do that."

Trinity took another step back at the hate and anger in Darak's voice. "He said-"

Kinnon interrupted her, moving close to take hold

of her hand. "He didn't answer that question. He answered an unspoken one."

"I would never kill my wife. We rode out day after day, looking for the three of you." Arwyn hesitated.

"Braeden lives," Kinnon said.

Trinity looked at each of them, remaining confused, trying to draw her hand from Kinnon's. "What is going on?" So much for thinking delivering a message would be easy. How was she meant to gain magic if no one knew where Lili was?

"Isn't it obvious?" Sarcasm dripped from Darak's words. "Our mother is missing, our father is imprisoned and we're under a Petrification enchantment."

"What are you doing using your magic while you're under that enchantment?" Arwyn demanded.

"Why would that be a problem?" Kinnon asked.

"That enchantment drains your magic until it runs out, taking your life with it."

Chapter Eight

Arwyn's words brought silence and Trinity once again found herself with her mouth hanging open and lost for words. For a split second she thought of the magic she'd probably never have before her gaze was drawn to Kinnon. "You'll die?" There was an unnaturally high note to her tone.

"No one will die."

She took a step back at Kinnon's fierce words, drawing her hand from his, hearing a hint of Darak in them. "But it's draining your magic and then you'll-"

Kinnon captured her hand again. "No one will die. I will not allow it."

"You must go," Arwyn urged. "The time draws near for Tarrant to bring my daily meal."

"And your daily beating?" Darak demanded.

"He must keep up appearances. Every day one of his men questions me on the location of your mother's body. Although there have been knights who've declined the dubious honour of being the one to make me confess."

Trinity opened her mouth, wanting to say something. Arwyn's emotionless tone spoke louder than if he'd filled his words with the pain each beating must have caused. But no words came. What could she say? When Kinnon's hand momentarily tightened on hers she met his gaze. At the look in his eyes, tears came to hers. How could he want to comfort her when he was the one in trouble? She threw her arms around him, the light from the torch splashing around the cell, wanting to comfort him. His body wasn't as solid as Troy's, but he felt equally strong, muscles shifting as his arms wrapped around her. "We have to find Lili. Have to rescue Arwyn."

Kinnon's arms tightened around her. "We will."

"No, you won't," Arwyn said. "You'll leave immediately and focus on breaking the enchantment. Take turns at remaining petrified. It won't drain your magic while you're stone."

Trinity drew away from Kinnon, feeling like she should apologise for her impulsive action. She faced Arwyn. "That will keep them safe?"

"We are not remaining under an enchantment. We might as well be dead." Darak glared at Trinity.

Arwyn held out his hands, the chains attached to the manacles at his wrists preventing him from coming closer. "Take my magic. Use it to keep you alive longer." A fine dust formed in his hands, paler in colour than Kinnon's, the same glitter to it. "Both of you take it." A mix of spices, possibly cloves amongst them, filled the air.

"No. What if you need it?" Kinnon took a step backwards.

"Take it," Arwyn ordered.

Darak glanced towards the door. "I hear something."

The magic sank back into Arwyn's hands. "Go. I don't want him to learn you're currently free of his enchantment." Arwyn glanced at the door. "Hurry." The mix of spices filled the air again. "Go."

"We'll return for you," Kinnon promised.

Before Trinity could add her assurances to Kinnon's, he drew her close and Arwyn and the dungeon disappeared in a shimmer. The world reformed, becoming her bedroom. The scent of mock orange and cloves faded as she tugged free of Kinnon's arms, moving towards Troy. "What happened?"

Troy looked up from where he leaned over Braeden who was lying in Trinity's bed. "I don't know. He collapsed. One minute he's doing the most amazing magic and the next he's hardly breathing and I can barely hear his heart beat."

"I will kill you." Darak drew a dagger and strode towards Troy, who backed away.

Arwyn's words came to mind and Trinity spun, diving for the curtains. She pulled the edge of a curtain back, flooding the room with afternoon light. Landing on the floor, she let go of the fabric as she twisted to see what had happened. She nearly groaned, staring at the dagger Darak held. "That is not going to be a good look when Dad gets home." She staggered to her feet, kicking off her sneakers and leaving them by the sliding door. "Maybe we can drape something over the dagger." Her gaze was drawn to Kinnon. Once again he was stone. And it was her fault.

"We could turn Darak into a coat and hat rack," Troy suggested.

A smile momentarily escaped before the fear and worry struck again. "We can't let them die." She looked at each of them. Kinnon between her and the bed, Darak in front of Troy with the dagger held out and Braeden stretched out on her bed.

"You can't always save everyone," Troy said.

Trinity raised her chin. "Want to make a bet?"

She'd saved them from being demolished, temporarily broken the enchantment they were under and stopped Braeden from dying. At least she hoped she had. "Well?"

Troy opened his mouth twice before he finally spoke. "No. I've got a feeling the odds aren't in my favour. Somehow or other you win more times than you should."

"And I'm going to win this time." She took a deep breath. "First we have to make sure Braeden doesn't come out of the enchantment."

"Why? What happened while you were gone?"

"When he runs out of magic he'll run out of life."

Troy dropped onto the bed to sit beside the Fae knight. "Why did he waste all that magic entertaining me?"

"Kinnon and Darak didn't know when their father told them. I guess he didn't either." She jumped when Troy's alarm went off on his phone. Pressing a hand to her heart, she took another deep breath, watching Troy send a message. "What are we going to tell Dad?" Things were worse than they'd been last night and he hadn't been impressed with the situation then.

Troy's phone beeped and after he read the message he held the phone up, the screen facing Trinity. "You better figure it out quick because he's halfway home."

"What time is it?" She started to reach for her phone.

"Nearly five."

She lowered her hand, leaving her phone in her pocket. "I'm dead." Her eyes closed as she tried to think what to do first.

"What happened while you were gone?"

Opening her eyes didn't help. The room remained the same. "Ah. Things didn't exactly go…" Her gaze was drawn to the dagger as she tried to think of a reply. "As planned. Not at all as planned." She rummaged in her built-in wardrobe, taking out a coat and cap.

"How bad is it?"

After hanging the cap from the dagger and draping the coat over Darak's arm, she faced Troy. She struggled to find words again, doubting telling him about the tally, drawn in blood, were the ones to speak.

"That bad, huh?"

"I didn't say anything."

"Exactly."

"Their father is a prisoner and has been keeping a tally of the days by using his own blood." The words escaped before she could stop them, needing to share them with someone.

Troy drew in a sharp breath. "You can't get involved. Do you want to get yourself killed?"

"They're mine. I found them. They were given to me."

"Owning someone is considered slavery."

"I don't care. They're mine. I'm not about to let them die."

"Darak might have something to say about your ownership." Troy glanced at the Fae Trinity continued to stand near.

A grin reluctantly formed and Trinity sighed heavily. "Probably. But that doesn't change anything. They're mine. I saved them from the dozer. Without me rescuing them they'd be dead." Her gaze was drawn to the cap and coat draped over Darak. "And there's nothing Darak can do about it right now."

Troy chuckled. "I'm sure he'll have more than enough to say about that once he's alive again. That and being turned into a coat rack."

She sobered. "I mightn't think much of him since he's always threatening us, but I'm not about to let him die. That wouldn't be right."

"They aren't strays you can bring home and keep."

Another grin momentarily appeared. "I did bring them home though."

"Fair enough. But you can't keep them. You have

to release them from their enchantment so they can find a way to end it properly. Except Braeden. He remains stone until he can be cured. You're right about one thing. We can't let him die."

Magic pooling in Arwyn's hands came to mind and a smile slowly formed. "Magic. I know how we can help Braedon. I need Kinnon to come back to life." She turned to check the curtain. It had fallen into place when she'd let the fabric go.

"How?"

"Bring magic to him. His father's magic." She shrugged. "Put it in a jar or something. But I need Kinnon awake so he can take me to Arwyn."

"Who is Arwyn?"

Trinity looked towards the doorway, trying not to wince when she spotted her father. "How was your day?" She smiled brightly.

"What happened?" Rod strode into the room. "Why are they stone again?" He stopped in front of Darak. "What are you hiding?" He lifted the cap, staring at the dagger. "Well?" He faced Trinity.

She tried to keep her smile in place. "Everything is okay. Or at least, I am." She waved vaguely towards the Fae. "Them, not so much."

Rod ran a hand across his forehead then through his

hair. "I've got a feeling I'm going to need a seat and a couple of beers to get through this explanation."

"Why don't you have a shower and Troy and I will start dinner?"

"Great," Rod muttered. "It's worse than I thought." He dropped the cap back into place. "Should have taken my sledgehammer to them." Still muttering he left the room.

Troy waited until Rod was out of earshot before he spoke. "How bad?"

She glanced at Kinnon. "Really bad."

"Think you can sum it up in a handful of words?" Troy rose to his feet.

Darak's words came to mind. "Their mother is missing, their father is imprisoned and blamed for her death and they're under a Petrification enchantment that drains their magic until it runs out. Then it takes their life."

Troy sat heavily on the bed again, speechless for a moment. "Oh, a walk in the park. Why didn't you say earlier instead of making me worry?"

She laughed softly. "Yeah. A walk in the park." Probably one filled with muggers and who knew what other dangers.

Troy brushed his knuckles across Braeden's cheek

before once more rising to his feet. "Let's get dinner started. We've got some planning to do."

It took a second for his words to sink in. She wound her way around furniture and Fae to throw her arms around him. "Thank you."

Troy's arms tightened around her. "I'm not about to let him die. Darak maybe, but not Braeden. He doesn't deserve that." He let her go and draped an arm around her shoulders. "What are we having for dinner?"

She walked beside him to the kitchen, making various suggestions until they found one to agree on. Dinner was prepared and cooking when Rod came out of his room and grabbed two beers from the fridge, handing one to Troy.

Trinity slowly walked to the table where they waited for her, trying to think of what to say. She made a production of sitting in the chair, drawing the moment out.

"Get it over and done with. I already know I'm not going to be happy about it," Rod muttered.

Chapter Nine

"How do you feel about dungeons?" Trinity asked.

"Depends. Do I get to lock you away in one to keep you out of mischief?" Rod asked.

"I don't know. You'll have to ask Kinnon."

Rod's mouth dropped open, his beer halfway to it. After a few seconds he placed the beer on the table. "They live in a castle?"

She shrugged. "I don't know. But I guess so since dungeons usually go hand in hand with a castle."

"Start at the beginning." Rod took a long drink of his beer and started to put it on the table. Halfway there he raised it to his mouth and took another long drink. "Maybe you should wait until I grab a second drink first. Or something stronger."

Trinity grinned at her father's dry tone. "Okay, the beginning. We were lying on my bed waiting for Kinnon to come alive again."

"Enjoying the scenery," Troy added.

"You're not helping." She gave Troy a pointed look before facing her father again.

"Weren't you meant to be by the curtain?" Rod asked.

"That came next." She hurriedly began to tell Rod, before Troy could add any more comments. But it didn't help. Troy, as well as Rod, regularly interrupted with questions, Troy needing to check the meal a couple of times during the telling. She was still going over everything when Troy served the meal, needing to answer some of the questions twice, Rod's disbelieving tone replaced by one filled with worry.

Rod pushed his empty plate away to lean on the table, his arms crossed in front of him. "You can't rescue everyone."

"Dad-"

"I'm serious, Trinity. This isn't some schoolyard bully or a teacher who's being unfair. You're not going back there."

She glared at her father. "I'm nearly eighteen-"

Troy interrupted Trinity. "I'll go with her."

"You shouldn't be going either. They're nothing to us. Understand? You don't know them. They're strangers."

"I know Braeden," Troy said softly. "I spent the entire day with him."

Rod pointed a finger at Troy. "When you were supposed to be with Trinity."

"Troy couldn't exactly stop Kinnon from using magic to take me to his realm."

"That isn't helping your cause," Rod said.

"It's not Troy's fault." She met her father's gaze. "He didn't do anything wrong."

Rod sighed heavily. "I'd like to say it was a lot easier when you were younger. But that'd only be wishful thinking."

Troy chuckled. "It'd also be wishful thinking if you thought it was going to get any better."

Trinity rose from the table. "I'm not asking to go."

"And if I said I wouldn't allow it?" Rod asked.

She continued to meet his deep blue eyes, steeling herself against the worry she could see in them. "This is my decision."

"So it'll be like last time? You'll run away?"

A giggle escaped, lightening the mood. "I was four-years-old." Her smile faded. "But yeah, it'll probably be like last time."

Rod pushed his chair back, slowly getting to his feet. "No wonder I have so many grey hairs." He came around the table to envelop Trinity in his arms. "Is there any way I can talk you out of this?"

She returned his hug, the familiar strength of his arms comforting. After a moment she drew away enough to meet his gaze. "You didn't raise me to walk away. How many times have you stood up for people?"

"Don't get in over your head." Once more he hugged her tightly before letting her go.

"I'll try not to."

He pointed a finger at her. "And you ask them what having magic will do to a human. Get the details before jumping in."

"Okay."

Rod turned to Troy. "You watch her back."

Troy nodded, rising to his feet. "Of course."

Once more Rod looked from one to the other. "You're certain-"

"Yes, Dad." She smiled. "Don't you always tell me I'm smart?"

"A little too smart for your own good. Should have known you only hear what you want to," Rod muttered.

Troy stood beside Trinity, draping an arm around her shoulders. "We've got this, Rod."

"I bloody hope so. Because if anything happens to Trinity…"

Troy gave a single nod. "I know." A wry smile formed. "You own a sledgehammer."

Rod nodded sharply.

Trinity pulled away from Troy. "We need to move Darak and Braeden so they don't come out of the enchantment."

"We'll put Braeden in my bed," Troy said.

"Really." She couldn't resist grinning at him.

Troy slowly shook his head. "Darak can go in my room too and I'll sleep on the couch."

"They're stone statues. Put him on the floor and take the bed," Rod said.

"You can't do that," Trinity said at the same time as Troy said, "He's not a statue. He can see, feel and hear while he's stone."

A moment of guilt struck Trinity. She'd have to apologise to Kinnon that she'd been mauling him when he couldn't tell her to back off. "You can share my bed, Troy."

Rod threw his hands up in the air. "Put yourselves out for a couple of statues. I don't know why I bother." He took a couple of steps towards Trinity's room. "You need a hand moving them?"

"I could use some help with Braeden. I don't want

to damage him and moving him around on the trolley while he's in a reclining position won't be easy." Troy led the way.

Trinity followed at a slower pace, setting the alarm on her phone to wake her before Kinnon came to life. She noticed a missed message and checking, found it was from Yvette asking her how working with her father was going. A grin formed. Nothing like she'd expected. She sent that as a message. Reaching her room she slipped her phone back in her pocket. The bed was empty.

"Out of the way, Trin."

She stepped out of her father's way, smiling when he tossed the cap and coat on her bed. Once Rod and Troy had carted Darak away, she shuffled Kinnon to a better location, straightening when she heard a noise at her door.

"Don't leave me wondering what's happening to you."

She hurried to her father, giving him another hug. "I won't. But time doesn't run the same between here and the realms of the Fae." She'd been surprised when she'd realised how much time had passed in her world in comparison to how long they'd been gone.

"Try."

"Okay."

Rod hugged her one more time before he stepped back, staring at her for a long, drawn out moment before he strode away.

She almost called out an apology. But she didn't. He would have thought it meant he could change her mind. He couldn't. Kinnon and his family needed rescuing. She smiled when Troy joined her in the doorway.

"What are you thinking?"

Her smile widened into a grin. "About strays in need of rescuing."

Troy chuckled. "These ones are a lot more interesting than a stray cat." He sobered. "Rod convinced me there's more than enough space in the bed. Not like Braeden is going to encroach on my side." A smile momentarily appeared. "Besides, Darak is there to chaperone us."

"You make sure they remain in starlight. I wouldn't be surprised if Darak uses that dagger when he comes out of the enchantment."

Troy nodded. "I'll rig a blanket in front of my door so I don't accidentally turn Kinnon to stone if I'm coming out of my room at the same time as you open your door."

She shuddered. "Thanks." There'd been more than

enough times that she'd accidentally turned Kinnon to stone. Hopefully he'd understand this latest time.

"I'll see you in the morning."

Her stomach lurched at the thought of what was ahead of them. "Okay." She tried to smile. "We can do this, right?"

"Of course we can." He drew her into a hug. "Aren't you the girl who can do anything?"

"Yeah." But she didn't feel like it. She felt too young, too clueless and too inexperienced. The only thing she had plenty of was determination. She didn't know if that'd be enough. "I better get ready for bed." With one more hug, she returned to her room, gathering her clothes for a shower.

While she readied herself for bed and returned her sneakers to their spot near her door, she kept going over all the things that might go wrong. By the time she was climbing into bed, she was starting to talk herself out of helping. Lying in the dark, she tried to think of something positive. Her lips curved into a smile when she found it. "There's no lightning." Her words were soft and the smile remained as she rolled onto her side and drifted off to sleep.

When her alarm went off far too early, she groggily reached for the bedside lamp, blinking at the overly bright light. She stared at Kinnon who stood at the foot of the bed. Was he awake the entire time he was stone? Or did he have periods of time where he slept?

A shiver went through Kinnon and colour returned to him. "No human owns a Fae knight."

She couldn't resist grinning. "Those are your first words?"

"A human is more likely to be the pet of a Fae. Not the other way round."

Her grin didn't dim as she got out of bed. "Really? I was the one who saved the three of you. The one who brought you home. And who is the one deciding when you're stone and when you're not?"

He crossed the space between them in seconds, his arms going around her waist and tugging her close. "We are going to talk about that."

She tried to draw back, her grin fading. "Stop doing that. Let me go." Before she could tell him she wasn't interested in a relationship with someone so arrogant, he spoke.

"You complain about this? I am the one who should be complaining. I'll accept that this time was to save my brother's life, but you will not turn me to stone again."

Chapter Ten

Trinity's chin rose. "Don't tell me what to do."

Kinnon's lips curved into a smile. "No wonder you and Darak argue. You're very much alike. I believe we're not the only ones who could be considered arrogant and overbearing."

A chuckle had Trinity turning in Kinnon's arms to glare at Troy. "Whose side are you on?"

"Always yours, but that doesn't make me blind to your faults." He looked past Trinity to Kinnon. "Your brothers are okay. Both are in my room with the curtains open."

Kinnon released Trinity so she was able to face him. "You want me to take you to my father so we can get magic for Braeden."

"Is it possible to bring some back for him?" Trinity asked.

"It can be stored in a glass container."

"We've got some old jam jars," Trinity suggested.

Troy slowly shook his head. "Only you would suggest storing magic in jam jars."

"The labels have been removed," Trinity said.

"They're still jam jars." Troy came further into the room. "We need to talk about what it means to have magic. For a human."

"I never offered magic to you," Kinnon said.

"Braeden did. Not long before you returned. He was trying to convince me to return to your world with him. That he wanted the chance to get to know me better."

Trinity stared at Troy for a moment. "You didn't tell me that."

Troy shrugged. "There were other things to worry about."

"You would become Demi Fae," Kinnon said.

"That tells us nothing. We don't know your world." Troy made a vague gesture indicating the area around him. "This is the world I know. There isn't anything magical about it."

Kinnon met Troy's gaze for a moment before he turned to Trinity. "You deserve to know. Now, rather than later like I'd planned to tell you. I was worried you might not help if you knew the drawbacks." He took her hand. "But I wouldn't have given it to you until I explained what it meant. That would be no way to repay you for your help."

Her gaze was drawn to their hands. It reminded her of the apology she needed to make. When his hand lightly tightened on hers she met his gaze. "I'll help. Regardless."

"I know." He drew her to the bed, sitting on the edge of it with her, gesturing to the space on the other side of Trinity. "Take a seat, Troy. This will take a few minutes."

"It's that bad?" Troy sat beside Trinity.

"I wouldn't ever want to give up my magic," Kinnon said. "The ability to travel to places in seconds, to fight and protect, to live more than a mortal's lifetime and have the ability to change the world around me more than compensates for the negatives."

"What are the negatives?" Troy asked.

"Iron sickness. You can't stay in this world, with all its iron, for long periods of time. You can of course drain off most of your magic if you do need to remain here for any reason, but that can weaken your power and slow it's growth and the improvement of your abilities."

"That's it? That's the only drawback?" Trinity asked. That didn't sound too bad to her.

"Iron sickness can kill. First it will send you mad and then you can die from it."

She stared at Kinnon. "Oh." It took her a few seconds to form a coherent question. "How long does it take?"

"That depends on how powerful your magic is and how much iron is around you."

"You're planning on taking her from me permanently?"

Trinity looked towards the doorway, where Rod stood. "I haven't agreed to anything."

"Yet," Rod said.

She rose to her feet, taking a step towards the doorway. "Dad-" She had no idea what to say to him.

He wrapped his arms around her and lightly patted her back. "Shh. It's okay."

She pulled back enough to stare up at him. "I didn't know."

"You'll figure it out. You'll make the right choice. The one that suits you." A wry smile formed. "Not necessarily the one that suits me."

His words surprised a chuckle from her. "I guess."

Rod let her go. "I'll make breakfast. It'll be ready in ten."

"Okay." She watched him go.

"Having magic doesn't mean you can't return to

this world. It only means you can't live here," Kinnon said.

She turned to find he'd risen to his feet and moved closer. She glanced at Troy, knowing she needed to apologise, but preferring not to do it with an audience.

Troy stood up. "Is that the only problem with magic?"

Kinnon shook his head. "No. You'll be forced to tell the truth. Some Demi Fae are able to lie, like Trolls, but most Demi Fae can't. Fae and humans that gain magic certainly can't. You can avoid the truth, use misdirection or skirt around it, but it must be the truth as you perceive it."

"As you perceive it," Troy stated.

Kinnon inclined his head.

"So if you believed a lie, then you could speak it."

Kinnon inclined his head again at Troy's words.

"That almost seems like cheating," Trinity said.

Kinnon chuckled. "Magic can't tell if something is true, it can only tell if you believe it's true. Many of the Fae have perfected the art of lying without actually lying."

"Have you?" Trinity asked.

"I haven't lived long enough to gain mastery of any skill, let alone that one."

For a second she nearly nodded and returned to the earlier topic. "Mastery doesn't mean you have no skill."

Kinnon stepped closer. "You're very observant." He glanced at Troy. "Do either of you have any other questions about magic? I can't think of anything else I'd consider negative or that humans generally consider negative."

"No," Trinity said at the same time as Troy shook his head.

"Can I go with you to collect magic from your father?" Troy asked.

"I need to conserve my magic. Taking two with me would use more than necessary," Kinnon said.

Trinity turned to Troy. "I'll be okay."

He held her gaze for a moment before he looked past her to Kinnon. "You will bring her back unharmed."

"I wouldn't want harm to come to someone who was helping me," Kinnon said.

Ever since Kinnon had said some Fae could lie without actually lying she'd been listening carefully to his words. "How long does it take to learn how to talk like that?"

Troy's eyes narrowed. "You didn't say she'd come back safely."

Kinnon took Trinity's hand drawing her close again. "Do you think I'd deliberately allow you to be harmed?"

"No, but it's not what I think that matters. You keep avoiding the question."

"I don't know what to expect when we return to the dungeon. It's impossible to say for certain that you'll be unharmed," Kinnon said.

Trinity grinned. "How hard was that to say?"

"Trin-"

She interrupted Troy, drawing her hand from Kinnon's light grip. "I didn't expect it to be safe." She held his gaze. "It's a dungeon. With a tally drawn in blood on the wall." That image would haunt her for a long time.

Troy was quiet a moment. "Breakfast is probably ready."

"I'll join you in a minute." She faced Kinnon. "Do you eat food?"

"Yes."

"Normal food?"

"I can eat your human food, but it isn't advisable for humans to eat Fae food unless they have magic."

"I'll bring something back for you to eat." Troy strode towards the kitchen.

Trinity waited until she could no longer hear

Troy's retreating footsteps. "I'm sorry I keep turning you into stone."

"Then don't do it again."

She stared at her bare feet. "I also didn't know you were real to start with. I thought you were a statue."

He raised her chin, meeting her gaze. "Why does that make you uncomfortable?"

"I wouldn't have touched you like I did if I'd known you were real."

Kinnon ran a finger across her lips and over her chin as she'd done to him while he'd been stone. "I have no complaints."

She opened her mouth twice before she could remember what she was going to say. "It wasn't right. You couldn't exactly tell me to stop."

He lifted her hand, placing it against his chest. "As I've already said, I have no complaints." He lowered his head, coming closer.

She pressed against his chest, shaking her head. "I don't think-"

"Breakfast."

At Troy's interruption, she momentarily closed her eyes. She would tell Kinnon later. A relationship wouldn't work between them. He accused her of being too much like Darak, but she thought it more likely she was too much like him. That she liked to have her own way as much as he did.

"Later." The word was whisper quiet. He reached past her, taking the plate from Troy. "Thank you for the food. I was becoming hungry."

"You coming?" Troy remained in the doorway.

She didn't answer straight away. She stared into Kinnon's tawny eyes a moment longer before she nodded. It wasn't going to be the later he expected. She grabbed a change of clothes and dressed in the bathroom before she joined Troy and Rod at the table where toast and fried eggs awaited her.

The meal was silent and she followed her father to the garage when it was time for him to leave, standing beside Troy as Rod drove away. She leaned against him, lowering her hand. It had felt like she was saying goodbye for longer than a day. "What do you think about getting magic?"

"That it might not be the best choice if you want to stay in our world."

"I don't know what the realms of the Fae is like. I've only seen a dungeon." A wry smile formed. "And if that's what the place is like I certainly don't want to live there." She thought of the magic that had pooled in Arwyn's hands. "But I really want magic." There was no point in getting rid of most of it to remain in her world. It would be pointless having something she couldn't use.

"Do you need to make up your mind immediately?"

She shrugged. "I don't know."

"Ask Kinnon." Troy stepped away from her, glancing over his shoulder before striding to the far end of the garage and shutting the roller door. He remained standing beside it, staring back at her. "Do you trust Kinnon with your life? Because I think that's what it's going to come to."

"I'm not sure." The memory of him placing her hand on his chest played over in her mind. "Half the time I don't know what to think about him."

"Ask him. Make him tell you the truth instead of avoiding it."

She was pretty sure that was easier said than done. "Okay."

Troy strode towards her. "Make him bring you home if things become too dangerous."

She nodded. "I need to get a jam jar."

Troy chuckled, slowly shaking his head. "Only you."

She walked beside him to the kitchen. "What else can I use? We don't have many empty glass containers."

"Almost anything would have to be better than an old jam jar."

Reaching the kitchen, she rummaged in the cupboard near the sink, finding a jar and matching lid. "This will have to do." Closing the cupboard, she rose to her feet to stare at Troy. "I wish you could come with us." She could rely on him. She didn't know what to expect from Kinnon.

Troy crossed the room, to grip her shoulder. "You don't have to do this."

Chapter Eleven

Too many images filled Trinity's mind. Arwyn chained to the stone wall, the tally drawn in blood, Braeden lying on her bed barely alive, Darak with his bow trained on them and Kinnon placing her hand on his chest. "I do. Who else will help them?"

"I can go. You can wait here."

A grin escaped. "When have I ever been the one to wait behind?"

Troy chuckled, his grip momentarily tightening on her shoulder. "Never." He let go of her shoulder to give her a hug. "Be careful. Don't trust anyone."

She returned the hug before drawing away. "I will be okay." She spoke the words firmly, sounding more confident than she felt. "You don't need to go to my room with me. I'll be okay." When he nodded, she smiled, reaching out to squeeze his hand before letting go and returning to her room. She paused in the doorway, slipping her feet into her sneakers. Her smile came more easily when she saw Kinnon held a picture of her and Yvette that had been on one of the bookshelves, leaning against a row of books.

He returned the picture before facing her, nodding towards the glass jar she held. "Are you ready to go?"

Troy's words came back to her. "Can I trust you with my life?"

Kinnon crossed the space separating them. "Yes." He took the jar from her, placing it on the bed before wrapping his arms around her. "You fascinate me and I'd love to trick you into becoming my pet so you'd always have to remain with me, but your willingness to help us won't allow me to throw away my honour to repay you in that fashion."

"I fascinate you?" The words escaped before she could stop them.

He ran a finger over her lips. "More than you can imagine. Are you ready to travel with me to see my father?"

She really needed to have a serious talk to him, but this wasn't the time. They needed magic to save Braeden. "About as ready as I'm likely to be."

"Don't worry. I always protect what's mine." He kept one arm around her, picking up the jam jar and holding it out to her.

"I think you have that wrong." She took the jar, grinning at him. "You and your brothers were given to me. I don't know who left you there, but Dad gave you to me. So that makes you mine."

"It was Tarrant. He expected us to be destroyed. But that doesn't make us yours. We'll discuss this when we get back. Grab your torch."

"That isn't all we need to discuss." She stepped away from him to pick up the torch that was on her bedside cabinet. "You and your brothers will get used to being mine. Troy did." She grinned. "He's learned it's easier to give in than to argue."

"I never give in. And don't compare me to Troy. It isn't your friendship I want." His arm went around her waist, drawing her back against him, the scent of mock orange filling the air. "Turn the torch on."

She pressed in the button. Before she could complain about the orders he was throwing about, he crushed a flower in his hand and the world shimmered and reformed, bringing them to the dungeon.

"What are you doing back here?" The chains rattled as Arwyn moved, coming as close to them as possible.

Trinity started to hold the jam jar out, but decided it might be best coming from Kinnon. Then she caught sight of Arwyn. She shoved the jar at Kinnon, hurrying over to Arwyn the moment Kinnon had hold of the jar. "What did they do to you?"

"Nothing that hasn't already been done." Arwyn took a step back from her.

Her hand was half stretched out to him, the light from the torch showing the new injuries. "Is he trying to kill you?"

"It's possible," Arwyn said. "But the better question is why it bothers you. I can hear the pain in your voice."

"No one should have to go through this." She turned to Kinnon who stood beside her, anger filling his tawny eyes. "We have to take him out of here. He can't stay."

Arwyn spoke before Kinnon could. "They plan to collect me at dawn. If you help me escape Tarrant will be looking for the one at fault. Would you have him kill an innocent? Or learn that the three of you are free?"

"That's not why we're here," Kinnon said.

"What happened?" Arwyn demanded.

Kinnon held out the jam jar once he'd opened the lid. "Braeden needs magic."

"What happened?" Arwyn's words were sharper

than before. "How close to death is he?" Magic pooled in his hands and he tipped it into the jar.

"He's been turned to stone again," Kinnon said.

Trinity watched the jar fill. "You're not giving us all your magic, are you?"

"It's a waste to take it to the grave with me." The jar was full and yet Arwyn continued to let his magic fill his hands.

"Do you really think any of us will allow you to die?" Kinnon stepped out of his father's reach, screwing the lid on the jar.

"You need to find your mother. Need to learn what happened to her. I didn't kill her, but when I awakened, surrounded by Tarrant and his knights, there was blood everywhere and she wasn't to be found. You're the only ones who believe she might be alive. I saw the shock in Emery's eyes. Even he thinks her dead." Arwyn stretched out his hands, the magic remaining in them. "Please, Kinnon." He tried to take a step forward, brought up short by the chain. "The last I remember was being attacked by magic and your mother's horse rearing. I was thrown from mine and knocked out. I don't know for how long, but it was enough time for it to look like a slaughter had occurred in the glade we'd been riding through."

"This is more than enough magic." Kinnon nodded

towards the jar he held. "I'm not going to take all of yours. How long do we have until dawn?"

"Wake Darak. He should be taking care of this. Not you. He'd listen to me."

Kinnon's lips thinned. "Even Darak wouldn't let you die. Besides, his anger isn't what we need right now."

"You would rather face it later?" Arwyn asked.

Trinity stepped closer to Kinnon. "I was the one who decided to leave Darak enchanted. Kinnon didn't have a choice in the matter. And he still doesn't. If he opens the door where his brothers are, he'll turn to stone."

Arwyn examined her. "Would you step between Kinnon and Darak like you have done between me and my son?"

"I didn't step between you. I'm standing beside him."

Arwyn pointed to her shoulder. "Not quite beside him. A little in front."

She glanced to the side, surprised to see Arwyn was right. Raising her chin, she met Arwyn's gaze. "I'll do what I need to." She had no idea how to explain the possessive feeling she felt for Kinnon and his brothers. She could only put it down to having claimed ownership of them when they were statues.

She didn't like it when people tried to take her things. Never had.

Arwyn inclined his head. "Then let me suggest that my oldest son is who you need for this task. He's the better fighter and more skilled than either of his brothers. He's also more practical."

It didn't surprise her that Darak was more skilled at fighting. He probably got into a lot of fights because of his attitude. "I'll think about it." Which would take her all of a few seconds. She wasn't about to change her mind. Darak couldn't help. They'd spend more time arguing than getting anything done. More than likely a time would come when his skills were needed, but it wasn't now.

"You might think on it, but you'll do what you wish regardless."

Trinity grinned. "So people keep telling me."

"Not always a good trait," Arwyn warned.

Her grin faded. "We need to get you away from here."

"You think you could force me to leave if I chose to remain?"

She tried not to smile at how arrogant Arwyn looked and sounded. She doubted many would be able to look so when they'd been incarcerated and beaten. "If your chains were removed could you use magic to appear somewhere else in the castle? Would there be something you'd collect where Tarrant's people would see you? Then use your magic to travel somewhere else."

"That still leaves Tarrant to wonder who helped me." Arwyn let the magic sink back into his hands.

"Take me with you." She took a step closer to Arwyn. "No one knows me so I have no ties to anyone here. They couldn't blame anyone innocent."

"We can't ask that of you," Kinnon said. "It's too dangerous."

"You didn't ask. I offered."

"Why would you offer to put yourself in danger for someone you don't know?" Arwyn's eyes narrowed. "Is this a trick?" He looked to Kinnon. "How did you meet her?"

"I don't believe it's a trick." Kinnon took Trinity's hand, clasping it firmly. "I trust her."

Arwyn looked from one to the other. "With all our lives?"

"Yes."

Trinity tightened her grip on Kinnon's hand, surprised he'd answered without hesitation. "We'll go back to my room and I'll get the bolt cutters out of the garage for you."

Kinnon turned towards her, continuing to hold her

hand. "I need to conserve my magic. It'd be too much to take you home and then back again. Does Troy know where they're kept?"

She didn't answer immediately, first needing to get past the urge to beg him not to leave her behind. "Yeah. Troy knows where everything is kept. Our place is his second home."

Kinnon released her hand to run a finger across her lips and over her chin. "You will barely notice me gone." The dungeon filled with the scent of mock orange and Kinnon took a step back before he vanished.

She held back a sigh. She really needed to have a talk with Kinnon.

"What is between you and my son?" Arwyn asked.

She stared at the spot where Kinnon had been before she faced Arwyn. There probably wasn't as much between them as Kinnon wished, but she couldn't tell his father that. Not until she'd talked to Kinnon first. A grin formed. She didn't need to tell him anything. "Where are we going to appear? What is it that you wouldn't leave behind?"

"My father's sword. It's hanging over the fireplace in the dining room. Tarrant's people are placed everywhere throughout the castle. One of them is sure to be in there."

"Your father's sword." Surely Tarrant wouldn't believe such a flimsy excuse. "Wouldn't you take money or something to help you live?" Didn't he realise the excuse needed to be believable?

"I have no idea what Tarrant did with my sword when he took it from me, but the one my father used during his lifetime will help me live. There's no way a knight would go anywhere without a sword."

Chapter Twelve

Hearing the conviction in Arwyn's voice, Trinity decided to trust that he knew what he was talking about. "How do you know the sword is still there? What if Tarrant has taken it down?" For all she knew Tarrant might want to use the sword himself.

"He gloated that he is now the one to sit in my chair, at my dining table, with my father's sword hanging behind him." Arwyn's hands tightened. "He will die for what he's done."

Trinity nearly took a step back from Arwyn. With the amount of anger in his voice, it reminded her of Darak. "Whose son is he?" She regretted the question the moment she asked it. What if Tarrant was his son? She didn't want to help someone kill their child. Actually, she didn't want to help someone kill another person no matter how they were or weren't related.

"My wife's stepson. Her first husband died in battle and she inherited him."

She was surprised by the amount of relief that washed over her. It was immediately pushed away by another thought. "You raised him?"

Arwyn inclined his head. "Since he was four-years-old and her first husband's squire brought him to us fourteen years ago."

His explanation confused her. About to ask what he meant, another question occurred to her. "You could kill someone you raised? Someone that was like a son to you."

"He has proven he's no son of mine. I offered him gold to secure his place in the world. My lands will go to my sons." Arwyn made a waving motion that encompassed the dungeon. "This is how he repays me."

She could think of no reply to his words. The thought of killing someone didn't sit right with her, but nor did what Tarrant had done to the man who'd raised him or to the brothers he'd been raised with. She had no idea what the answer was. And a dungeon certainly wasn't the place to be dwelling on uncomfortable thoughts. "How long do you think Kinnon will be gone?"

Arwyn lifted a single shoulder. "Time passes

differently between the realms." He was silent a moment. "Do you regret your offer already?"

She was beginning to with his talk of killing. "I'll help." She held his gaze, seeing the anger in his eyes. "And you'll help break your sons' enchantments."

"You think I'd turn my back on them?" Arwyn demanded.

Trinity had no idea how to answer and before she could come up with a reply, there was the sound of footsteps headed towards them. "Is it dawn?" She kept her voice low, moving closer to Arwyn.

"Put your light out and hide it. We don't have such things in our realm."

She turned the torch off and slipped it into a pocket of her jeans, the darkness closing in on her. "You didn't answer my question." She wasn't about to let him avoid it.

"It shouldn't be dawn."

She heard him move away from her, the sound of his feet and chains revealing his location. Her gaze was drawn to the door, light increasing through the barred window. Why hadn't she checked every corner in the dungeon to see if there were hiding places? It was too late now. And what if Kinnon returned? He'd be caught. She almost hoped something had happened to cause him to be turned to stone again. Twelve hours as a statue had to be better than being discovered trying to rescue his father.

The sound of a key turning in a lock came a few seconds before the door was swung open. An armed man stepped in, holding a lantern. He remained to the side of the door, a young man following him in. He was tall and blond, his narrow frame richly dressed, his long hair pulled back to show his slightly pointed ears.

He stopped abruptly, his gaze on Trinity, his hand going to the hilt of his sword. "Who are you and what are you doing in here?" He turned to Arwyn. "How did she get in here?"

"She's a human. I'd never be unfaithful to my wife with a human," Arwyn said. "You should know me better than that, Tarrant."

Having Arwyn confirm it was Tarrant had Trinity eyeing the doorway. There was no escape. A guard was outside the door as well as the one inside the cell holding the lantern. She took a second look at the one with the lantern, realising he looked as young as Tarrant, his short hair an impossible white colour she'd only ever seen on toddlers. She didn't know if he looked to be around her age because he was young or because the Fae didn't age like humans. His sky blue eyes were drawn towards her, holding her gaze a moment before he returned his attention to Tarrant. Trinity's gaze again scanned the dungeon, confirming there was no escape.

Tarrant strode towards Arwyn, stopping in front of him. "You say you wouldn't be unfaithful to your wife. The wife everyone believes you killed."

"The wife I have no memory of having killed," Arwyn said.

Trinity pressed her lips together to prevent herself from staring at Arwyn slack jawed. Why had he worded his denial so ambiguously? No wonder everyone believed he'd killed his wife. She wanted to demand that he tell them in a way that left no doubt he was innocent. But she didn't dare draw Tarrant's attention.

"It doesn't matter. Tomorrow at dawn you'll be shot unless you tell us what we want to know. I've chosen a dozen of the best archers." Tarrant gestured for the guard to come inside before turning back to Arwyn. "I considered giving you a final meal, but decided on having a last drink with you. In honour of the years you allowed me to remain in your home."

"As if I'd drink with you. I raised you alongside my sons and this is the way you treat me." Arwyn looked past Tarrant to the guard with the lantern. "I thought better of you too. Lili would be disappointed."

Trinity glanced at the guard who looked at a point past Arwyn, his lips pressed tight together. When Tarrant spoke, she returned her attention to him and Arwyn.

"I thought you might decline a drink. I considered letting you know a different death would await you if you chose to drink, but I know you well enough that it wouldn't make a difference." Tarrant shrugged. "So I guess you won't mind if I kill one of your people every hour between now and dawn until you agree to drink with me." He glanced at Trinity. "Starting with her. Although it will be a pity to kill such a pretty creature."

It took a second for his words to sink in. She froze when she would have preferred to run. It wouldn't have helped. Another glance around the dungeon showed her what she already knew. There was nowhere to hide and two guards who'd chase after her. Her gaze was drawn to the swords hanging at their sides. If they moved as fast as Kinnon she didn't stand a chance. Her gaze clashed with that of the light haired guard who remained by the door and she could have sworn she saw pity. A fleeting emotion that went as quickly as it had arrived, his gaze returning to a point past Arwyn. There'd be no help from him. She looked at Arwyn, not expecting any help from him either.

Arwyn glared at Tarrant, gesturing to the guard who held a jug and two cups. "Pour the drink. It will mean nothing to me. There's no honour in you. I want your word, bound by magic, that if I share a drink with you all my people will live to see sunrise."

Tarrant's lips curved into a smile. A humourless one that promised nothing good. "We all have our own version of honour. None of your people will die before sunrise if you drink every drop in your cup." He glanced at Trinity. "Do you claim her too?"

Arwyn nodded. "All in the castle who've remained faithful to me are mine. She I expect you to keep from harm for as long as I live."

The air filled with the scent of sandalwood. "Done. But once dawn arrives you will die and your people will be my people. Then I can do with her as I wish." Tarrant's smile lingered as he looked Trinity up and down. "The first task will be to find out what she's doing in here. By whatever means necessary." He took the cup the guard held out to him, raising it. His gaze met Arwyn's. "To honour. Or what each of us sees as honour."

Trinity drew in a shaky breath, edging away from Tarrant. He might be far better looking than Kinnon and his brothers, but there was no warmth in his manner. Her legs ached with the need to run. Another glance at the guard by the door showed he hadn't moved.

Arwyn finally took the cup the guard held out to him. "Dawn is hours away." The scent of his magic filled the air as he raised the cup to his lips and drained it, watching over the rim as Tarrant did the same. Once he was finished, he held the cup upside down. "You and I are done. I owe you nothing more." He let go of the cup. It shattered when it hit the floor, the sound echoing around them.

Trinity backed further away, tempted to run while everyone's attention was focused on the broken cup. A glance at the guard showed his attention was on her, his sky blue eyes momentarily colliding with hers. She looked away from the guard when Tarrant spoke, worried about what he might do in retaliation.

Tarrant indicated the broken cup. "You think that bothers me?" He let go of the one he held so it too smashed against the floor. "If anything, now no other will drink from the cups we used for our last drink. Quite a fitting end." He turned to the guard beside him, taking a key from a pouch on his belt and giving it to him. "Take the human to my chamber and lock her in. I'll question her after dawn." He strode from the room, leaving silence in his wake.

When the guard went to grab hold of her arm, Trinity hurried after Tarrant, not wanting to be restrained in case she saw an opportunity to escape. They also needed to get out of the dungeon as soon as possible. Then she could stop worrying about Kinnon returning and being caught. Behind her she heard the door being locked and it caused her to quicken her pace. She stayed near Tarrant, glancing at him when he withdrew a small glass bottle from the pouch on his belt, taking a sip from it before returning it to the pouch, the guards well behind them. "What did you drink?"

Tarrant barely glanced at her. "I will be the one who asks the questions. Not you." He stopped at the end of the corridor where a guard stood. "Open the door."

"Did you give Arwyn poison? What happened to waiting until dawn?" Trinity followed Tarrant up a set of stairs. Unless it was a slow acting poison and he wouldn't die until dawn. Was this the different method of death Tarrant had hinted at?

Tarrant kept walking, not even glancing at her.

She stared after him, unable to keep up with his pace. By the time she'd reached the top of the stairs, and left the dungeons behind, Tarrant was nowhere in sight. Only the two guards remained with her. When one of them tried to grab her arm again, she pulled away. "I'm not about to try and escape. Besides, there's two of you."

"Are you willing to bind that promise with magic?" the light haired guard asked.

Trinity nodded, frantically trying to think of a way to word it that wouldn't cause her problems later. There was no way she was about to remain Tarrant's prisoner. "I'll go to Tarrant's room without trying to escape."

The smell of old campfires filled the air. "This way." The guard gestured to the left, the second guard taking his lantern and giving him the key, walking away after a nod to his companion.

Chapter Thirteen

Trinity walked beside the guard, taking note of the path they took. Maybe she could escape from Tarrant's chamber and find her way to the dungeons. Not that she knew how she could get in there. And what about the bottle Tarrant had drunk from? If he'd poisoned Arwyn, she had to get it from him. Or somehow let Kinnon know. If it was a slow acting poison, she had until dawn. Not that she knew how much time that was. The guard led her up two more flights of steps and down another corridor. Their way was lit by candles and lanterns.

The guard stopped in front of a door and used the key to unlock it. "Inside." He swung the door open, stepping back to let her pass.

She held his gaze for a moment, looking into sky blue eyes. "Are you faithful to Arwyn or are you one of Tarrant's men?"

"I once served Tarrant's father as his squire."

She slowly nodded her head, calculating his age from what Arwyn had said. Nineteen. Two years older than her and serious enough that he might have been twice her age. "Tarrant only promised that Arwyn's people would see sunrise."

He nodded. "I serve Tarrant as faithfully as I served his father. Without question. I swore an oath to him as his knight."

She tried not to show her surprise at learning the young man she'd mistaken as a guard was actually a knight. "Does that mean you helped Tarrant put an enchantment on his stepbrothers and tried to kill their parents?"

The Fae gestured towards the room. "You can't run. A promise bound with magic is impossible to break. Inside."

"I'm not running. I'm talking to you."

"No, you're trying to make me question my loyalty. Tarrant would never have harmed his stepbrothers. He scoured the countryside along with everyone else when they went missing. He was as sad as the rest of us when Arwyn went crazy and killed his wife."

She saw sorrow in the knight's eyes. He truly believed what he said. His magic and the conviction on his face made that clear. She spoke softly so that he leaned forward to catch her words. "What will you do if you find out everything you thought true was lies?"

He jerked back, as if struck. "As if I would believe a human. You are notorious liars."

She tried to keep her gaze on his, fighting the urge to check the room he wanted her to enter. Once she was locked inside, she doubted she'd get to see anyone other than Tarrant. And he wasn't about to let her go. "I've been told the Fae can tell a lie while seeming to tell the truth. How trustworthy is that?"

"No Fae can lie. Not if you know how to listen properly."

She decided to try a different tactic. "My name is Trinity. What's yours?" She smiled at him, her smile widening when his gaze was drawn to her lips.

"If I give you my name, will you enter the room without another word?"

"Are you going to bind that with magic too?" She grinned at him when she would have preferred to beg him to help her escape.

"Well?" When she didn't answer, he spoke again. "I have other tasks that need to be done."

"Yes. There's no need to bind that with magic."

"Emery."

With a nod, she entered the room, turning back in time to see Emery close the door. She heard it lock. It hadn't helped. All her words had been a waste of time. "Emery? Are you still there?"

"You'll be safe until dawn. You might want to use that time wisely."

Leaning against the door, she listened to the soft sound of his retreating footsteps, surprised by his words. Had he told her to escape? Why? She didn't know how far away dawn was. But it didn't matter. She wasn't about to die in some strange land. There were too many things she wanted to do with her life. An image of the magic filling the jam jar came to mind. How would having magic have changed things for her?

Facing the room, remaining against the door, she checked out her surroundings. She was in a large room with a four poster bed to one side, a timber trunk at the foot of it. There was a lantern hanging from a hook in the middle of the room and two armchairs beside a fireplace. On the wall opposite the bed was a dark timber dressing table with a hairbrush and a timber box placed on it. Curtains were drawn back from a set of glass paned doors that led onto a shadowy balcony, both doors closed.

What had Emery meant by making the most of

her time? Had he been letting her know there was a way to escape? She crossed the room and checked the doors leading onto the balcony. They were locked. Outside she saw the night sky was filled with stars, none of the constellations looking familiar. Turning her back on the doors, she looked around the room once more. Even if she broke the glass of the doors, it wouldn't help. Each individual pane was surrounded by thick panels of timber that wouldn't be so easily broken.

Further along the wall from the doors was a window. Checking it, she found it was open. It was a dizzying drop to the ground below, but there was a ledge that ran under the window and ended not far from the balcony. She eyed the distance. It might be possible to step across to the balcony rail and hop down. But where could she go next? There was another balcony past the other one, but she wasn't certain she could reach it. And if she did leave the room, how would Kinnon and Arwyn find her? She was safe until dawn. Surely Kinnon would be back before then. Time couldn't be that different between the realms.

She paced the floor, having tried to sit in the armchairs. It was impossible for her to sit still. Several times she checked out the window, staring into the sky as she tried to figure out what time it was. All she knew was that it was dark. Dawn could arrive at any time.

The scent of magic filled the air, a mix of spices, as Arwyn appeared in front of her while she was taking a step away from the window. He instantly turned to stone. She stood gaping, a hand pressed to her mouth. A step back had her running into the wall, the breeze coming in from the window cool against her back. "No." The word escaped as little more than a sigh. "Arwyn." She slowly shook her head, closing the distance between them to place a hand against his arm. He was stone. There was no mistaking it. She closed her eyes, drawing in a deep breath as she shut her mouth. This couldn't be happening.

It hadn't been poison. The realisation struck her, causing her to stand with her mouth open again. "He has the antidote." She kept her voice low, not knowing who might be walking past in the corridor outside. "Tarrant has the antidote." She had to figure out how to get it from him. Her gaze darted between Arwyn and the door to the corridor. Not that it would help if he spotted Arwyn. She had to hide him. Another look around the room showed the only place it would be possible to hide the Fae would be under the bed. But first she needed to close the curtains to keep out the starlight. Twelve hours was a really long time to wait.

After the curtains were closed, Trinity pushed and shoved at Arwyn until he was beside the bed. Her gaze was frequently drawn to the door, half expecting Tarrant to come bursting inside. She eyed the distance between Arwyn and the floor. "Why do you have to be so tall? Aren't there any short Fae?" She grabbed pillows off the bed, along with the quilt, placing them on the floor to cushion Arwyn when she attempted to lower him to a reclining position.

Standing behind him, she pulled on his shoulders, nearly dropping him when he came towards her. Luckily she'd had plenty of practise lugging heavy plants around and she managed to lower him to the floor without dropping him. She remained kneeling at his head, taking a deep breath before she slid him off the quilt and under the bed. A sound had her looking towards the door. She froze for a minute before she dumped the pillows and quilt on the bed, pushing the rest of the linen towards the foot of the bed, remaining kneeling in the middle of the mattress as she stared at the door.

It stayed closed. There were no other sounds. Her heart raced and she waited, unable to move. Nothing happened. She sat back on her heels, not caring that she wore her sneakers in Tarrant's bed. What had the noise been? She clambered off the bed, crossing the room to the door, pressing her ear against it. All was quiet in the hallway. She peered through the keyhole. The wall opposite the room came into view. She had no idea what the sound had been. Wandering across the room, she tried to think of what had to be done next.

Escape wasn't an option. The first thing Tarrant was likely to do was look for her and he'd find Arwyn under the bed. She stopped in front of the window, wanting to see if it was nearly dawn. But she couldn't open the curtains without risking Arwyn remaining a statue for longer than twelve hours. They had to escape as soon as possible. Tarrant would destroy Arwyn if he found him. Then she'd no longer be safe from Tarrant. She shuddered when a memory of his smile surfaced. She didn't want to know what he planned to do to her.

Returning to the bed, she started to take the quilt so she could cover Arwyn. She stopped, her hand above the quilt. He'd notice it gone. She had to find something else. Rummaging in the trunk at the foot of the bed, she found two more blankets and some old clothes. She used one of the blankets, hoping it was thick enough to keep the starlight off Arwyn when the curtains were opened. Sitting back on her heels, she surveyed her work. Not a single bit of the statue was visible.

Trinity checked out the window, not sure if she should be happy there was light in the sky or terrified about what Tarrant would do when he learned Arwyn was missing. She barely had time to move away from the window when the door was flung open and Tarrant stood in the doorway, Emery and another Fae behind him.

She nearly glanced at the bed. Or under it. Could Tarrant see Arwyn from where he stood? Worried he could, she hurried forward. "Have you killed Arwyn already?"

"No." The word was sharp. Tarrant turned to the Fae next to Emery. "Find him. Someone else must have helped Arwyn escape." He faced Trinity taking a step towards her. "How did you get inside the dungeon?"

Chapter Fourteen

Trinity wanted to retreat from the anger she could see in Tarrant's eyes. "Why would I tell you anything?"

Tarrant took another step towards her. "Tell me now." He raised his hand, drawing it back.

She wanted to remind him that he'd promised not to hurt her while Arwyn lived, but maybe he'd found a way around it. Had he worded it in a way he could break the binding?

"Now." Once again the word was sharp. "Tell me." He tried to strike her, growling when he couldn't. He pointed a finger at her. "When he dies, you will pay for your insolence."

Emery came closer. "My lord, maybe she doesn't know who left her in the dungeon."

Tarrant spun, drawing a dagger that hung from a sheath on the opposite side to his sword. "Is it you? Are you conspiring with her against me?"

"Why would I conspire against you after how well I've served you these many years?"

Tarrant took another step towards Emery, keeping the dagger pointed at him. "Someone helped her. She's human. How could she have managed to get in there on her own?"

Hearing the threat in Tarrant's voice, Trinity feared he'd attack the knight. Like Arwyn, she didn't want anyone innocent harmed. Drawing in a shaky breath, she stepped between them. "He didn't help me. No one in this castle helped me."

"Why would I trust you? Humans can easily lie." Tarrant glanced behind her before once more meeting her gaze. "If you aren't helping him, why try and save him?"

She almost closed her eyes and barely managed to keep from groaning. She'd made it worse. "Because I am human. We care about what happens to others." A few people she'd met over the years came to mind. "At least most of us do."

"My lord, I am your knight."

Tarrant looked past Trinity. "You can work against me even if you are my knight."

"My loyalty hasn't changed."

"Are you saying you've always been disloyal?"

Trinity wanted to push Tarrant away from her.

The dagger was too close and at this rate he'd push her out of the way and attack Emery. She doubted the knight deserved that. "Give me magic. You want to make sure I can't lie? Then give me magic and ask me if he had anything to do with me being in the dungeon." She didn't know if she wanted it, but it seemed preferable to letting an innocent person, or Fae, be killed. Especially in front of her.

"I wouldn't waste magic on a human." Tarrant strode from the room, slamming the door behind him, the sound of it being locked breaking the silence.

Trinity looked towards Emery, who appeared to be stunned by Tarrant's actions. "I guess he doesn't normally act like that."

"He has been raised to be a knight. Someone the lord of the castle can call upon to protect his people and lands. I was so proud of the Fae he'd become when he told Arwyn he didn't need his gold. That he'd make his own way in the world." Emery slowly shook his head. "Surely he won't go mad with sorrow too. The loss of his stepbrothers has been devastating."

She continued to stare at Emery, initially surprised at the way he'd spoken. He acted like he was years older than Tarrant, not a single year. Then the rest of his words sank in. Was Kinnon wrong? About everything. Surely not. But Emery seemed certain Tarrant didn't normally act like this. The thought of Arwyn, under the bed, brought a halt to her doubts. It was too much of a coincidence that Tarrant had used that enchantment on Arwyn.

"You don't believe me."

"Tarrant used a Petrification enchantment on his stepbrothers. They were turned into stone statues."

"How do you know this?"

She looked between Emery and the door. Had it been an act? One to make her think Emery was on her side. She shook her head. With his sky blue eyes, impossibly white hair, sculptured features and wiry body he was as stunning as the rest of the Fae she'd met. But that didn't mean he wasn't as evil as Tarrant. "I'm sorry. I don't trust you. How many times have you said you're loyal to Tarrant?" She turned away from him, glancing under the bed. It was a relief to find that the shadows from the large bed made it impossible to see all the way underneath. Hopefully that wouldn't change if the curtains were drawn open.

Emery stepped around her so he could face her. "If you don't trust me, why protect me?"

That was another question she couldn't answer. At

least not the full truth. "You don't deserve to be hurt for something that wasn't your fault. No one does."

"The only way you could know it wasn't my fault is if you know who is at fault."

"Do you really think I'm going to answer that?"

"Only Tarrant can't harm you to find out the truth."

She nearly pressed a hand to her heart, going as far as to move her hand a fraction. "Did he tell you to do this?"

Emery shook his head. "If it was by his order, it would be impossible for me to harm you. The magic wouldn't allow it. But there are many who'd harm you because they thought it might be what Tarrant wants, even if he never speaks a word to give such an order."

She tensed, ready to move if he went to attack her. "Are you planning to hurt me?" She couldn't take her gaze from his sky blue eyes, but she could clearly picture the sword that hung at his side. It was likely to be as sharp as the dagger Tarrant had drawn.

He didn't answer her immediately. "No. I owe you that much for your protection of me." He stared at her silently for a moment. "I never would have expected such courage from a human."

She didn't feel very courageous. And she certainly wasn't courageous when there was a thunderstorm.

"I don't understand your motives."

She half shrugged. "I guess you're going to have to believe me when I say it's a human thing."

"Can you tell me, without a doubt, that Tarrant harmed his brothers?"

"No. Not without a doubt. But there are a few things that make me believe I was told the truth about what he's done."

"Thank you." He gave her a single nod before striding to the armchairs and sitting in the furthest one.

She stared at him for a moment before she walked on shaky legs to the bed. Dropping onto it, she lay back to stare up at the material canopy above. What had Emery been thanking her for? How long would it be until Tarrant returned? Where was Kinnon? Were his brothers safe? And what about Troy? What was he doing while she was trapped here? There were so many questions and absolutely no answers.

She had no idea how much time had passed, other than it was long enough for her to become extremely bored, before the door opened. A warrior remained at the door while a human brought a tray of food in and held it out to her. She placed it on the bed while the human retreated.

Before Trinity could pick up a pastry from one of the two plates, Emery's hand was closing over her wrist keeping her from touching it. "This is Fae food. Don't eat it." He looked to the human who'd reached the door. "Did Tarrant order food sent?"

The human nodded.

"Then bring human food. Otherwise Tarrant would be considered to have harmed the girl and the backlash from the magic will be terrible. He would make you pay for causing him such a problem."

"I was told to bring you both food," the human said. "Not which type of food."

Emery let go of Trinity's hand to stride towards the door, taking the tray with him. "Bring back food suitable for a human. I will inform Tarrant who is to blame otherwise."

The human glanced at Trinity before nodding, taking the tray and leaving the room. The warrior stepped forward and closed the door, the sound of it locking clearly heard from where Trinity stood.

She stared at Emery. "Why did you stop me? Aren't you angry with Tarrant?"

"No. He has much to cope with."

"Is that the only reason you stopped me from eating?"

"Were you expecting there to be another reason?"

"It's really annoying the way you Fae answer a question with a question. What's the problem with telling the truth?"

"Information is power. If you're going to remain in this realm you should at least learn that."

She started to say she wasn't staying in this realm, but stopped. "I don't understand this realm. Or the people in it."

"I can offer you some magic to help you survive here. It will allow you to eat what you wish without worrying over the problems it will cause."

She slowly shook her head. "That won't help me when I return home." She didn't know enough about this world to decide if she was interested in living here.

"You're imprisoned. How do you think you'll be able to return home when you're being held here?"

It took all her self-control not to glance under the bed. "Hope. And positive thinking." She smiled. "It always works in difficult situations."

Emery looked startled for a moment. "Do you really believe that?"

She was about to give him another flippant reply,

when something in his expression stopped her. She held his gaze. "No. I believe in not giving up. No matter the odds."

"That is a good trait to have."

"Why do you act far older than your age?"

"I'm nineteen."

"I know. That doesn't change my question. What made you so serious? Was it becoming a squire at five?"

"How do you know this?"

It took her nearly a minute to decide what to say. "Arwyn spoke of you. Not by name. But as the squire who brought Tarrant to him. You were five. How could anyone have expected that of you?"

"I was the son of one of the knights who served the same lord Tarrant's father served. Five is the typical age to become a squire if you want to be a knight. Tarrant was four when I became his father's squire, having lost his mother when he was a baby. I was the squire of his father for only a few weeks when he died fighting at the side of his lord."

She had no idea what to say. She felt sorry for the baby who'd lost his mother and the young child who'd lost his father. She couldn't imagine what it would be like to grow up knowing her parents had died. "Who looked after Tarrant?"

"Lili did what she could, but she had her own life. Her own children. Kinnon was the same age as Tarrant."

"Kinnon's mum?"

He inclined his head. "Yes. Not exactly Tarrant's stepmother, but she was both the friend and the first wife of his father so technically that is what she is. It was logical for him to ask me to take his son to her since he had no family."

"If Lili didn't always look after Tarrant, then who did?"

"Servants helped take care of him."

"But who did he turn to when he had a problem?" She stepped closer to him, her voice low, determined to learn the answer the more he avoided it. She stared into his sky blue eyes, trying to figure out the glimpse of emotion she saw in them before it was masked. "When he was hurt who did he ask for?"

"Why do you insist on knowing?"

Chapter Fifteen

"He isn't a baby in need of protecting anymore." Trinity watched Emery carefully, but his expression didn't change. "He doesn't need you. There's a year between you. He shouldn't expect to come running to you with his problems." She almost missed the slight change in his expression that told her she'd figured out the truth.

The door opening had Emery stepping away from Trinity, his gaze holding hers a moment longer before he strode over to the servant and took the tray. He remained in front of the door until it was closed and locked before striding to the armchairs and balancing the tray between them on the arms.

Trinity joined him, looking at the two plates of pastries. "How are these any different from the previous ones?"

"Humans should be able to eat these without side effects." Emery sat in one of the armchairs.

Trinity hesitated before sitting in the second armchair. She took one of the pastries. "What sort of side effects?"

"All other food becomes dust and you're unable to eat anything else. It also makes it impossible for you to return to your world for more than a day or two without becoming sick."

She finished off the pastry. "Then why would you eat it?"

"For those with magic it makes no difference to them."

They fell silent as they finished off the pastries and Trinity licked her fingers clean. "Now I'm thirsty."

"One moment." The scent of old campfires filled the air and Emery vanished.

Trinity stared at the empty armchair. Why had he remained with her if he could leave so easily? It didn't make sense.

Emery appeared in front of Trinity holding out a glass of water.

It took her a few seconds to take it. "Why did you return?"

"This is where Tarrant wants me."

She took a mouthful of water as she tried to think

of a polite way to word her question. There was none. "That doesn't make sense. If he can't keep you here, why remain?"

"I have no reason to run from him." Emery returned to the armchair.

It still made no sense. Tarrant wasn't exactly the nicest person. She'd be running as far as she could. The image of Tarrant returning the bottle to his pouch came to mind. She wouldn't run either. But not because she didn't know any better. The moment she could, she was getting away from here. It took all her effort not to glance towards the bed.

Feeling restless, she rose, pacing back and forth. A few times she glanced under the bed, but only when her back was to Emery. Once again it felt like a ridiculously long amount of time passed before the door opened again. She faced it, expecting a servant.

Tarrant strode inside, gesturing towards Emery. "Out."

Emery strode towards the door.

Tarrant grabbed hold of Emery's arm as he walked past him, turning him to face him. "Wait outside the door. Close it on your way out."

Emery nodded.

Trinity glanced through the doorway. The corridor was empty. Her attention was drawn to

Tarrant when he continued to walk towards her. She held her ground. He couldn't hurt her. He'd promised. With magic.

"I can keep you here as long as I like. There's nothing to stop me."

She remained silent. There was nothing she could say to his statement.

"Don't you want to go home?"

"What do you think?" She didn't bother keeping the sarcasm from her voice.

"I already know what I think. I'm interested in learning what you think."

"I guess you'll have to keep wondering then." She wasn't about to tell him anything. Look what he'd done to Arwyn.

Tarrant took several steps forward, stopping centimetres from her. "Do you think you'll always be safe from me?"

"How safe am I from you now?"

"I am unable to harm you. You're a lot safer than you would normally be."

She was tempted to smile, but didn't think Tarrant would take it well. "You're wasting your time. I'm not interested in telling you anything." She did smile this time, a phrase of her father's coming to mind. "Not even the time of day."

"That is something I can figure out for myself."

Her smile didn't slip. "Exactly." It was an effort to keep her smile in place when she saw the anger flare in his eyes.

"You want to be very careful."

She clearly heard the threat in his voice. But Arwyn was alive, of a fashion, and Tarrant couldn't do anything to her. "You might as well let me go. You're wasting your time keeping me here."

Anger flared in his eyes again before he turned and strode from the room, slamming the door behind him. A few seconds later the sound of the door locking proceeded two sets of footsteps travelling along the corridor.

Trinity glanced at the bed, tempted to check on Arwyn. But anyone might arrive, using magic to appear in the room. She returned to pacing, the time slowly passing. After a bit, she dropped onto the bed, staring at the canopy. She drifted off to sleep, startled awake by a sound. Opening her eyes, she found the room filled with shadows and a figure sitting on the bed beside her. It took her a few seconds to realise it was Tarrant. She remained still, staring up at him, only a dim light reaching them from the lantern that hung from the ceiling.

He captured a lock of her hair, running it through his fingers. "How do you know Arwyn?"

His voice was soft enough she barely heard it. She nearly asked him the time, but doubted he'd tell her considering what she'd said to him earlier. "Why do you hate Arwyn? What would have happened if he'd refused to raise you?"

"He's too weak to eliminate rivals before they become a problem."

His tone had sounded too ordinary for what he'd said. Trinity wanted to demand if he was crazy. She slowly sat up, remaining beside him. "Would you have killed a child?"

"I was nothing to him. And he showed me I was nothing by giving my stepbrothers everything and me nothing of equal value."

She almost pointed out that he was eighteen yet sounded like a petulant toddler who hadn't got his own way. It took her a few seconds to contain the words that wanted to escape. "What did he owe you? I would have thought it'd be the other way around." She almost missed his reply when she realised the pouch was not far from where her hand rested on the bed.

"You think I should owe him for something I had no say in?"

Even with how softly he spoke she couldn't miss the anger in his voice. She didn't have a clue how to answer and nearly smiled when she realised the only way to answer was with a question. Like the Fae did. "Why should you care what I think? What do you think?"

He leaned closer to her, brushing her hair back from her ear, his finger tracing the curve. "One could almost believe you were Fae with the way you speak."

She held his gaze, looking deep into his pale blue eyes. "I guess you've never met a politician before." She inched her hand closer to the pouch.

His hand closed over her wrist. "What do you think you're doing?"

"Where's the key?"

"You think I would carry it with me? How would you keep it from me if you managed to find it? The moment I tried to lock the door I'd know it was missing."

She pulled out of his grip, shrugging. "I didn't say I'd thought it through."

Tarrant rose, stepping away from the bed. "There's food on the tray for you." He gestured towards the armchairs before striding from the room.

She stared after him a moment before checking the room. She was alone, but didn't know how long that would last. Slipping onto the floor, she peered under the bed. "Are you awake?" She'd nearly asked him if he was alive, but after all he'd gone through it hadn't seemed like the best way to word her question.

Arwyn drew the blanket off, holding it out to her. "Put it somewhere else and I'll take you from here."

"I can't leave. Tarrant has the antidote." She shoved the blanket onto the bed.

"I promised Kinnon I'd bring you back. With magic. If you don't leave, neither can I."

She slowly shook her head. "Magic sounds like it's more of a problem than it's worth."

Instead of replying, Arwyn took hold of her arm and the scent of his magic filled the air.

Before she could argue, they were in the dungeon, sitting on the cold stone floor. She pulled away from him to stand up, taking the torch from her pocket. "I don't like being dragged places without my permission."

"Trinity."

"Kinnon?" She turned on the torch and pointed it in the direction his voice had come from. "What are you doing here?"

"Waiting to take you home." He crossed the space between them in seconds, wrapping his arms around her waist, pulling her close. "Did he hurt you?"

"He can't. Didn't your father tell you?" She tried to pull away from him.

His arms tightened around her. "There can be ways around magic. Not always, but often."

"He can't harm me." This time when she drew away he let her go. "We have to get out of here. Tarrant used the Petrification enchantment on your father."

Kinnon turned to Arwyn. "When?"

"Take your human home and come back for me. We'll discuss it when we're somewhere safe."

Trinity took several steps away when Kinnon tried to take her hand. "Tarrant can't hurt me, take your father first. If he dies then I'm in danger. Tarrant will go after me if something happens to break his promise."

"If I return without you, Troy said he'd turn me to stone and use your father's sledgehammer on me," Kinnon said.

Trinity grinned. That sounded like Troy.

"He wasn't joking," Kinnon said.

"How long will it take for you to leave your father in my room and come back for me?"

Kinnon sighed heavily. "Likely less time than it will take to convince you to let me take you first." Kinnon rested a hand on his father's shoulder, the two of them disappearing.

Chapter Sixteen

For a moment Trinity regretted telling him to take Arwyn first. She checked the dungeon, the light from the torch not bright enough to show her all of the area at once. It looked the same as last time she was in here. Right down to the closed door. When Kinnon appeared in front of her, she jumped back with a gasp. "I didn't think you'd be that quick. You were barely seconds."

"Ten minutes." He took hold of her hand. "Time doesn't always pass the same between the realms."

The world shimmered and reformed as her room, Troy speaking angrily to Arwyn. "I'm safe." She pulled away from Kinnon, running to Troy.

His arms wrapped tightly around her. "You've been gone too long. I was starting to think you'd been killed or something. So was Rod. He didn't get any sleep last night."

"He…" Her voice trailed off. "How long have I been gone?"

"It's the next day." Troy's grip didn't loosen.

"But…" Again her voice trailed off. "I didn't think I was gone that long." She tried to pull away from Troy. He held her a moment longer before he let her go. "How long were you awake under the bed?" She faced Arwyn.

"A couple of hours. I didn't know if I should come out. Then I heard Tarrant come in." Arwyn was silent for a few seconds. "I never knew he felt that way."

"None of us knew how much he hated us," Kinnon said softly.

"We have to find Lili. She can't be dead," Arwyn said. "And wake your brothers." He turned to Trinity. "You need to wake my sons. They need to know their mother is missing."

She nearly gave in to him. "How much magic do you have to spare? Do you want your sons to die?" She turned to Troy, a glance for Kinnon. "What did you do with the jar of magic?"

"It's in the kitchen," Troy said.

For some reason she found that funny and couldn't help giggling, dropping onto the bed as she struggled to be serious.

"Cauldrons?" Troy asked.

She tried not to grin, but his questioning tone made her realise exactly why she'd found it funny. "Yeah." Seeing the confusion in Kinnon's expression she was finally able to push aside her laughter. "I need to go back."

Kinnon shook his head. "No one will take you back. It isn't safe."

Troy spoke at the same time. "No. Are you crazy?"

She could see that both were determined not to let her go. Needing a few minutes to organise her thoughts, she grabbed a change of clothes, leaving her sneakers by the door. "I need a shower. When I'm finished, you're taking me back to the realms of the Fae." She pointed at Kinnon before retreating to the bathroom.

The time she spent in the shower didn't help to organise her thoughts, only had fear wanting to swamp her each time she considered facing Tarrant again. But she couldn't come up with any other plan. Returning to her room, she stopped not far from the doorway, looking at each of them. They'd broken off their discussion when she'd entered and she wouldn't have been surprised to learn they'd been talking about leaving her behind. "Tarrant has the antidote. He carries it with him in a pouch on his belt."

"Then there's no reason for you to return," Kinnon

said. "He only removes that when he goes to sleep or bathes."

"How else are you meant to get the antidote?"

"I'll get it," Troy said.

She looked at each of them. They'd obviously made their own plans while she'd been in the bathroom. "How?"

"I'll take him to our treasure room where we can get enough gold to pay for it and then I'll take him to the Fringes. You can buy almost anything there," Kinnon said.

"Is the Fringes somewhere without starlight? And are you guaranteed to be able to buy the antidote there?" Trinity slipped her feet into her sneakers, determined to return.

"This is the best plan," Kinnon said. "None of us want to put you in danger again."

Trinity stepped close, her eyes narrowing. "Don't avoid the questions. Will you turn to stone if you take Troy to the Fringes? Can you definitely buy the antidote there?"

Kinnon gathered her hands. "None of us want you harmed."

She refused to be distracted by his avoidance of the questions. "You aren't taking Troy. Take me to the room next to Tarrant's. The one on the left when you're in the corridor facing his door."

"My room?" Kinnon asked.

She shrugged. "I don't know whose room it is. But I could have escaped to there if Arwyn hadn't been turned to stone or I hadn't wanted to try and get the potion." At least she guessed she could have.

Kinnon smiled fleetingly. "Any other time I would willingly take you to my room."

Before she could argue Kinnon's comment, she heard her father speak behind her.

"Don't go, Trin."

She pulled away from Kinnon to face the doorway. For a moment she remained where she was before running to her father and throwing herself into his arms. "I'm sorry you were worried."

Rod crushed her to him, letting go after a moment. "But it won't stop you from going."

She didn't answer straight away. "No." As scared as she'd been at times, everything had made a strange kind of sense. The kind of sense she'd been searching for with every career she'd considered.

"I should have raised you to be self centred."

Laughter burst from her. "Then you shouldn't have set an example by helping out your mates."

Rod gestured towards Kinnon and Arwyn. "They aren't your mates."

She slowly turned, glancing at Arwyn before her gaze was drawn to Kinnon. Her lips curved into a smile. "Aren't they?" None of them wanted her to return. They wanted to protect her. That sounded like mates. "I don't need any of you to protect me. I can protect myself."

"You don't understand our realm," Kinnon said.

"Tarrant could trick you into cancelling the magic keeping you safe," Arwyn said.

"I've watched enough political debates over the years." She glanced at Rod. "And listened to your commentary on their words." She faced Kinnon again. "Promise nothing, question rather than answer and trust no one." She returned to Kinnon. "I can do this. Look at all I've done so far." She took hold of one of his hands, about to ask him to take her back when something occurred to her, filling her with a sense of accomplishment. She didn't know what she'd do with her future, but it had to be something that made a difference. Like what she'd done in the realms of the Fae in helping Arwyn escape. Something worth doing.

"She's as canny as the Fae," Arwyn said. "Quick thinking."

"Of course she's quick thinking," Rod said.

"You're not helping to keep her here," Troy pointed out.

She kept hold of Kinnon's hand and faced Troy, grinning at him. "Do you really think you can convince me to stay?"

"Then take me with you," Troy said.

"No." She tightened her grip on Kinnon's hand. "We have to conserve magic until we can get antidotes." She didn't want Kinnon, or his father, to end up the same as Braeden. Or worse. She faced Kinnon again. "Is there somewhere in your room that starlight doesn't reach?"

"There's one corner, possibly two."

She held his gaze a moment. "Take me to your room." A smile slowly formed. "Now."

"Trinity–"

She ignored the protests behind her. "I can do this."

Kinnon opened his mouth as if he was about to protest, then returned her smile. "Maybe you can."

She started to say that of course she could, but the world shimmered around her, reforming as a room similar to Tarrant's. The only difference was that a woman was chained to a chair that was placed in the sunlight streaming through the doors leading to the balcony, her back to the balcony doors. A goblet rested on the arm of the chair, her hand wrapped around the stem. On the floor at her feet was a sword.

"Mother!" Kinnon tried to move towards the woman.

Trinity pushed him back into the corner. "Starlight. The sun. Don't, Kinnon."

"I have to–"

Trinity interrupted him. "I'll draw the curtains."

The woman had turned her head to look at them when Kinnon had spoken, her head barely visible over the high backed chair. "You're alive." Her voice was filled with relief, her smile echoing her tone.

Trinity kept her hands on Kinnon's chest, pressing against him. "Will you stay out of the light?"

"What happened to your brothers?" Lili asked.

"Kinnon?" Trinity didn't want to move until she was certain he wouldn't step out of the corner.

"They live." Kinnon looked down at Trinity. "Leave the drapes open. Someone might notice if they're closed."

"You'll stay here? You won't move?"

Kinnon took her hands from his chest. "Check on my mother for me. There's no longer any need for you to take her a message, but I'd appreciate you seeing that she's unharmed."

When he let go of her hands, she took a step away,

glancing between him and Lili. "You should get the bolt cutters."

"I can't leave here," Lili said.

When Trinity stepped around in front of Lili, she tried to keep her expression neutral. There was blood splattered across the front of the Fae's gown and bruises around her throat. Her long blond hair was tangled and knotted, her pale skin smudged with dirt and the flesh of her wrists underneath the manacles was torn and bloody. Large blue eyes shimmered with tears.

"What's wrong?" Kinnon demanded.

Lili's gaze held Trinity's. "The two of you need to leave. I'll not put Arwyn's life in any more danger than it already is."

"He's safe from Tarrant where he is," Kinnon said.

At the same time, Trinity asked, "What do you mean?"

Lili looked over her shoulder. "He's safe?"

"None of them are really safe. They're under a Petrification enchantment." Trinity eyed the light coloured liquid in the goblet that was on the arm of the chair. "What is that?"

Lili faced Trinity again. "Poison."

Chapter Seventeen

Movement caught Trinity's attention and she took a step towards Kinnon, her hand stretched out. "Don't you move."

"Get rid of it. I will kill Tarrant for what he's done to our family." Kinnon's voice was low, his tone filled with anger.

Trinity looked from Lili to Kinnon and then to the sunlight streaming through the doors. "It's almost like he expected one of you to try and save your mother."

"It's a trap. But not because he would have expected us. I'm sure he's done something in Darak and Braeden's rooms in case they returned." Kinnon paused a moment. "Why did he leave poison with you?"

Lili's gaze was drawn to the goblet. "He placed Arwyn's sword at my feet and said that if I drank it, he promised to let him go. He said he'd allow Arwyn to walk out of the castle alive and neither him nor his people would raise a weapon against him. I couldn't do it. As long as he continued to negotiate with me, I knew Arwyn lived. But I haven't seen Tarrant for two days. I feared-" Lili's voice broke.

"Arwyn escaped." Trinity looked to Kinnon. "You have to get the bolt cutters. We need to get your mother out of here before someone checks on her."

"Sunrise and sunset. Tarrant brings me food. I haven't seen anyone else since I've been chained here."

"He hasn't fed you in two days?" Kinnon demanded.

Trinity felt the same anger she heard in Kinnon's voice. She didn't know Lili, but no one deserved to be left chained without food or medical attention. "Go, Kinnon. Get the bolt cutters."

"I'm not leaving you here. Look what happened last time."

"Nothing will happen. You need to conserve your magic. Now go and get the bolt cutters." For a moment Trinity thought Kinnon might argue again. He nodded and vanished, the scent of his magic filling the room, dissipating as quickly as it had come.

"Thank you."

Trinity frowned, trying to figure out what Lili meant. "I didn't do anything."

"You didn't tell Kinnon how bad a shape I am in."

"He might have stepped into the sunlight."

Lili smiled slightly. "Exactly."

A noise in the corridor had both of them falling silent. Trinity crept closer to the door. She froze when she heard Tarrant yelling.

"Search again. She's human. She can't have gone far. Keep searching until she's found."

"Yes, my lord," Emery said.

Trinity rushed to the door, pressing her hand against it as she listened to footsteps striding away before Emery had finished speaking. She opened her mouth to call out to him, but what if he didn't help? What if he called Tarrant?

"Don't. He would do anything for Tarrant." Lili's words were soft, barely loud enough for Trinity to hear them.

She closed her eyes, her hand still resting on the door, half convinced he'd left too. She heard slow footsteps start to move away. "Emery." The footsteps stopped.

"Please. Don't call him in." Again Lili's voice could barely be heard.

"Trinity? Where are you?" Emery asked.

Her hand tightened into a fist, still against the door. "Promise me one hour before you consider going to Tarrant."

Emery moved closer to the door. "Are you in Kinnon's room?"

"Promise me."

Emery appeared in the room, the scent of old campfires fading away. "I owe-" His words ended abruptly when he caught sight of Lili.

"Emery, please." Trinity tugged on his arm, trying to gain his attention.

He pulled away from her, striding to Lili, kneeling on one knee in front of her, the sword between them. "My lady, who did this to you?"

Lili smiled sadly, trying to hold out a hand to him. The chain prevented her from reaching him. "One who I never would have expected it from. One who came upon us while we were looking for our sons and offered to help. Someone we trusted and accepted a drink from when we took a few minutes break to rest the horses. They attacked us with magic, causing our horses to rear and Arwyn to be knocked unconscious. The drink had something in it to make me drowsy and when I woke, I was chained in this chair and the person I trusted held out a goblet of poison. He said if I drank it he would let Arwyn walk out of the castle."

"My lady…" Emery slowly shook his head. "My lady…" Again his voice trailed off.

Trinity wanted to tell Lili to give him a name. To tell him before he had the chance to leave and bring Tarrant back.

"Emery, my first husband would have been so grateful for all that you've done for me and his son. But I'm afraid the two of us have failed my first husband. He was there for me when I needed to escape an arranged marriage, promising to take me as his wife until one of us found the right partner. Yet the one thing he asked of me, years later, I failed in doing for him."

Emery continued to slowly shake his head. "No. It isn't possible. You must be mistaken." He took Lili's hand that she continued to hold out.

"I wish that I was." Tears gathered in her eyes again. "When you first brought him to me my heart broke that he should never know his mother and had lost his father after knowing him for so few years. I vowed to do my best by him."

"You always did. None could fault how you treated him. Even though you had your own children to raise you often made time for him," Emery said.

"And yet he isn't the man we tried to raise. He has failed us as much as we've failed his father," Lili said.

Trinity's heart ached at the tone of Lili's voice, wishing she could comfort the woman. But she didn't want to interrupt the two of them. Nor was there anything she could say or do that would help them face so great a betrayal.

Emery bent his head, his shoulders lowering. "He has never–"

The scent of magic filled the room, bringing Emery's head up. Kinnon appeared in the corner, dropping the bolt cutters and reaching for his sword the moment he saw Emery.

Trinity raced across the room. "No. Don't come out of the corner." She flung herself at Kinnon, his sword half unsheathed.

Kinnon slid the sword back into the sheath, moving Trinity to the side. "Never do that again. You might have cut yourself." His gaze was on Emery who'd risen to his feet.

"Stay where you are, Kinnon," Lili ordered. "Do you want to turn to stone?"

Trinity felt Kinnon tense. "You can't help anyone while you're stone. And Emery won't hurt your mother."

"Never," Emery said. "I swore to Tarrant's father

that I'd protect Lili and look after his son. I tried to save him, but the wound was too great and all I could do was promise him what he asked and sit by him on the battlefield for the few minutes he had left."

"No one attacked you?" Trinity asked.

"The battle was moving away from us, but I was a child. No one would have bothered with a child."

Trinity pulled away from Kinnon, picking up the bolt cutters, her gaze on Emery. "Will you help us? Or isn't that possible with the promise you made Tarrant. Oath or whatever you called it."

"I swore an oath to help him protect Lili, he swore an oath too." Emery looked to Lili. "Which is why I can't understand how he could hurt you. He swore to protect you."

"What did he say exactly?" Lili asked.

Trinity went to Lili's side, trying to cut through the manacles. It was impossible so she tried to cut the chain.

Emery took the bolt cutters from her, hissing when his hands touched the metal. He shifted his hands to the plastic grips before cutting through the links close to the manacles. "Tarrant swore to always protect his mother and to speak well of her and never allow others to speak ill of her."

Lili rose from the chair, holding the goblet. She

stumbled and would have fallen if Emery hadn't steadied her. "He has never called me mother. How old was he when he made the promise?"

Emery let the bolt cutters fall to the floor. "Six."

"Then it wasn't us who failed him. He is more like his grandfather than his father. A man no one mourned when he was killed," Lili said.

Trinity picked up the bolt cutters. "What was his grandfather like?"

"He killed by a knife in the back or poison. There was nothing honourable about him. Tarrant can't be like his grandfather," Emery said.

Lili held out the goblet. "Can't he?"

"We don't have time for this. We have to leave." Trinity strode to Kinnon's side. "Take these with you."

He took the bolt cutters. "Why can't you carry them?"

"Because you're taking your mother back. I have something else to do. Remember?"

"We'll find another way. Emery can help," Kinnon said.

Emery took the goblet from Lili and placed it on the chair before picking up the sword and helping Lili over to Kinnon. "What do you need help with?"

Kinnon stared at his mother, shock on his face at his first proper look at her. "He will pay."

Lili nodded, taking the sword from Emery, clinging to Kinnon. "I can wait here until you take Trinity to safety."

"I'm fine. Emery can help me while Kinnon takes you back to my place," Trinity said.

Lili laughed softly. "Someone who throws around as many orders as you, Kinnon. That must be interesting to watch."

The smell of magic had them facing the middle of the room where Tarrant appeared in front of the chair, a tray of food in his hands. He let it fall to the floor, crockery smashing and food scattering as he drew his sword. "You would betray me, Emery?"

Trinity stepped away from Kinnon. "Go. Now."

"I won't leave-"

"Don't be stupid. Go. There's nothing to stop him from hurting your mother. Look at her." Trinity stepped further away from Kinnon. "Hurry."

Tarrant took a step towards them. "Leave and I will kill Arwyn."

"That's a little hard to do since we have him," Trinity said.

"Once I have him back I'll kill him," Tarrant warned. "Then you won't be safe either."

"I swore to protect Lili." Emery wrapped an arm around Trinity's waist, taking her from the room. When the world came back into focus, they were in a small room with a single bed and a trunk at the foot of it.

Chapter Eighteen

Trinity pulled away from Emery. "What about Kinnon and Lili?"

"You were all that was keeping Kinnon from saving his mother." Emery took a cloth rucksack from the trunk and put the clothes from the trunk into it, along with a pocket watch. He stripped the blanket from the bed and rolled it up to strap it to the top of the rucksack before slipping his arms through the straps.

"What are you doing?"

"Leaving. I can't stay here. What is it that Lili's sons need?"

"An antidote for a Petrification enchantment."

The scent of Emery's magic momentarily filled the room and he held out what looked like a piece of bark. "I'll leave you somewhere safe, but if you need me, call my name and it will help me find you."

She slipped the bark into a pocket. "Is there anywhere safe in this realm?"

Emery smiled. "Most don't look for safety when they come to the realms of the Fae."

The scent of magic filled the small room as Tarrant appeared, dragging Trinity behind him. "You're too predictable, Emery."

"Let her go, Tarrant. What use is she to you when you can't harm her?"

"If Arwyn ever dies I'll be able to harm her until she begs for death. But for now, I'll put her somewhere none of you will be able to find her. I'll see how many of you are willing to exchange yourselves for her safe return. Give them my message, Emery. Tell them if enough offer to take her place I'll set her free."

She tried to pull away from Tarrant. He was too strong. As he took them to another location, she grabbed the dagger he wore, striking out at him with it when the world reformed.

He knocked the dagger from her hand and tried to hit her. It was as if something stopped him. Lowering his hand, he stepped close. "One day I'll be able to do that and you'll regret everything you've tried to do."

"I regret nothing. Not now and not later." She met his angry gaze, the wind blowing her hair back from her face.

"So you say now." Tarrant stepped away, making a sweeping gesture. "But can you really say that when this is where you'll remain until Arwyn dies? For I doubt they'll be willing to offer me enough of them to make me want to let you go."

Trinity wanted to tell him he was wrong. Not a single one of them would exchange themselves for her, but she couldn't be certain of that. There was always the chance Kinnon would do something stupid. To keep herself from blurting out the words, Trinity looked around, barely managing to control her expression when she realised where she was. They stood atop a mountain, a sheer drop over the edge she stood beside, a green valley below. The plateau where they stood was about five metres across and the drop to the valley had to be at least three hundred metres. There was no escape. Glancing in the opposite direction, she saw foothills in the distance, but nothing close. The land dropped away on this side, less steeply than it did on the other side. Although not by much. In the direction of the hills dark clouds formed.

"Speechless?" Tarrant collected his dagger, sheathing it.

"I was admiring the view." There was no way she

was about to let him know how terrified she was. What if that was an electrical storm?

Tarrant stepped close to the edge overlooking the valley. "See that bent and twisted tree with the boulder at the base?"

She nodded.

"That's where my father died. Emery brought me here when I was six. He tried to make me promise to protect Lili, but I tricked him. He thought he was so clever at seven. As if that single year made him wiser than me. But he wasn't clever enough."

She stared at the grassy patch, unable to imagine someone dying there let alone a battle raging in the peaceful valley. "Do you miss him? Or miss the fact you never had the chance to know him?"

Tarrant laughed. "Him dying like that saved me the need to kill him."

Her gaze was drawn to him, shock filling her. "Kill him?"

Tarrant grinned. "I can see that bothers you. The sons in my family tend to kill their fathers. My grandfather killed his father and my father killed my grandfather. I'm sure I would have done the same one day."

"Why?" The thought of something happening to

her father was bad enough. She couldn't imagine wanting to kill him.

Tarrant's only answer was a smile before he vanished.

She glared at the spot he'd been. There were more questions she'd wanted to ask. Growling in frustration, she drew out the piece of bark, speaking Emery's name. Nothing happened. Was anything supposed to happen? How did it work? She held it closer to her lips. "Emery."

The breeze increased and dragged the bark from her hand, swirling it away and out of sight. She stared in the direction it had gone, seeing only the valley surrounded by a forest. Her gaze was drawn to the place where Tarrant's father had died. Why would he have killed his father if he'd lived? She couldn't imagine there to be any good reason. A man who would save a friend from an arranged marriage didn't sound like the type of person others would want to kill. And especially not their own child. Maybe Emery would know. She glanced around. Emery was nowhere in sight. She examined the mountaintop.

Nearly every side was a sheer drop, on the far side there was the slightest of slopes and plants struggled to grow in the mostly rocky soil. She checked them over, examining the root system. Some would pull easily from the ground, others would cling tenaciously, even with part of her weight dragging at them. Her gaze was drawn to the ever darkening clouds. If Emery didn't hurry, she was getting out of here. There was no way she could remain out in the open in a thunderstorm.

Pacing the mountaintop, she kept checking the sky. Back and forth she went, crossing the distance in six or seven steps, five if she took unnaturally large ones. Emery didn't come. She stopped on the side of the mountaintop with the foothills, staring down the slope. It was almost vertical, barely worthy of the name slope. Yet she couldn't remain on the mountaintop until Arwyn died. He was likely to outlive her. She didn't want to spend the rest of her life here.

She crouched at the edge. Some of the plants looked like ones they'd planted in a rock wall garden, a couple of years ago, for one of her father's clients. The bark was gnarled and the leaves fine, but in spring they were covered in dainty flowers. There were no flowers now and she didn't know if they were the same plant, but they looked like they'd take part of her weight.

Easing over the edge, she took a deep breath, trying not to think about the clouds forming behind her. Finding a toehold, she eased further over the edge. Then she was clinging to the side of the mountain, wondering at her sanity. It reminded her of abseiling, but without the rope and harness. She tried not to think of how far below the nearest foothill was. Not as far as the valley had been on the opposite side, but probably somewhere between a hundred and fifty and two hundred metres. A drop she wouldn't survive if she fell. A pity Troy hadn't taken her mountain climbing instead of abseiling. It would have been a lot more useful right now.

Reaching for another plant, she tugged on it before she let it take part of her weight. Metre by metre she made her way down the slope, rocks slipping out from beneath her feet, but the plants always holding. The day grew darker and she hoped it was because the sun would set soon. Then she changed her mind, not wanting to be stuck out here in the dark. A crack of thunder sounded and she froze, closing her eyes tightly, reminding herself to breathe.

This couldn't be possible. Stuck on a mountaintop was bad enough, but in an electrical storm? Maybe it was only thunder. She forced her eyes open and turned her head to scan the sky. Lightning forked out of the clouds, thunder following several seconds later. The clouds rolled across the sky, rapidly approaching.

"No." The word was a whisper, but it wouldn't have mattered if she'd shouted it. There was no one to hear. She flinched as lightning lit the darkening sky, thunder following.

She drew in a sharp breath. If it rained, there was a good chance the plants would come loose and she'd plummet down the mountain. "I can't do this." Again the words were a whisper. But she had to. She couldn't continue to cling to the side. Looking upwards, she doubted she could return to the mountaintop. Each time lightning lit the sky she flinched, remaining where she was.

Her only option was down. Looking for another plant to cling to, she reached for it, trying to focus on what was close, not the oncoming storm. Humming didn't work. What she needed was earplugs. Or music. Anything to block out the sound of the thunder. And probably something to block the flashes of light.

What had happened to Emery? Had Tarrant found him? He'd followed Emery to his room easily enough. Surely he was okay. But then that would mean he'd deserted her.

Thinking over the problem helped her descend another ten metres. She glanced down, surprised she was around a quarter of the way. Thunder and lightning had her flinching again and this time she slid down a metre. Her heart pounded as she clung to a plant, trying to slow her breathing. She didn't want to hyperventilate and pass out. That would kill her. She fleetingly wondered what that would do to Tarrant since he was the one who'd left her here, but didn't want to find out.

Prying her hand away from the plant, she reached for another one, the light barely visible. Shortly she wouldn't be able to see anything, except when lightning lit the sky. A shudder ran through her. Now that was something she'd never thought to think about positively. Not in the slightest.

"Keep moving," she ordered herself. Her hands didn't obey. The sky lit up and she remained frozen until the roll of thunder faded away. She managed to travel another couple of metres before lightning flashed across the sky again, freezing her in place. It was going to take her forever to climb down the mountain. Droplets of rain fell on her.

A groan escaped. She was dead. The rain was likely to become heavier and she'd be washed down the mountain. Her gaze was drawn upwards. There was absolutely no way she could return to the top. Lightning lit the sky and she drew in a shuddering breath, her grip tightening on the plants. Was she halfway? She looked down. It wasn't bright enough to see. She could barely see a metre away.

Grabbing another plant, she inched lower, struggling to see in the rapidly fading light. Then it was impossible and she was blindly reaching for another plant, screaming as it tore from the dirt and she slid what felt like metres, but was probably barely one, before she grabbed hold of a plant, her hands stinging, but the plant holding.

Chapter Nineteen

Lightning forked across the sky and Trinity saw blood on her fingers. Seconds later she heard Tarrant yell her name from atop the mountain. She pressed herself close to the slope, barely daring to breathe. Would he see her if he looked over the edge? Looking up she stared into the dark.

"Trinity!"

There was no way she was about to answer him. She'd rather be struck by lightning. It'd probably be safer in the long run.

"Answer me. Where are you? How did you hurt yourself in a way to cause it to rebound onto me? Trinity! What did you do?"

When the sky was filled with light, she saw him silhouetted at the edge, looking out towards the foothills. It went dark again. When the lightning lit the sky once more, he was gone. The thunder rumbled away, bringing silence. Had he left? She couldn't tell. And she couldn't stay here. She had to move. She almost smiled at the thought of her injuries hurting him. Almost. If there hadn't been an electrical storm she might have managed a smile.

When the sky brightened again, she stared at the nearby plant that looked like it would support her weight. She tried to move while the sky was lit, but it was impossible. It wasn't until the thunder quietened that she was able to move, holding her breath as she reached for the plant she'd seen. Her fingers closed around it and she tugged. The plant held and she went a little lower.

Bit by bit she made her way down the mountain, trying to move during the displays of light and noise. It was impossible. She tried to remind herself it was a miracle she could move at all. Yet it didn't help. "Idiot," she muttered. The lightning filled the sky again and she caught a glimpse of a ledge below her, about three metres away.

Scrambling for it, she collapsed onto the ledge, huddling against the dirt of the slope as the rain went from large random drops to light but steady. She couldn't go any further. Closing her eyes, she breathed in deeply. At least she hadn't been on the mountaintop when Tarrant came back. During the next flash of light, she stared at her hands, finding that they were grazed, the blood washing away in the light rain.

The scent of magic filled the air and Emery appeared in front of her, the lightning highlighting him as he fell over the edge. She automatically grabbed for him, the thunder rumbling around them, pain causing her to gasp. She clung to him tightly with one hand, worried he'd slip down the rest of the slope, trying to keep her tone even. "What took you so long?"

Emery grabbed hold of the ledge before letting go of her hand. "I went to the Fringes to see if I could buy the antidote." He pulled himself up beside her.

"Could you?" She pressed herself against the slope of the mountain, trying not to think of what had nearly happened. But like the tree struck by lightning, the moment played over again in her mind. Would he have died? If it hadn't been for the amount of time she'd spent frozen, pressed against the slope, she might have been in the foothills by now.

"I was told to visit a Troll village if I wanted any."

"And it took you all this time to find out there was none." She tried not to flinch as the entire sky was lit up. It didn't help. If there'd been a bed nearby, she'd have likely been under it. Something she hadn't done in a decade.

"I was waylaid by someone Tarrant had upset. Someone Tarrant likely misled me about."

"Did they hurt you?" She couldn't see him in the dark. But didn't want to see badly enough that she wanted lightning to strike again.

"I convinced him I was no longer Tarrant's knight. That I was protecting Lili from Tarrant." Emery was silent a moment. "In the end he agreed to let me go if I took him and half a dozen of his knights into the castle so he could go after Tarrant. He didn't trust me not to find a loophole so I was forced to transport him back and forth each time I took one of his knights."

She rested a hand on his arm, flinching at the lightning. "I'm sorry."

"Why?"

"That you were betrayed by Tarrant." She could only imagine how painful an experience that must be, but was certain the reality would be worse than she could imagine.

Emery met her gaze during the seconds light filled the sky. "You're a strange creature."

Laughter burst from her as she glanced at the slight point to his ears during the next burst of light. "Yeah, sure." Thunder cracked and her laughter faded. For a moment the lightning hadn't frozen her in place. She'd been too surprised by Emery's comment.

"Are you all right?"

"I've had better days."

Lightning filled the sky again and he took her hand, looking at her palm when she breathed in sharply. "You're injured."

"That's my fault. I tried to get off the mountaintop." Although if the magic was anything to go by, it was actually Tarrant's fault.

Emery drew her to her feet. "I'll take you somewhere safer."

"Somewhere without a thunderstorm?"

The scent of magic filled the air and the world reformed as a town. "I'll arrange a room for you in the tavern." He let go of her hand, gesturing towards the nearby building. "I'll have them prepare a bath and food for you while we decide what needs to be done next."

"What is this place?" She shivered in the cool night air, her wet clothes not helping.

"It's a human village. You'll be able to eat the food here."

She glanced at the sky. The stars were out and there was no sign of the storm. "How far are we from the mountaintop? And from Arwyn's castle. Will the storm reach here?"

"Possibly. Eventually. Or it might be over before it can arrive. The mountaintop is only a few hours from Arwyn and Lili's castle."

"Tarrant said his father and grandfather had both killed their fathers and he would have killed his too if he hadn't died. What did he mean?"

Emery didn't answer immediately. "Tarrant's grandfather was an evil man. When his own father tried to kill him, he killed him instead."

"What about Tarrant's father?"

"He was forced to kill his own father to keep those he cared for safe."

Trinity had no idea what to say and silence stretched between them.

Emery gestured towards the tavern. "Do you want to get cleaned up and eat?"

She looked down at herself, a nearby lantern showing her how terrible she looked. The rain hadn't washed away the mud, probably only made it worse. "Yeah." If anyone saw the state she was in now they might blame Emery. "Thank you for coming to get me." She certainly didn't want to get him killed after all he'd done for her.

"I should have been there sooner. I'm sorry." The

scent of his magic filled the air and he held out a piece of bark. "In case you have need of me again."

She stared at it for a few seconds before pocketing it. "Thank you."

Emery inclined his head before turning and leading her inside.

She gazed at the inside of the tavern and the customers. It was what she'd imagined a medieval tavern to look like, right down to the barmaids weaving between the crowded tables serving drinks. "They're humans?"

Emery nodded towards the corner. "There are a couple of Fae here." He led the way to the bar, talking to the bartender in a low voice.

Trinity was too fascinated by the people around her to worry about what Emery and the bartender were talking about. She wanted to show Troy this place. And her father. Surely there was no reason why he couldn't visit the realms of the Fae to see how amazing it was. She watched as a barmaid slipped past customers, headed for the bar, her tray empty. She turned and listened to the barmaid list off the drinks that had been ordered.

"You show this girl to a room while I pour the drinks." The bartender gestured towards Trinity.

"Give her fresh towels. A bath is being sent up for her. Put her in room eight."

The barmaid nodded, glancing at Trinity. "This way." A smile made a brief appearance. "Looks like you could do with a wash."

Trinity glanced at Emery, who nodded, before she followed the barmaid through the crowd and up a set of timber stairs. The woman unlocked a door partway along the hallway to reveal a storage cupboard. She handed Trinity a well-worn towel before locking the door and continuing along the hallway.

The woman opened another door, gesturing inside. "Your bath won't be too long." She hurried back the way she'd come before Trinity had the chance to speak.

Stepping inside the room, Trinity saw it contained a single bed, a trunk at the foot of it, and a table and chair beside a window. The room was sparse, but clean. A noise had her spinning to face the door.

"Want it anywhere in particular?" A boy carried a wooden tub over one shoulder.

Trinity shrugged. That was not what she'd expected when Emery had suggested she might want a bath. "You don't have running water?"

The boy placed the tub on the floor in the middle of the room. "We're not that fancy. You want fancy, you chose the wrong place." He headed for the door, pausing as he reached it, looking over his shoulder. "Water is on the way."

She remained where she was standing, even after the boy had walked away. Surely they weren't going to lug water up the stairs. A few minutes later, she learned that was exactly what they planned to do. She watched as buckets of water were tipped into the tub by two young men, steam rising from the water. The boy returned with a pile of clothes and a plate of food, leaving them on the bed and handing over a bar of soap before he left.

Chapter Twenty

Alone, Trinity closed and locked the door, sliding the bolt into place. It was a few seconds before she could bring herself to strip off her clothes and climb into the tub. She breathed in sharply, the water stinging her grazed hands. The rest of her body welcomed the warmth, aching muscles easing slightly.

She felt dazed. And more than a little confused. This realm was full of strange and unexpected places. The castle came to mind, quickly followed by Tarrant and the antidote. She didn't know what Trolls were like or if they'd give them an antidote, but she knew where one bottle was to be found. Was the storm there? It'd cause enough noise to mask her breaking into Tarrant's room. That was if she could bring herself to move and not crawl under the bed.

She ran the bar of soap over her arms, watching as suds and dirt made the clear bathwater become cloudy. She'd frozen on the mountain slope. But at least she'd been able to focus and plan her next move. It had surprised her. She'd never been able to do that before. No other ideas came to mind, and as clean as she was likely to get, she left the soap on the edge of the tub and clambered out, drying herself on the towel.

The clothes had a medieval look to them and she was pretty certain the trousers and long sleeve shirt had been hand sewn. Since there was no underwear with the garments, she put her own back on before dressing, relieved she hadn't been soaked through to the skin. Slipping the piece of bark into a pocket of the trousers, along with her phone, she turned towards the food. After eating, she bundled up her clothes and headed downstairs, finding Emery at the foot of the steps, patiently waiting for her.

Without a word, he took her clothes and put them inside a calico drawstring bag, slipping the string over one shoulder once he'd pulled it tight, closing the bag. He looked her up and down. "Are you fine? Do you need to rest?"

She shook her head. "No. We need the antidote."

"Where do you wish to go?"

She took a deep breath, trying not to think of the storm. "When will Tarrant go to sleep?"

"Have you forgotten there are others also waiting for him to sleep?"

She had. It took her a few seconds to rethink her plan. "What if we see what they're doing? We might be able to use them as a distraction."

"We'll find the antidote another way."

"Can you promise me that?"

Emery didn't answer immediately. He inclined his head. "Once you have the antidote, where do you wish to go?"

"Home."

"Where is home?"

She wasn't sure what she should answer. A moment ago she'd been certain she knew the answer to that question. Not that it mattered. They needed to get the antidote to Kinnon and his family. "Brisbane, Australia."

"I've visited that city before. There were a few of us, Tarrant one of them. We danced in a garden along the riverbank, watching fireworks in the sky."

The pain in his voice made her want to comfort him, but there wasn't the time. "That will do." She held out her hand. "Can we see if the men have attacked yet?"

"It will be better for us if they haven't." Emery took her hand.

Her grip tightened. "Wait."

"What is wrong?"

She hesitated. "You said they were angry with you."

He inclined his head again.

"Will they… I mean…" She struggled to find the words. "I don't want you hurt."

He was silent, his gaze roaming over her face. "You mean those words. It would bother you if I was harmed."

A wry smile formed at the confusion she heard in his voice. "Sometimes I think it's a failing. Or at least it seems to get me in trouble a lot of the time."

He clasped his other hand around the hand he held. "If Tarrant had a fraction of your compassion he would have been a knight worth following and protecting. I will keep you safe."

She was startled by the fierceness of his words. "Who'll keep you safe?"

"The same person who's always had that task."

"Who?"

"Myself."

She wrapped her hand around his, ignoring the pain from her grazes, wanting to tell him she was sorry. Meeting his gaze she saw nothing in his eyes to let her know he was bothered by the situation. It made her ache for him. Her hands tightened around one of his that cupped hers, automatically leaning closer. "You aren't alone anymore."

"Kinnon is very lucky."

Before she could protest his words, the world shimmered around them, reforming as Emery's room.

He pushed her behind him when several Fae drew swords. "We've come to help."

A Fae sheathed his sword, motioning for those with him to do the same. "Earlier you said we're on our own."

"There's something we need. I can take you closer to Tarrant's room once he's asleep," Emery offered.

"How close?" the Fae demanded.

"His balcony."

The Fae looked to his companions. One of them shrugged. "How do we know this isn't a trick?"

"Because I'm going too," Trinity said. "I'll be entering the bedroom with you."

"As will I," Emery said.

"How many of us will fit on the balcony?" the Fae asked.

"You and about half your knights," Emery said.

There was a long silence and Trinity fought the urge to break it, watching as Emery and the Fae held each other's gazes. Eventually the Fae nodded.

Emery dropped the drawstring bag of Trinity's clothes on the chest at the foot of his bed. "I'll return as soon as Tarrant retires for the night. If you harm the girl, I will warn the castle's inhabitants that you're here."

Before Trinity could protest being left behind, Emery vanished, the smell of old campfires fading. She nearly took a step backwards when the Fae eyed her up and down.

"What's your name, human?"

"Trinity." She met his gaze, not impressed with his tone. "What's yours?"

"Tomas." He paused. "What is it you need from Tarrant?"

She wasn't about to trust him. He was well armed and planned to secretly attack. "Once I have what I want, I won't be staying. We're leaving the moment I find it."

"That doesn't tell me what you're after."

"No, it doesn't." She met his hazel eyes, holding her ground. She was surprised when he laughed.

"I'll have to ask Emery if he'll part with you. I wouldn't mind a pet like you."

Her chin rose and she glared at Tomas. "I'm no one's pet."

"Then what are you?"

She had no idea what to tell him.

One of his knights turned away from the window he was looking out. "There's a storm rapidly approaching. We're likely to be drenched going in through the balcony doors."

She wanted to close her eyes and sink to the ground. They didn't need the storm for cover. They had these Fae. Or at least half of them. Keeping her eyes open, she crossed the room, turning sideways to get through the press of bodies. "How far away is it?" Looking out the window she saw stars above, none further away. The clouds were moving in, obscuring the stars. She tried not to shudder, but couldn't help it.

"What's wrong?" Tomas demanded.

"A cool breeze." She wasn't about to tell him she was terrified of lightning. Not that she could see any yet, but if it was the same storm she'd been in earlier, it would arrive quicker than she liked. She remained at the window, staring off into the distance, still there when she saw the first lot of lightning fork across the sky, thunder following. Forcing herself to remain where she was, she counted the seconds, her hands gripping the window ledge. Why couldn't the storm have waited? A shiver ran through her when lightning filled the sky again, lighting it up bright enough it could have been day.

Tomas grabbed one of her hands, tightening his grip when she tried to pull away. "You're cold. Why stand there when you're cold?" He tugged her away from the window, looking to one of his knights. "Close the window. I won't be accused of letting her sicken because she has no sense."

She finally managed to drag her hand from his grip. "What else is there to do while we wait, other than see what's happening outside?" She barely managed not to flinch when thunder sounded directly overhead.

Emery arrived, the scent of old campfires accompanying him. "Tarrant has retired for the night." He drew Trinity close to him. "You're unharmed?"

She nodded, surprised at the relief she felt at his return. "We're going now?" Maybe they'd get in and get the antidote before the storm came too close and anyone learned how terrified she was of lightning.

"Yes."

Tomas grabbed Emery's arm. "Take me with you."

"Make him leave the girl behind." One of his knights grabbed Emery's other arm. "He might be leading you into a trap."

"I give you my word," Emery said.

"But your word about what." The knight continued to hold Emery's arm.

Trinity reluctantly pulled away from Emery. "Take me next. I'll wait for you."

Emery held her gaze, nodding after a few seconds. "I will come for you."

He disappeared before she could say anything in reply, taking Tomas and his knight with him, leaving her to wonder at what his expression had meant. He returned in less than a minute, appearing centimetres from her, gently taking her hand. She smiled up at him. "That was quick."

"I apologise for taking so long earlier." He held out his hand to a nearby knight. "Will you join us?"

She wanted to tell Emery that she hadn't been referring to earlier. It had been surprise that had made her comment. But the world shimmered and reformed, large drops of rain falling down on them. She looked upwards when Emery let go of her hand and disappeared. The stars were almost completely hidden, only a handful struggling to show through the cloud cover. Around her the darkness pressed in. The sounds of the two who'd been left on the balcony earlier were soft as they whispered quietly to each other, the third knight joining them.

Emery returned, bringing another one of the knights. He stood in front of the Fae. "If something happens to me, can you take Trinity to the human world? I've brought you closer than we originally agreed upon."

The night lit up behind her, thunder sounding in the distance, silencing the protests she'd been about to make.

"This is for you," Tomas said.

"It benefits you. We chose to bring you with us. If we didn't, we might have made it difficult for you to go through with your plan," Emery said.

"Where in the human world?" Tomas asked.

"Brisbane, Australia," Emery said.

Tomas didn't answer immediately. "I'll leave her in the city. I've been to a park there."

Regaining her speech, she started to protest again. She wasn't about to leave Emery behind. He spoke before she could say anything.

"That is acceptable."

Chapter Twenty-One

Trinity wanted to argue it wasn't acceptable to her. She didn't want anything to happen to Emery because he was helping her. Once again she missed the opportunity to protest. He opened the door and stepped inside. Lightning lit up the sky again, thunder on its heels. She froze, barely able to breathe. She couldn't do this. She'd been crazy to think she could.

Emery turned, taking her hand and drawing her forward with him, keeping her close, his grip on her hand tight.

She held on equally tight, ignoring the pain as she struggled not to drag her hand from his grip and look for the nearest hiding place. She should have known better than to think she was capable of doing anything during an electrical storm. She stumbled against Emery.

He pulled her tight against him, staying motionless. His breath brushed across her cheek. "Not far. We'll be able to leave soon. I will protect you."

The room lit up and thunder sounded again, chasing all words from her mind. She could only cling to Emery, his wiry strength reminding her of Kinnon's and Troy's. Yet being pressed against his body felt nothing like being held by either of them.

Lanterns sprang to life, the scent of Tarrant's magic filling the room as he came out of the bed towards them, a sword in his hand. Tomas intercepted him and Emery dragged Trinity with him to the dressing table. He grabbed the pouch, pressing it into her hands.

She clutched it against her chest, Emery's hand drawn from hers. She spun to see Tarrant had dragged him back, guards having entered the room to attack the Fae with them, the different scents of magic mixing. Balls of fire were thrown by one of the guards. Emery raised a hand to block it, a gust of wind swirling around him.

Emery pulled out of Tarrant's grip, drawing his sword, attacking with both the weapon and gusts of wind. Tarrant blocked, grinning as he sent his own gust of wind at Emery, taunting his skills, or what he considered lack of skills.

Trinity remained frozen for what felt like far too long before she realised she should be doing something. She plunged a hand into the pouch, finding the potion bottle and shoving it in her pocket, her fingers brushing against the bark and her phone. There was nothing else in the pouch that could help so she let it drop to the floor, frantically looking for a weapon. Not that she had any idea how to use one. She spotted a blanket lying on the chest at the foot of the bed and ran towards it, grabbing it and facing Tarrant and Emery who continued to fight. Both held their own, neither advancing nor retreating. But that was about to change. Two guards strode towards Emery, swords ready. She ran back to Emery, throwing the blanket at Tarrant.

With a roar, Tarrant burst from the folds of the material, reaching for Trinity. Emery grabbed her hand first. With another roar, Tarrant attacked Emery, blood coating his blade before Emery was able to take them from the room.

The world reformed around them and Trinity grabbed hold of Emery as he collapsed against her, late afternoon light startling her. She felt a dampness against her hand and drew it away from his side, staring at the blood. "Emery." The word was a whisper as his weight dragged her to the ground, his sword falling from his grip. She pressed her hand against his side. "No. Don't…" Her voice trailed off as she met his gaze. His sky blue eyes were filled with pain.

"I'm sorry."

She leaned close to hear his words. "What for?"

"I didn't return you to Kinnon."

Anger raced through her. "I don't belong to him. If anything, he and his brothers belong to me since they were given to me." She kept her hand pressed against his side. "Tell me what to do. Can't you use magic to stop the bleeding or something?"

"If I had more power. I've exhausted what I had available."

She thought of the jam jar in her kitchen that was filled with magic. "Don't you dare die on me." Her words were fierce and she glared at Emery when he momentarily smiled. "I'm serious." Wiping her hand against her trousers, she took out her phone, calling Troy.

"Where have you been?"

"Use the lost phone function to find me and bring the jar of magic. Hurry."

"What's wrong?"

"I don't have time to explain. I have the antidote." She hung up, returning the phone to her pocket before pressing her hand against Emery's wound again. A glance around showed they were in a backyard, washing hanging on a nearby clothesline and the curtains at the windows of the house drawn closed. She felt too exposed. There was a shady tree near a timber garden shed at the back corner of the yard. "Can you move?"

"I can try." Emery struggled to rise.

She helped him to his feet, supporting part of his weight as they stumbled their way across the yard and collapsed in the shadows between the tree and shed. "Stay here." She ran to the clothesline and grabbed a couple of t-shirts, running back to him. Her breath froze in her throat when she saw the spread of blood across his shirt. She dropped to her knees in front of him. "How bad is it?" She drew up his shirt, gasping at the gash angling across his side, swallowing hard when she thought she might have caught a glimpse of bone. Was that his rib?

"Will you stay with me to the end?" He took hold of her hand, his grip weak.

"You're not going to die." She drew her hand from his, pressing one of the shirts against the wound, putting pressure on it in the hope it'd stop the flow of blood. "Why didn't I learn first aid?" Although this looked beyond that. What she needed was a surgeon.

Someone who could stitch him up. Wild ideas raced through her mind.

"Why are you so concerned? You've called for someone to come fetch you. Tarrant is in the realms of the Fae. You're safe."

Her gaze was drawn to his. "Because you aren't safe. Why aren't you more concerned?"

A slight smile appeared, before disappearing as fast as it had arrived. "Who is there to miss me when I'm gone?"

Pain arrowed through her and she tried to blink back tears. She started to say she'd miss him, but didn't think it would matter to him. "Lili will."

The slight smile made another brief appearance. "Tarrant won't."

Anger chased away the ache in her chest. "Don't think about him. He's not worth wasting a single second on."

"So fierce. It no longer surprises me that Kinnon is interested in a human."

"You better not say I'm his again. Because I'm not."

"Then why fight so hard on his behalf. And on my behalf."

The world shimmered and she realised it was tears ruining her vision. Not wanting to take pressure off his wound, she turned her head to first one side and then the other to wipe her eyes against her shoulders. "I only fight for those worth saving."

"You might not want me to think of Tarrant, but what of all those I've punished on his behalf. Ones I believed were guilty. I've thought of everything he's ever told me and all his statements could be taken more than a single way. How many of them were innocent?"

"Emery..." She wanted to protest the blame she could hear in his voice. The words wouldn't form.

"Even you know I'm guilty."

"All you're guilty of is keeping a promise to a dying man. Even I'd do that."

Emery placed a hand over one of hers, blood coating it. "Would you keep a promise to me?"

She leaned close, his voice growing more faint. She felt his breath brush across her face and she closed her eyes, struggling not to let tears fall. "It isn't fair."

"What isn't fair?"

She met his gaze again. "What have you done that is for you, not a dying man?" Where was Troy? How far were they from her home? She couldn't look away from Emery to see if anyone was coming to help.

"The time of a landless Fae knight belongs to their lord."

That was what she'd feared. While she'd spent her

life living it the way she'd wanted, he'd spent his protecting others. How had the three brothers spent their lives? "And your childhood? Or were you too busy being a squire?" She wanted to scream for Troy. What was taking him so long?

"I only have one regret." His gaze was drawn to her lips. "Possibly two." His gaze returned to her eyes. "If you want that magic I once offered, then ask for it before it's too late."

"What can I do to save you?" The sound of running feet caught her attention and she drew back to see Troy coming towards her, a jar of magic in one hand, his phone in the other. Relief rushed through her. "Troy!"

He came to a skidding stop, crouching beside her. "What happened? Who is this?"

"Emery." She looked from her hands to the jar. "Open it for me."

Troy opened the jar. "What do we do with it?"

Her gaze was drawn to Emery's face. His eyes were closed. "Emery." No reply came and fear raced through her. "Emery. You have to tell me what to do." There was only silence.

"He's lost a lot of blood," Troy said softly.

She shook her head, refusing to accept the meaning behind his words. "He will be okay." She grabbed the jar from Troy, drawing the shirt away from the wound. She ignored Troy's indrawn breath, tipping magic into the wound. It sank in, but nothing else happened.

"I don't think it works like that."

She tipped more into the wound. "He can't die. I won't let him."

"I'll get a blanket from my ute. We can't take him away looking like this. Someone is likely to call the cops. And there's no way we can easily explain the existence of the Fae." Troy waited a few seconds before he walked away.

"Emery. Please." She tipped more magic into the wound, watching as it sank into him. "Emery." When he still didn't answer, she pressed her ear against his chest. For a moment she couldn't hear his heart over the roar of sound in her ears. Then she heard it. A faint sound that had another rush of fear washing over her. "Do not die on me." Drawing away from him, she looked from the wound to the jar of magic. She had to try something else. This obviously wasn't working. Taking a deep breath, she held out a bloodstained hand, tipping magic into it.

Chapter Twenty-Two

For a moment the magic remained on Trinity's hand, pins and needles prickling her skin when it sank in. Not knowing if that was enough, she tipped more onto her palm, watching as the magic slowly sank in while she poured it over her hand. There was only a quarter of a jar left when she stopped, putting the lid back on so it didn't get tipped over, bloodstains on the outside of the glass and lid. Placing it in the dirt, she tried to figure out what to do. She didn't have a clue.

Leaning close, she pressed her lips against his ear. "Emery. What do I do?"

He turned his head towards her. "Trinity?"

Her lips were near his. "Tell me what to do. How do I use magic?"

"Feel it. Will it."

She pressed a hand against his wound. "Help me."

He placed a hand over hers. "Feel it."

She was about to say she couldn't when she realised that she could. "I can feel the magic."

"Will it. What you want to happen. Will it."

"That isn't-"

"Will it."

She looked into his sky blue eyes. "Okay." A fierceness rushed through her and she thought of him whole, his wound healed. A rush of energy filled her, his skin moving beneath her hand. The sensation caused her to lose concentration, but it didn't matter. She felt the wound close, blood still coating her hands. "Did that work?"

"Thank you."

A smile briefly appeared before she pressed her lips against his. She felt his hand wrap around hers, his other going to the nape of her neck, his fingers threading through her hair. Hearing a sound, she drew back, glancing over her shoulder to see Troy walking towards her, a blanket thrown over his shoulder. When Emery's hand tightened on hers, she returned her attention to him.

"Why?"

"I'm not sure what you're asking. Why I healed you? Why I kissed you? Or something else."

"Both."

"How could I let you die?"

"And the other?"

She grinned, almost giddy with relief that he lived. "One less regret for you?"

"Trinity?" Troy stopped beside them. He carried both the blanket and Emery's sword.

She looked up at him, still grinning. "I've got the antidote." Letting go of Emery's hand, she took it from her pocket and held it out to him, blood smearing the bottle, sunlight shining through the glass to show how little was in it.

"Two doses. There isn't enough," Emery said.

Troy took the antidote, looking at it for a moment before putting it in his pocket. "I'll take the sword out to my ute first. Probably best not to carry it around the streets. We don't need that kind of attention."

She nodded, turning back to Emery. "Think you can stand? We can meet Troy at the corner of the house."

Emery glanced at Troy's retreating figure, his sword now wrapped in the blanket. "How will I ever repay you for my life?"

"You saved me too." She helped him stand, realising that neither of her hands ached from the grazes. She stared at one of them, her palm smooth beneath the blood.

"What is wrong?" Emery cupped her hand.

"It's healed."

"Humans of old used Fae magic to do blood magic. A powerful, ancient magic that's drawn to evil. A little bit of blood is fine, but your hands were drenched in it. Be very careful until your magic settles in properly."

"What do you mean?"

He placed his other hand over hers that he cupped. "Don't kill anyone."

"I couldn't."

"You say that now, but you don't know what you might have done. Wielding nature isn't all that your magic might be drawn to."

"What if you kill someone?"

"It's different for the Fae. Magic is natural to us."

Before she could ask him further questions, the scent of magic filled the air and she spun to see Tarrant standing nearby, his sword drawn and his hand raised. Her mouth dropped open, the demand to know how he'd found them remaining unspoken.

Emery moved her to the side, stepping closer to Tarrant. "Go, Trinity."

Her mouth closed and she stepped around him. She wasn't about to let Tarrant try and kill him twice. "How did you find me?"

"A strand of hair." Tarrant glanced at his hand.

She noticed the hair wrapped around his finger. "How did you get that?" A sound caught her attention and she saw Troy enter the backyard. Fear raced through her again. Rapidly followed by anger. She was sick of being afraid. Sick of worrying about those she cared for. "What do you want, Tarrant?"

"A few deaths, but I'm willing to start with the traitor's." Tarrant nodded towards Emery who had stepped to the side of Trinity.

She wasn't about to let that happen. Somehow she had to get Tarrant away from Emery and Troy. Her hand closed into a fist and she thought of how it had felt to use magic. Spices filled the air, reminding her of a Christmas cake, and she felt something form in her hand. Throwing herself at Tarrant, she wrapped an arm around him. "Not going to happen." She met Tarrant's startled gaze, opening her hand and closing it on what she held, unwilling to break contact with his gaze to see what it was. "Not today. Not ever." The only location she could bring clearly to mind was the bent and twisted tree with the boulder at the base. The scent of spices filled the air again and the world shimmered, reforming.

Tarrant pulled away from her, the sky behind him filled with dark clouds, the sun barely above the horizon. "You think you can stop me? I can be back there in seconds and you won't be able to do anything."

"That's what you think." Beneath her feet she felt the roots of the tree, making them snake up out of the ground and wrap around Tarrant's legs.

Tarrant laughed. "A child's trick." With a wave of his hand, the roots began to unravel.

She focused on the roots, forcing them to tighten and rise higher. Something twisted through her and anger had her gritting her teeth. The roots crept higher and she smiled at the flare of fear she saw in Tarrant's eyes. "A child's trick?"

Tarrant raised his hand high, lightning forking out of the sky. It struck above his hand, close enough that the strand of hair wrapped around his finger burned. He flung the lightning at her.

She stumbled back, the anger swamped by fear. The lightning veered away from her, striking the ground with a crack, the smell of singed grass and burnt hair hanging in the air. Before she could recover, Tarrant vanished, the roots sliding back into the earth. She dropped to the ground, focusing on her breathing. "I'm alive." The word was a whisper, all she could focus on for a moment. Then it hit her. Tarrant had controlled the lightning. Wonder raced through her. She didn't have to be afraid. All she had to do was learn how to control it, like she'd controlled the roots.

Another thought hit her. She'd wanted to kill him. She began to shake. Never before had she felt such an emotion. Emery's warning came back to her and she drew the piece of bark from her pocket, raising it to her lips. "Emery." The bark was dragged from her hand by a gust of wind. Emery appeared before her, seconds after it vanished from sight, missing his shirt, his sword again at his side and dried blood smeared across his torso.

He dropped to the ground, his hands wrapping around her upper arms. "Did he hurt you?"

Tears pooled in her eyes at his fierce words. She shook her head. Fear fought with relief at seeing he was safe.

"Trinity." His grip on her tightened. "What happened?"

She flung herself against his bare chest. "You're okay?"

His arms wrapped around her, his head resting on hers. "Yes."

"Troy?"

"I sent him to safety."

She momentarily closed her eyes, not wanting to

let go of Emery. "I wanted to-" She took a deep breath, trying again. "He was threatening me and I-" The words wouldn't form.

"I'll hunt him down for you."

She drew back enough to meet his gaze, seeing the concern in his sky blue eyes. "No. I don't want him to hurt you again."

A slight smile made a brief appearance before Emery spoke. "I won't allow him to hurt you. I'm certain there are others who feel the same."

"I tried to kill him." The words burst from her and she gestured towards the nearby tree. "With the roots of the tree." Seeing more worry in his eyes, she drew further away, his hands moving to her shoulders. "He attacked me with lightning and left."

The scent of old campfires filled the air and Emery opened his hand, closing it immediately on the piece of bark that had formed. The world shimmered around them, becoming a room that looked in need of repair, several tin buckets half filled with water sitting around the edges of the otherwise empty room, a single window letting the early morning light inside.

"Where are we? Why did you bring us here?" She stumbled to her feet, the wooden floorboards creaking at her efforts. She stared down at them. "Will they break?"

An elderly man shuffled into the room before Emery had the chance to speak, a smile lighting his face. "Young master. We weren't expecting you."

"Emery?" She stepped closer to him, her gaze on the elderly man. "He's human?" She stared at the ears that weren't pointed.

Emery slid an arm around her waist. "Put the kettle on, Roland."

The elderly man dipped his head. "Yes, my lord." He shuffled back out of the room.

"Emery?"

He faced her, his hand resting on her waist. "Welcome to my home. What little there is left of it." A wry smile formed, vanishing as quickly as it had come.

Chapter Twenty-Three

Trinity stared at Emery, temporarily speechless. "Didn't you say you were landless?" She frowned. "You lied to me?"

"I might as well be landless for all the use this place is. The mansion hasn't been in good repair since my grandfather made enemies of a powerful family. The main house is falling down, the out buildings aren't much better and the ground was sown with salt, which led to erosion and nothing being able to grow. It will take more gold than I am likely to earn in a lifetime to repair the place and my magic isn't strong enough to make a difference. I wouldn't wish this burden on a descendent."

She stared up at him, her heart once more aching. "Is there anything in your life that isn't a burden?"

"Why does that thought bother you so much?" He

brushed his thumb across the skin beneath her eye, spreading the dampness of her tear.

She couldn't bring herself to answer that question. "There are plants that grow well in saline conditions and that can help with erosion. You can mulch the plants and bring in topsoil, or make your own with composting."

"There is fifty acres. Some of the surrounding forests have encroached on my lands, but not enough to make a difference."

The size gave her pause. It was two hundred times bigger than the land their house was built on. She met his gaze, seeing he didn't believe anything could be done. "If it's one thing I know, it's plants. I've heard Dad and Troy talk enough about them over the years. And what I don't know, they would."

"It's a nice thought, but there are other things that must be done."

She thought of Tarrant and the problems he'd caused. "It won't take forever to sort Tarrant out."

"You don't know exactly how many problems he's caused over the years. Even I don't, although I fear his victims number everyone he's ever come into contact with."

She started to protest his need to clean up Tarrant's

messes, when another thought occurred to her, causing her mouth to drop open.

"Trinity? Is something wrong?"

"What if he tracks down Kinnon and his family?" They were in her home, with her father and Troy.

"They wouldn't have left strands of hair lying around to be used against them. Us Fae know better than that. Something personal like hair is what allows someone to track another."

"What about Lili's blood on the chair?"

It was Emery's turn to remain speechless for several seconds. "Blood is personal."

"We have to warn them."

"We'd be better off taking a Tracking Concealment enchantment to Lili."

"A what?"

"It's a Troll enchantment that prevents a tracking spell from finding you. They usually put it on jewellery to be worn by those wishing to hide themselves."

"How do we get one?"

"There's one in Arwyn and Lili's treasury. They bought it for Tarrant when someone went after him a few years ago. They paid a servant to steal a strand of hair and used that to keep track of him so they could catch him alone. Tarrant called for my help, otherwise he might have been killed. That's when Tarrant learned how to track people. He went after the one who was tracking him. He had their blood on a dagger he'd used to defend himself."

"A pity you didn't arrive too late to rescue him." It would have changed so many things. Shock raced through her. No, it wasn't a pity. How would she have met them without the Troll enchantment?

"I'm sorry."

She frowned. "What are you sorry for this time?"

The smell of old campfires filled the air and Emery held out a piece of bark. "I will try never to be late again when you call me."

She took the bark, slipping it into her pocket, slowly shaking her head. "I've forgotten about that. I only meant it would have stopped so many other things from happening." She took hold of his hand, holding it in both of hers. "Then I realised I wouldn't want to have missed all of this." She held his gaze. "I wouldn't have wanted to miss meeting you and Kinnon." A grin escaped. "I could have done without meeting Tarrant and Darak though."

"I–"

"Tea is ready, my lord," Roland said from the doorway.

Emery met her gaze a moment longer before he faced Roland. "We'll have it in the kitchen."

"Very good, my lord." Roland shuffled away.

"How old is he?"

"He served my grandparents. Him and his wife. I don't know his exact age, but he'd have to be well over a hundred."

"Oh."

"Maybe a hundred and fifty."

Her mouth opened several times, yet no sound escaped. How was that possible?

"We'll have something to eat before we search for the necklace." Emery drew her towards the doorway.

She caught sight of the land through a window, pulling away from him to look outside. "What necklace?" She was distracted by the view, anger causing her hands to curl into fists. How could anyone destroy land like this?

"The one the Troll enchantment was placed on."

She slowly shook her head, trying to focus on the conversation. The barren land, trees in the distance, made it hard to follow what Emery said. "Enchantment?" Turning her back on the bleak scenery, she met his gaze. "Oh. Yes." She paused a moment. "What about warning Lili that Tarrant might come after her?"

Emery took her hand, leading the way through a dark corridor. "It will be at least eight to ten hours before Tarrant can do such complicated magic again without completely exhausting himself. He won't want to leave himself vulnerable."

They stepped into an old fashioned kitchen and Trinity's gaze was drawn to an elderly woman who was placing a plate of biscuits and slices of cake onto an old timber table. Two teacups were already on the table, a teapot sitting in the middle. After washing her hands at the kitchen sink, Trinity sat in the seat Emery drew out from the table for her.

The elderly woman curtsied. "It is good to have you home, my lord."

"I can't stay, Naida. I have things to take care of."

"You have things to take care of here," Naida said. "Tarrant is old enough to take care of his own life. He doesn't need you to run around after him. There are others who can be his errand boy."

"Naida." Emery's tone had a warning note to it.

"Never should have given your oath to him." Naida poured the tea. "Would have been better to have given it to one of the other boys. Even that hot tempered one. Or to Arwyn himself." Naida placed the teapot on the table. "Do you want some honey to sweeten your tea, miss?"

She shook her head, having been too caught up in learning more about Emery to have declined the tea. It wasn't something she liked to drink.

"This is Trinity." Emery sat at the table across from her, picking up a slice of cake.

Trinity glanced around the room, wanting to protest the need to eat something when they should be finding the necklace. Her stomach rumbled and she grabbed one of the biscuits, about to take a bite. She lowered her hand. "Is this Fae food?"

"That isn't an issue for you any longer."

"Oh." She'd forgotten that magic would allow her to eat the food. "Of course."

"You gave her your magic?" Naida looked her up and down.

"The magic came from another," Emery said.

"Arwyn." She looked at each of them when she caught their startled expressions. "What?"

"You're Arwyn's pet?" Naida asked.

A sound of exasperation escaped. "I'm no one's pet." She sent a glare in Emery's direction. "Not Arwyn's and not Kinnon's either. No one's." She took a bite of the biscuit, the burst of flavour distracting her.

Naida turned to Emery. "Why would he have given her magic?"

"She saved his life. And his is not the only life she saved."

"Whose life?" Naida demanded.

"Lili's and mine."

Trinity finished her mouthful. "Braeden's too." She reached for another biscuit, stopping when she realised they were staring at her again. "You're going to have to stop doing that."

"Stop doing what?" Emery asked.

She took another biscuit. "Staring at me like I'm strange."

Emery smiled fleetingly. "You are strange. Do you not realise what it means to have so many Fae who owe their lives to you?"

"That I might get really good presents on my eighteenth birthday?" She grinned then took a bite of the biscuit.

"She doesn't understand our ways, does she, my lord?" Roland asked.

"You'd be better off not telling her," Naida muttered.

Trinity started to say it wasn't that big a deal, but to them it would be. "Anyone would have done it."

Emery reached across the table, capturing her hand before she could take another biscuit. "No. Not in this realm. Not unless they can see a benefit to themselves."

She had no idea how to reply to that comment. Telling him that sounded sad probably wasn't very polite. "I like the biscuits. Who made them?"

Naida beamed. "You should taste my roast dinner. Now Roland has put in those raised vegetable gardens out the back I've been able to grow fresh vegetables." She turned to Emery. "You bring her back and let me know so I can make her a decent meal."

Roland spoke before Emery, who'd opened his mouth, could. "Then don't go complaining about them gardens being where the old mistress once had her flower gardens and rose arbour. The way you go on about the state of the land!"

Trinity used her other hand to grab a biscuit, smiling as she watched the good-natured arguing between Roland and Naida. Her gaze was drawn to Emery and her smile faded when she found he watched her intently. She wanted to ask him what he was thinking, but doubted he'd tell her with Roland and Naida in the room. She thought of the bark he'd given her to call him if she needed him. Finished another biscuit, she closed her hand and was surprised when what looked like a large, dark coloured seed formed. The scent of spices faded away, a hint of them remaining on the seed.

"Are you going somewhere?" Emery asked.

"How do I make this work so you can call me?"

Emery didn't answer immediately. "It already does."

She held it out to him, waiting nearly a minute for him to take it.

"Thank you." He pocketed the seed and captured her other hand. "Why did you give me the means to summon you?"

"You gave one to me. And what do you mean by summon?"

"Request someone to come to you. It can be used to travel to the one you gave it to."

"How?"

"By willing it."

Chapter Twenty-Four

Trinity grinned. "I should have known." Pulling from Emery's grip, she grabbed another biscuit. "These are amazing. I wish Troy could taste them."

"They're Fae food."

"I know. I wouldn't give him any." She finished off another biscuit. "And I probably shouldn't have any more or I might make myself sick."

Naida broke off from her arguing with Roland. "You're welcome to help yourself to my biscuits any time." When Trinity thanked her, Naida nodded before returning to her argument.

Trinity eyed the nearly empty plate, barely managing not to take another biscuit. "We should go. Before we run out of time and Tarrant tries to track Lili down."

Emery rose from the table, continuing to hold her hand. "We have plenty of time."

"What does the anti-tracking device look like?"

"The-" Emery slowly shook his head. "The enchanted necklace is a stone hung on a leather cord. It was made by mountain Trolls."

"Okay." She drew the word out, not sure she should ask exactly what a mountain Troll was and if there were different kinds of Trolls. "How will we get it?"

Emery stepped around the table, continuing to hold her hand. "I'll take us to the dungeon entrance. At the start of the corridor. We need to take the key from the guard. I'm not one of the family. I can't use my magic to transport us directly inside."

"When will you be back, young master?" Roland asked.

"I can't tell you that." Emery paused. "Take care while I'm gone."

"Thanks for the biscuits." Trinity tried to smile, but worry over what they were about to face made it falter.

"You didn't drink your tea, miss," Naida said.

"Uhmm…" The words that she'd have tea next time wouldn't come, reminding her it was impossible to lie.

"Stay behind me." Emery opened a hand, a piece of bark in it, the scent of his magic filling the kitchen.

He closed his hand on the bark and the world shimmered and reformed. They were in the dungeon corridor. He let go of her hand, drawing his sword.

The guard drew his sword, the exit door behind him, a lantern hanging above him, and advanced on Emery.

"I need the key to the treasury," Emery kept his sword up.

"Tarrant would kill me if I gave it to you," the guard said.

The scent of magic filled the corridor and Emery launched himself at the guard, colliding with him, both of them disappearing.

Trinity took a step forward. "Emery?" The word was soft and there was no reply. "Emery!"

"Trinity?"

She spun, frowning as she tried to place the voice.

"Trinity? Is that you out there?"

"Tomas?"

"Yes."

She hurried forward, peering through the bars of the first cell. It was too dark to see anything. "Tomas?"

"You didn't happen to see a key lying around anywhere."

She shook her head. "How did you end up in here? And where are your knights?"

He didn't answer immediately. "Tarrant used a Petrification enchantment on them. He's getting more for me as he used up the last of his supply."

She momentarily closed her eyes. What was with Tarrant and his love of that enchantment?

"Is something wrong?"

A wry smile formed. "Don't you think I should be the one asking you that question?"

Tomas chuckled. "I think we've already established that there is definitely something wrong with my situation."

She heard a rattle of chains and guessed he was chained to the far wall like Arwyn had been chained in the other cell. "When will Tarrant be back?"

"I don't know."

"What is he going to do with you once you've been turned to stone?"

Again Tomas didn't answer immediately. "I don't suppose it matters what I tell you. My situation is a little impossible and it isn't like anyone is going to be rushing to my rescue since you're the only one who knows where I am."

Trinity frowned, about to ask him what he meant when he spoke again.

"Tarrant plans to use us to decorate his gardens if we don't fight him and willingly drink the potion. It seemed the better option since I'm chained and can't escape. If I don't, he'll force the potion on me anyway and push my stone body off the highest point of the castle."

"It's a wonder he has any friends." Her words rang in her mind. "Enemies." It came out as a whisper.

"Sounds like you thought of something."

She wanted to deny it, but her magic wouldn't let her. "Just because an idea occurs to me it doesn't mean it'll be useful."

Tomas chuckled. "Oh I have a feeling it is useful. What do you want in exchange for helping me out of this predicament?"

She thought of Emery's land, one more burden for him. "Can salt be removed from the earth with magic? Can magic make barren ground fertile?"

"Nearly anything is possible with magic and enough Fae to wield it."

"Could you fix Emery's land?" The smell of old campfires surrounded her and she turned to see Emery stride towards her, alone.

"Who are you talking to?"

"Tomas."

"You can't ask that of him." Emery stopped beside

Trinity, looking through the barred window. "My apologies. She doesn't know."

"Know what?" Trinity demanded.

"It was one of his uncles who called for the destruction of my family's land in the first place."

"So? I had a great uncle I didn't mourn when he died. Being family doesn't guarantee that you'll like them."

"I'm currently feeling more inclined to like Emery than I ever liked my uncle," Tomas said.

"You would expect me to trust you on my lands?" Emery asked.

Chains rattled, a jerky sound that proceeded Tomas' words. "Do you think I'm in a position to bargain for my favour?"

The scent of magic filled the corridor and Tarrant appeared by the exit door, a small potion bottle in his hand. He reached for his sword. "Have you come to let me finish the job of killing you, Emery?"

Emery shoved a ring of keys in Trinity's hand. "The treasury is at the end of the corridor. Find the necklace."

She kept her voice at a whisper like he did, conscious of Tarrant advancing on them, sword drawn. "I don't know what it looks like."

"You'll recognise it." Emery drew his sword. "It

looks like it's of no value." He faced Tarrant, raising his voice. "The only reason you got the better of me was that you tried to harm Trinity." He strode towards Tarrant, meeting him a couple of metres from the cell door, their swords colliding.

"What did you do with my guard?"

Emery drove Tarrant back towards the exit. "He's alive."

"Trinity."

She looked between the cell door and the fight.

"Name your price. I've run out of time to bargain with you."

She stared at the cell door a second longer before looking at the keys she clutched. Stepping forward, she tried to keep her voice low. "You know what I want. I've already asked it of you, but I won't hold you to it." She spun, racing along the corridor, the sound of swords clashing behind her, Tomas calling after her.

There were enough lanterns hung sporadically along the corridor to help her find her way to the end. The door looked little different from the cell doors, other than there was no barred window. She tried half the keys until she found the correct one. Swinging the door open, she peered inside, surprised to find it was well-lit. Slipping inside, she closed the door behind her. The sound of swords clashing and Tomas calling after her were silenced.

Along one wall were large timber chests, their lids closed. In the middle of the room were several statues and a couple of busts on plinths, all covered in jewellery. Her mouth dropped open at the display. More wealth than she'd ever seen in one place in her entire life other than inside a jewellery shop that catered to the very wealthy. Her and Yvette had entered one in the city a couple of years ago, feeling like criminals with the way the security guard had shadowed them. Closing her mouth, she took several steps towards the nearest statue, her hand outstretched. Stopping, she reminded herself of Emery in the corridor fighting for his life.

She turned her back on the display of jewels, striding to one of the chests and flinging it open. Once again she stood stunned, staring at the mass of gold coins, a handful of gold necklaces and bracelets scattered through them. Chest after chest she found the same. In some were golden goblets and tableware along with a couple of candlesticks. She slowly shook her head. What did Arwyn plan to do with all this gold? No one would be able to spend it in a lifetime. She stumbled as she remembered the Fae lived a lot longer than humans. She had no idea how much it cost to support yourself during a Fae lifetime. Shaking her head, she tried to focus on why she was in the treasury room. A seemingly impossible task. She strode across the room, heading for the tall woven baskets that were haphazardly arranged on the opposite side of the room. Slipping past the statues and busts, a simple necklace caught her attention, half hidden by one dripping with rubies and diamonds. She slipped it over the head of the statue.

The leather cord was well worn, the stone a simple river pebble with a hole through the centre, the leather cord threaded through it. "No value." It certainly looked worthless. Particularly next to the wealth displayed. She shoved it deep in her pocket, her fingers brushing over her phone and the bark. She kept her fingers pressed against the bark a second longer, her thoughts turning to Emery. He better be okay.

Chapter Twenty-Five

Trinity strode for the door, stepping into the corridor, locking the door behind her. Frowning at the increased noise, she ran towards Emery, anger rushing through her when she saw he fought Tarrant and two guards. A hand curled into a fist, while the other rose. There were no roots in here to call up, or lightning. The air rushed back towards her and she drew more of it, wanting to gather enough to knock them off their feet when she forced it at them.

"Trinity. No." Tomas gasped the words out as she slowed near his cell door.

She had no idea what he was trying to tell her so gathered more air.

The Fae staggered, the guard closest to her dropping his sword, his hands tearing at his throat. The other three stopped fighting, using their swords to keep themselves upright.

"Emery?" She strode to him, her fist opening so she could grab hold of him. She kept the air close, not wanting to release it yet.

"Can't breathe. Let it go."

Her mouth dropped open as she realised what she'd done. But she couldn't let the air go. The look in Tarrant's eyes promised pain. And he couldn't take his anger out on her. That only left Emery. She formed a seed, releasing the air as she crushed the seed, picturing her bedroom. At the last second the bent and twisted tree invaded her mind and the world reformed, becoming the glade where Tarrant's father had died, lit by the midday sun.

Emery crushed her to him. "Why did you bring us here?"

Her hands cupped his face. "Are you okay? I didn't mean to do that. I didn't know what I was doing."

Emery's lips slowly curved into a smile. "Imagine what you'll be able to do when you know what you're doing."

"Are you serious?" She couldn't keep the fear from her voice. "I nearly killed you."

He took hold of one of her hands, turning it to raise it to his lips. "Once again I owe you for saving me. Three Fae against one are not good odds."

"Emery-"

"We have to leave here. Go somewhere less dangerous."

"I tried to travel to my bedroom, but it didn't work."

He drew back from her, clasping one of her hands. "Picture where you wish to go. Focus on it and nothing else. Let me be the one to take us there." The scent of old campfires filled the air.

When she could clearly see her room, she nodded. Before she had a chance to say anything, the world reformed and they were in her room. Kinnon paced the floor, Lili and Darak conversed softly, the bedroom light created a soft glow and the curtains were drawn back to show the night sky. Her phone beeped, warning her of messages. Ignoring the messages, she grinned, relief rushing through her to see they were okay. With a glance at Emery, she let go of his hand to draw the necklace from her pocket, ignoring Kinnon's exclamation at the sight of her. "This is for you." She held the necklace out to Lili.

Lili rose to her feet. She'd bathed and wore a t-shirt and jeans that Trinity recognised as her own. "Why do I have need of this?" She took the necklace.

Trinity glanced at the jeans that looked like they might slip off Lili, too short at the ankles. "To keep

Tarrant from tracking you down with the blood you left on the arms of the chair."

Lili slipped the necklace over her head. She looked from Trinity to Emery. "Who do I have to thank for this?"

Trinity interrupted Emery, expecting him to find a way to deny the help he'd given her. "Both of us. Emery kept Tarrant busy while I looked for the necklace. I had the easy task." She looked from Lili to Darak and back again. "What were you plotting when I came in? And where are Braeden and Arwyn."

"Stone." Darak growled the word, glaring at her.

Kinnon stepped closer to Trinity so that he was between her and his brother. "We were trying to figure out how to get two more doses of the antidote. They didn't like my suggestion." He looked her up and down. "You're unharmed?"

She nodded before glancing at each of the occupants of her room, wondering where Troy was. The neighbourhood was fairly quiet so she supposed he was sleeping. Her gaze returned to Kinnon. "We need nine doses of the antidote."

"No," Emery said. "No bargain was reached."

She stepped closer to him, a smile forming when she saw the concern in his sky blue eyes. She placed her hand against his chest. "Do you think that will stop me from getting the extra doses?"

"I would like to think it would, but I fear I'll be left wishing for the impossible."

She laughed. "I fear you will be too." Staying close to him, she lowered her hand, turning to face the others who carefully watched them. "What plans have you come up with?"

"Nothing that isn't without too much risk," Lili said.

"Life is a risk," Darak muttered.

Kinnon took a single step towards Trinity. "Can I talk to you?" He gestured towards the bedroom door that was closed.

She hesitated, not sure she was up to the coming conversation. "I need to clean up first." She glanced down at her blood stained clothes.

Kinnon nodded. "Once you've washed."

She hesitated once more. "Okay." Gathering clothes, she left her sneakers by the door before using the bathroom, returning to the bedroom once she was clean, letting Emery know he could use the bathroom to clean the blood from himself.

Emery held her gaze a moment before he nodded and headed to the bathroom.

"Can we talk now?" Kinnon asked.

Doubting it would become any easier by putting it off, Trinity nodded. She followed Kinnon to the door and stepped through when he held it open for her, the hallway light on.

Kinnon closed the door and moved further into the short hallway. "You do know Emery might as well be landless for all that he can offer you."

Trinity grinned, moving closer to him to keep her voice low when she saw that the door of the spare bedroom was closed, not having noticed it when she'd used the bathroom, too caught up in images of blood and wounds. Her earlier guess was looking like it might be right and Troy was probably sleeping. And more than likely her father too. "Do you think that would bother me? Someone being landless, or broke as we'd put it in this world."

He stared at her for a moment. "I wish I could say yes, but then if I could, you wouldn't be the person I'm fascinated by."

She looked away from his piercing gaze. "How many days have passed?"

"Two since you were last here. Troy didn't want to do anything until you returned." He reached for her.

She captured his hand before he could make contact. "Kinnon…"

"Is there any hope you might change your mind?"

A smile formed, tinged by sadness and a second of regret. "We wouldn't suit." A touch of wryness curved the corners of her mouth further. "You're too arrogant and overbearing to cope with someone you say suffers from those same traits." Not that she believed she was arrogant or overbearing.

Kinnon chuckled, humour filling his eyes for a couple of seconds. He sobered. "Our debt to you is great. There's very little you could ask of me that I'd ever deny you."

Her grip tightened on his hand. "All I ask is for us to find nine doses of the antidote."

He remained silent, examining her. "Why does that worry Emery?"

"You'd have to ask him."

He grinned. "You have magic."

"Yeah."

"My father's magic."

She nodded.

"You know why he's worried. Which is why you avoided the question."

"I have a feeling Emery spends a lot of his time worried." She didn't need to see Kinnon glance behind her to know the bathroom door had opened and Emery was not far from her. She faced him with a smile, letting go of Kinnon's hand to reach for him.

"I think I'm going to have to teach you that not every worry is yours to shoulder."

"He's always been the sensible one, trying fruitlessly to keep us out of trouble," Kinnon said.

Trinity laughed softly. "Don't you recognise a hopeless case when you see one?"

"Every time I look in the mirror."

She threw her arms around Emery. "I think you need a new mirror."

Emery met her gaze. "I see something different reflected back at me from your eyes to what I see when I look in a mirror."

Her mouth opened, a soft sound escaping, her arms tightening around him. "Emery-"

"Trinity!"

She was crushed between the hard planes of two bodies, grinning at the startled look she caught in Emery's eyes before it was masked. She almost told Troy to loosen his grip, that she couldn't breathe. The words were too close to what she'd done to Emery so she left them unspoken.

"Are you all right?" Emery asked softly.

"I will be." She raised herself enough to lightly brush her lips across his before letting go and twisting in Troy's grip to be able to return his hug.

Troy drew her away from Emery, spinning on the

spot with her, her feet off the floor. "I was terrified he'd kill you."

"I was terrified I would kill him."

Troy loosened his grip so he could meet her gaze. "You can't lie."

"I know."

"How is that possible?"

Chapter Twenty-Six

Troy's question was ambiguous enough that Trinity chose the one she wanted to answer. "Magic makes it impossible for me to lie."

"Don't, Trinity. Don't hide from me. Not now." He crushed her against his chest. "Surely you can't believe you'd have been able to kill him."

She fought the urge to cry, taking a deep, shaky breath. "It wasn't planned. I was angry. I nearly killed Emery too." Thinking Troy might believe she was talking about the same time, she added, "The second time I nearly killed Tarrant."

Troy drew back, his arms continuing to encircle her. "You nearly killed Tarrant twice?"

"Yes. The first time I tried to strangle him with the roots of a tree." She looked over her shoulder to find Emery watched her. She gave him a reassuring smile before facing Troy again. "Can we bring life to barren land?" She couldn't rely on Tomas to help. Nor would she hold it over him in exchange for rescuing him. That wasn't her. Not that she was exactly herself lately.

"What was done to it?"

"Sown with salt. Then erosion finished it off."

"Sure, but do you think we can focus on the current problem first?"

"Trinity, it isn't necessary for you to take on my burdens," Emery protested.

She waved his concerns away, escaping Troy's arms to face him. "Didn't you hear Troy? We have other things to focus on first. You'll have to wait until later to talk about your land."

Troy chuckled. "Let me give you some advice."

Emery met Troy's gaze. "Freely given, nothing expected in exchange?"

"The advice isn't worth that much."

Emery inclined his head.

"When her mind is made up it would take a force of nature to change it."

Troy's words brought a smile to her lips, making her think of how Emery had fought. A sword in one hand, wielding nature with the other.

Emery's gaze collided with hers and he smiled back before turning his attention to Troy. "It doesn't surprise me it'd take one force of nature to alter the course of another force of nature."

Troy stared at Emery, a startled expression crossing his face before he burst out laughing. He turned to Trinity, laughter still in his voice when he spoke. "I like this one. He suits you."

"I know." Her words were soft and she glanced at Emery again once she'd spoken them. Returning her attention to Troy, she asked, "Where's Dad?"

"Asleep. Not that he's been sleeping well. You should let him know you're back. We've been worried. I had to tell him what happened."

She sighed heavily. "I know." She didn't need anyone lying for her. Holding out her hand to Emery, she took a step towards him. "I want you to meet my dad."

Emery took her hand. "I'd be honoured, but you should see him first. He might not want a stranger at your side for your reunion."

She nodded, guessing he was probably right. She pointed a warning finger at Kinnon and Troy. "No making decisions about our next step until I'm back." She headed into the connecting hallway, stopping before she reached the kitchen when she remembered the unread messages. Drawing her phone out, she stared at it, surprised to see how many days had passed. She hadn't thought to ask how much time had passed while she was in the realms of the Fae this time. She shied away from thoughts of Emery injured. The initial rush of her return left and tiredness tugged at her, making her feel ill, an ache in her body that she could find no reason for.

She tried to focus on the time. What had happened while she'd been gone? It was Sunday. Almost three in the morning. Half the school holidays were over and it didn't feel like they were anywhere close to solving all the problems. Tomas' pleas for help came to mind. If anything there were more problems than they'd started with. No, there was still only the one problem. Tarrant.

Hearing soft footsteps Trinity turned to see Emery coming towards her. "Did you change your mind about meeting my dad?"

"What is wrong?"

"What do you mean?"

"You're standing here when you'd planned to see your father."

"Oh." A smile formed and she went to him, holding him close. "I remembered I had messages on my phone and noticed the date when I checked them."

"Messages?"

She held up the phone, surprised at how little charge it had. Frowning she tried to remember how much there'd been before. "I think something is wrong with it. There was more charge earlier."

"Magic."

"Huh?" His word made no sense. "What do you mean?"

"Your magic is draining it. Just like this world is probably making you feel drained and ill."

"Oh. I thought it was from lack of sleep." She checked her messages while her phone had power. One was from her mother asking if she wanted to join them for dinner one night next week and the rest were from Yvette demanding why she was ignoring her. She placed it on the kitchen bench in the hope the battery wouldn't die so quickly if she wasn't holding it. She'd have to answer the messages later. Hopefully her magic wouldn't prevent her from lying through texts because there was no way she could tell either of them the truth.

"You should sleep once you've talked to your father. You look tired. But not here. You won't rest the way you should by staying in this world. None of us will." He ran his fingers across her cheek, cupping her face with one of his hands.

Closing her eyes, she rested her head against his

hand, not wanting to move. "I don't regret it." She opened her eyes. "Saving your life."

"Do you regret having magic?"

She grinned at him. "It'll take time to learn the answer to that question."

"So you regret it."

She stepped close to him, her hand resting on his chest, his heartbeat beneath her palm. "I doubt I'll ever regret something that kept you alive." She still wasn't certain if she'd have chosen to have magic, but as she'd said, she didn't regret keeping him alive. Far from it.

He stared down at her, his gaze holding hers before he lowered his head. His lips met hers.

She clung to him, trying not to think of how close he'd come to dying. She drew back enough to gaze at his face, lingering on his impossibly white hair, sky blue eyes and serious expression. "You caught my attention the moment I saw you in the dungeon." A grin escaped. "Now that's going to be an interesting answer whenever anyone asks where we met."

Emery chuckled, his arms tightening around her momentarily. "It might be in your world." Letting go, he took a step back. "Let your father know you are currently safe."

Nodding, she headed towards her father's room,

looking over her shoulder to smile at Emery before she knocked on the door. Her smile widened when he returned hers. When the door opened, she faced it, surprised at how tired her father looked.

"Trin." He crushed her to him.

"Dad. It's okay. I'm currently safe." She repeated Emery's words, knowing that she couldn't tell him that she'd been safe all the time she'd been gone or was likely to be safe when she left again.

"That doesn't reassure me." He held her at arm's length. "You look tired."

"So do you."

"Is it any wonder?" He paused a moment. "What happened while you were gone?"

She didn't want to tell him about trying to kill Tarrant. Not once, but twice. How would he accept that news? She angled so she could gesture towards Emery. "I have someone I want you to meet."

Emery came forward, holding out his hand. "It is an honour to meet you, my lord."

Rod's gaze rested on Emery's ears before he took his hand and shook it. "Rod will be fine. I'm not a lord of some castle."

Emery inclined his head. "Nor am I."

"This is Emery."

Rod stepped back, looking from one to the other. "This is the one you saved from dying?"

Trinity nodded.

"The one you got magic to save."

She grinned at her father. "I don't regret what I did." As she'd said to Emery, she didn't regret saving his life. And she never would.

"How long are you home?"

"Not long. I need you to send some messages for me." She gestured to her phone she'd left on the kitchen bench. "It'll need charging too."

"Are you coming back?"

Chapter Twenty-Seven

Trinity threw herself into her father's arms. "Of course I am. And you have to visit the realms of the Fae. If we can't get Emery's property fixed by magic I'm going to need yours and Troy's help to turn barren land into fertile land."

"What happened to it?" At her grin, Rod frowned. "Are you trying to distract me?"

"No." She stepped away from her father, standing beside Emery. "It was sown with salt and erosion finished off the job. It's Emery's family home. Fifty acres and a mansion."

"A mansion?" Rod looked from one to the other.

Trinity grinned again. "Nowhere near as fancy as it sounds. I'm surprised I didn't fall through the floorboards."

"I would never have taken you there if I thought you might have come to harm," Emery protested.

"How far has this relationship gone?" Rod's eyes narrowed.

"I owe her my life. More than once."

"I'm not counting." She held Emery's gaze before turning to her father. "I can't stay here. I need to return to the realms of the Fae." A reassuring smile made a brief appearance. "But I will be back."

"You better be."

She gestured towards her phone. "Send Mum a message to say I've made other plans and let Yvette know I've been so busy I've barely had time to sleep." She grinned at him, surprised she'd been able to speak the truth without actually giving away anything that had been happening.

"That grin better not be about your plans."

"Nope. It's about learning to speak the truth like a politician. Or the Fae."

Rod slowly shook his head. "Only you would think something like that."

Laughter escaped. "Stop worrying, Dad." She hugged him again before drawing away. "I'm going to work on a plan to solve the current problems."

Emery moved closer to her. "We'll work on a plan."

She slipped her hand in his, holding her father's gaze. "Yeah, that too." She glanced over her shoulder.

"I better go and make sure no plans have been made without me."

Rod followed them to Trinity's room, muttering, "What a pity that'd be."

She barely managed not to laugh at his words. Reaching her room, she opened the door, pausing to listen to the argument between Troy, Kinnon and Darak, Lili adding the occasional comment. They needed Braeden. He was obviously the peacemaker of the family. But they couldn't wake him without having the antidote. "None of us should stay here. This world isn't helping any of us." She turned towards her father. "You'll make sure Braeden and Arwyn are safe until we can come for them."

Rod nodded.

Trinity faced the room. "Good. So none of us need to be left behind. All we have to figure out is where to go so we can rest before we deal with Tarrant."

Darak pointed a finger at Trinity. "You can't tell us who goes and who stays."

"They'll be safe here." She was tired. And the longer she stayed in this world, the worse she felt. "We have to rest. No one knows about this place. So no one will come here looking for them."

Lili stepped forward. "We'll stay in the cottage

where Tarrant was born. He'd never think to look for us there. Nor would he ever return to his first home."

"Why wouldn't he?" Trinity asked.

"The lord of the estate can barely afford house servants so many of the estate cottages are empty and in need of repairs. Tarrant found the cottage lacking back when it was in reasonable repair, he'd find it more distasteful now and have no reason to return."

"How do we get there?" Trinity asked.

"I can take two with me." Emery moved to her side, offering his hand.

She took Troy's hand also. "I'm ready." She was ready for bed.

"We will see you there." Lili took hold of Darak's hand, waiting until Kinnon slung an arm around his brother's shoulders before leaving.

Trinity barely had time to glance at her father, sending him a reassuring smile, before the world shimmered and reformed, a cottage in front of them that was in severe need of repair. She squeezed Troy's hand at the soft sound of surprise he made, her attention caught by Lili and her sons, relieved everyone had arrived safely.

"This is the realms of the Fae?" Troy drew his hand from hers, slowly turning as he looked around the area. Late afternoon light showed fields gone to grass and a small herd of cows ambling towards the castle that could be seen in the distance.

"One small area of it." Darak's expression was one of distaste as he eyed the cottage. "Do not judge all the realms by this lord's lack of care."

"Like our world there are areas of beauty and ones of devastation." She couldn't help thinking about Emery's lands as she took a step towards the cottage. "Will it be safe to stay here? What if someone notices us?"

Emery stepped past her. "I'll check that the cottage is unoccupied. Wait out here."

She wasn't about to stand back while he took all the risks. "We can both check that the cottage is unoccupied." She tried to follow Emery inside, glaring at Troy and Kinnon who both tugged her back from the doorway.

"Stop rushing into danger all the time," Troy said.

"Let me go." She spoke through gritted teeth, taking a step away from them when they released her hands, surprised at the amount of anger that rushed through her.

Emery returned to the doorway, looking at Trinity, Troy and Kinnon before he spoke. "It's safe." He stepped to the side to allow everyone to enter.

Trinity remained outside, her gaze on Emery. She

didn't speak until they were alone. "I don't need you to protect me. I can look after myself."

Emery stared at her, finally inclining his head.

She stepped closer. "I don't want you hurt again."

He smiled at her. "Have you considered that I might not want you hurt either?"

"Tarrant can't hurt me. Not as long as Arwyn lives."

"He's not the only danger in this realm."

Troy appeared in the doorway before Trinity could say anything else. "There's a single bed and a double. You might want to come and stake your claim if you have a preference."

She looked from Emery to Troy, barely holding back a sigh. "Okay." She pushed past Troy and looked around the cottage. There was a layer of dust over everything. Not that there was much in the room. To her left was a small timber table, the remains of three chairs scattered across the floor, part of one in the fireplace, the chain of a cooking pot that had hung over it, broken. The pot was on its side amongst the ashes and charcoal. At the other end of the single room cottage was a double bed in one corner and a single bed in the other corner. The linen was long gone and the mattresses were covered in dust and crumpled brown leaves. There was a window at the side of each bed, both too grimy to see through.

Lili moved closer to the beds, clouds of dust and leaves swirling around and towards the door. Darak joined his mother, resting a hand on her shoulder. She glanced at him with a smile.

Trinity closed her mouth the moment she realised she was staring, gaping again when Emery sifted through the remains of the chairs, the timber repairing itself. She took a step towards him, mouth still open as a chair reformed, raw timber looking aged and scarred, but intact enough to use. "How did you do that?"

Emery turned to her with a smile, placing the chair beside the table, the dust having been sent from the area by Darak and Lili. "Nature is easy to work with."

"You shouldn't waste your magic on unnecessary things. You'll need every bit of it when we face Tarrant." Kinnon stepped inside with a bundle of sticks and branches in his arms.

Trinity glanced around the dim interior, surprised she hadn't notice him leave. But she supposed the magic had been enough to distract her. Catching sight of Troy's expression, she grinned. Had she looked that shocked? She hoped not.

Emery moved the chair closer to Trinity. "I'll be

back with blankets and bedrolls. There aren't enough beds for all of us."

Before Trinity could ask to go with him, the smell of old campfires mingled with the scent of spices and flowers that lingered in the air. She sat on the chair, not knowing how to help. The three Fae seemed to have everything under control. Darak and Lili were cleaning the place with their magic and Kinnon was making a fire in the fireplace. She looked up at Troy when he came to stand beside her.

"I thought it was all tricks and entertainment. That's all Braeden showed me."

She clasped Troy's hand tightly. "It can kill too." She tried not to think of her fight with Tarrant, but the memories washed over her, bringing with them dark feelings.

Troy looked her over. "Are you okay?"

She couldn't say yes. Her magic prevented her from lying to him. Instead she smiled, briefly tightening her grip on his. "You're the one who looked shocked."

Troy grinned fleetingly. "You didn't look much better."

Kinnon stood up from the fire he'd lit, the cooking pot in his hand. "There's a stream nearby. Naturally running water. I'll bring some back for drinking."

Trinity frowned. "Running water?" Why had he made a point of mentioning it was running?

Kinnon nodded, heading out the door.

She stared after him, turning to Lili, curious. "Why did he mention it was running water?"

"Was that to let us know it's clean?" Troy asked.

Darak slowly shook his head. "We should have left them behind. They're going to get themselves killed and us along with them."

Lili smiled gently, brushing her hand across Darak's cheek. "She's more resourceful than you believe."

"You don't know her," Darak stated.

"She has the heart of a knight. You're the one who needs to learn to know her." Lili turned towards Trinity. "It's for your friend. He can't eat or drink Fae food. If it is washed in naturally running water it will allow him to eat it without harm."

"Harm?" Troy asked.

"All other food would taste like dust and you'd crave our food to the point you would eat nothing else. Unless you chose to have the magic my son offered you."

"I'd starve to death," Troy said.

Lili inclined her head. "Yes." She glanced at the doorway. "I'll see if there are any vegetables left in the overgrown garden beds out the back." A smile curved her lips slightly, a sad faraway look in her eyes. "I doubt anyone has taken care of them in years."

Darak placed a hand on his mother's arm. "Rest. I'll search."

Lili placed her hand over Darak's. "You were the one under a Troll enchantment recently."

"Rest." Darak's tone was firm.

Troy followed Darak. "I'll help."

Reaching the doorway, Darak turned to face Troy. "I doubt I'll need your help."

Troy grinned. "You sure digging in the dirt isn't beneath you? Too much like what a peasant would do?"

"You think I am incapable of foraging?"

Troy shrugged. "I guess we'll find out."

With narrowed eyes, Darak stalked off.

Lili sighed. "Sitting around waiting is difficult for one born a warrior, raised a knight."

Lili's words reminded Trinity that Darak had told her to rest. She rose from the chair, gesturing towards it. "You look tired." The Fae looked far better than when she'd been imprisoned, but that wasn't saying much.

Lili shook her head. "No, Emery fixed the chair for you." She sighed again. "I fear we're a terrible burden to him. One he shouldered far too young. But he never seemed young. He always appeared capable of shouldering the burdens he took on."

Chapter Twenty-Eight

Trinity's lips tightened on the words that wanted to spill. She didn't know all the details. He'd been a child. Five-years-old. Surely the Fae didn't expect their children to shoulder such responsibilities so young. She couldn't help thinking about what she had been doing at that age. Beginning school. Playing with friends, getting into mischief. When this was done, she was going to show Emery how to have fun.

"You look like you don't approve. Such a fierce expression."

"He was a child." The words escaped before she could prevent them.

Lili nodded. "He was always serious." Laughter drew her attention, a smile forming. "I often said he needed to swap some of my younger boys' mischief for his seriousness."

Another lot of laughter drew Trinity to the window and she knelt on the bed so she could look through it. She recognised Troy's laughter, followed by Kinnon's. Rubbing at the glass with the heel of her palm, she peered at the three of them, a smile forming as she noticed Darak was glaring at both Troy and Kinnon. The two of them grinned, sharing a look. She wondered what they'd done to deepen Darak's constant glare.

Troy tossed what looked like a clod of dirt to Kinnon who grabbed it, his other hand keeping the cooking pot resting against his hip. Trinity giggled when Kinnon looked like he might throw the clod at Darak who reached for his sword.

Kinnon glanced towards the cottage, turning back to Darak, his words indistinct before he tossed his clod of dirt on a pile they'd created. Facing the cottage, he walked towards it.

"I had thought you were interested in my youngest."

Trinity slipped off the double bed to face Lili. "As intriguing as he is, we'll do better as friends."

Kinnon stepped inside the doorway in time to catch her words. "What she's really trying to say is that we're both too arrogant and overbearing to have a harmonious relationship." He grinned. "And we both like to win." He placed the cooking pot on the table.

Troy came inside. "Sounds like he knows you pretty well, Trinity."

She faced Troy. "Whose side are you on?"

Troy's grin faded, a serious expression taking its place. "Always yours."

She was across the room in seconds, taking hold of his hand, accustomed to finding dirt on it. "I know." She held his gaze, staring into his green eyes, barely enough light left in the cottage to see the clear colour. "The same goes for me."

Troy tightened his grip on her hand, loosening it as he grinned. "Doesn't mean I'm blind to your faults though." He ran a dirty finger across her nose.

She pulled away from him. "Did you have to?" She wiped at her nose, feeling the dirt he'd left behind.

"Yep." Troy continued to grin.

Darak stopped in the doorway. "We're running out of daylight. Were you both expecting me to be the one to wash the vegetables in the stream?"

"You found some?" Trinity asked.

Kinnon chuckled. "You could say he found some. Or they found him."

Trinity frowned, trying to make sense of his words.

"Don't torment your brother," Lili said.

Kinnon's answer was laughter, echoed by Troy. "I guess only you are allowed to throw vegetables at him."

Trinity realised what the dirt clod must have been. "I'll help wash them." The light was fading rapidly and they needed rest. Although she'd stopped feeling so ill when they'd returned to the realms of the Fae.

"We do not need your help. When Emery fixed the chair for you I'm sure he was expecting you to use it." Darak headed outside.

Trinity strode after Darak. "Then he'll have to get used to being disappointed. I'm not the sort to sit around waiting." She heard Troy chuckle and ignored the sound even though she was tempted to make a comment. Reaching the pile of root vegetables that Darak was already at, she grabbed a handful. For a few seconds she was surprised to find ordinary potatoes. It was the realms of the Fae. She'd half expected something else. Something exotic.

Troy reached her side as she finished gathering some of the potatoes. "I saw herbs that would go well in a stew. I'll collect some then wash them in the stream."

"Not on your own," Kinnon said. "I'll go with you."

Trinity stopped following Darak. "Do you-"

"Darak will protect you," Kinnon said.

She wanted to protest that she didn't need anyone to protect her, but Kinnon and Troy had already headed off, leaving her to hurry after Darak before she lost sight of him in the fading daylight. She caught up with him by the stream where he was washing the potatoes in the flowing water, placing them on the bank beside him. She couldn't resist taking in the view, mesmerised by the beauty of the place. A flicker of movement caught her attention and she saw a Fae drawing back an arrow, partially hidden by the greenery on the far side of the stream. His golden coloured hair was all that gave him away. It took a couple of seconds for her to realise he had his bow aimed at Darak.

Her heart raced and she dropped the potatoes she carried, automatically reaching for the shrubs around him with her magic. Their thin branches grabbed at the bow, pulling it upwards. The arrow flew skywards, drawing Darak's attention. He rushed across the stream, reaching the Fae who fought against the shrubs that were wrapping tightly around him.

Darak looked over his shoulder. "Let him go."

Trinity was so focused on forcing the branches to tighten around the Fae that Darak's words didn't sink in immediately. Her eyes narrowed. He wanted her to let the Fae go? After he'd tried to attack? Opening her mouth to argue, the sounds of laughter penetrated the anger that swamped her. Troy's laughter. She sank to the ground, horror replacing the satisfaction, trembling as she let the shrubs free to return to their usual state.

"Trinity?" Troy knelt beside her, rubbing her hands.

She stared at him blankly for a moment, not sure how he'd reached her side. A glance around showed Kinnon stood close, Darak a few metres from her with the Fae restrained. She threw herself into Troy's arms, burying her face against his chest, trying not to shake at the thought she'd once again tried to kill someone. Troy's arms wrapped around her and she clung to him, not answering when he repeated her name.

"What did you do to her?" Troy demanded.

"If you wish to know what happened, why not ask her yourself instead of throwing accusations around." Darak's tone was equally angry.

Trinity pulled away from Troy, shaking her head. "He didn't do anything to me." She met Darak's gaze, surprised to see no anger in his hazel eyes. She nearly asked him why he didn't tell Troy she'd tried to kill his prisoner, but there was no friendliness in his gaze either. It was neutral.

"Then what happened?" Troy looked from Trinity to Darak and back again.

She shook her head, not wanting to talk about it. "What are we going to do with him?" Her gaze was drawn to the prisoner who remained defiantly silent. She knew what Tarrant would do. Decorate the gardens with another statue.

Kinnon shrugged. "We'll see what our mother says. Maybe she recognises him since she lived in this area years ago."

"He won't talk. I've already questioned him and he's not said a word," Darak said. "We might as well kill him. We've got enough problems to deal with."

She was tempted to ask Darak why he'd stopped her from killing the Fae, but that would cause questions she didn't want to answer. "We have to go back to the cottage." She could barely see anything. The shadows had lengthened and there was only a glimmer of light left in the sky.

"The vegetables are by the stream. Someone will have to collect them." Darak nodded towards his prisoner. "I can't be expected to do everything."

"I'll get them." Trinity gathered up the potatoes she'd dropped and hurried to where Darak had left his. She glanced at Troy who walked with her, his expression worried each time he looked at her.

Troy took some of the dirt clad potatoes from her, washing them in the stream. "What happened back there?" He kept his voice low.

She tried to say that she'd tell him later, but the words wouldn't come. They'd have been a lie. "Do you think we should wash all of them? How will we find our way back to the cottage in the dark?"

"Trinity."

She washed potatoes, glancing at him again, barely able to meet his gaze. "Troy-" She broke off, not sure what to say.

He washed the last potato, gathering them up. "Have you forgotten already that I'm on your side?"

A smile reluctantly formed at the teasing tone he used. She picked up the handful of potatoes he'd been unable to carry. "Did Kinnon go with Darak?" She walked at his side, trying to see where she stepped. Twigs and leaves crunched beneath her feet.

"Trinity-"

"I haven't forgotten. I just don't want to think about some things for now. And I certainly don't want to talk about them." She needed to ask Emery what would happen if she did kill someone. Exactly what would happen.

"Kinnon didn't think it was safe for only one of them to watch the prisoner. Especially since they were taking him back to their mother."

When Trinity stepped inside the cottage, it was to find the fire steadily burning and the prisoner tied to the chair. The chair made her worry about what was taking Emery so long. Had he exhausted himself fixing it?

"If we let him free when we leave tomorrow we won't be able to return here if we need to," Darak argued.

"We can't keep him imprisoned forever. It's quite likely he's meant to be on these lands." Lili left unspoken that they were trespassers.

"You can't take in every stray you feel sorry for," Darak said.

Lili looked at her son until he glanced away. "That was uncalled for, Darak. None of us could have known how Tarrant would turn out."

"You know what Tarrant is like?" the prisoner demanded.

Trinity came forward, dumping the potatoes on the table before facing the prisoner. "He wants most of us dead."

"You're hiding from him?" The prisoner glanced at Lili. "All of you?"

Trinity's lips twisted into a wry smile. "That's one way to look at it. I prefer to think we're resting in preparation for taking him down."

"You're going to fight him?"

Chapter Twenty-Nine

Trinity held herself still when she would have preferred to take a step back from the look in the prisoner's eyes. It reminded her too much of how she'd felt when she'd attacked Tarrant with the tree roots. "We need to find a way to stop him from destroying those we care about." Realising her hands were clenched into fists she relaxed them.

The prisoner looked at Lili. "You think you can face him after being fooled by him all these years?"

"You know who I am." Lili's words were soft, no question in them.

"My father serves the lord of these lands. One of the few knights who remained at his side when he lost his last battle. I've seen you visit my lord occasionally."

"You don't like Tarrant. At all." Trinity stepped closer. "You could join us when we go after him."

"Why would I fight for you? I don't know you."

Lili stepped forward, stopping next to Trinity. "You know me."

He shrugged. "You visit my lord occasionally. That doesn't mean I know you."

"Then what are you willing to do?" Trinity demanded.

"You let me go free and I'll tell you who hates Tarrant the most. The one who'd like to see him held accountable for what he's done."

"We'd want more than that," Kinnon said.

"I'm not about to get myself killed. No one survives Tarrant. There isn't anything he isn't willing to do. And his knight is no better than him."

Trinity had a bad feeling about the answer, but had to ask the question anyway. "His knight?"

"Emery. He does whatever Tarrant asks of him."

She wanted to argue, but Emery's words rang in her mind. 'What of all those I've punished on his behalf. Ones I believed were guilty.' She wanted to close her eyes in the hope this was a bad dream. But she knew it wasn't.

"He didn't care if they were innocent."

The prisoner's words were echoed by the memory of Emery's. 'How many of them were innocent?' She wanted to tell him to stop talking, but Darak spoke before she could.

"Your bound promise that you'll not tell anyone we're here, that you saw us or that we plan to go after Tarrant. You're to give us five full days."

"Two."

Troy grinned. "You don't look like you're in much of a position to bargain. "Why don't we throw your life into the deal too? We won't kill you for trying to shoot one of us."

"But you will kill me for something else?" the prisoner demanded. "Anyway, you were the ones who invaded my lord's lands. For all I knew you were spying for one of his enemies."

"Unless you come against us we have no reason to go against you," Lili said.

The prisoner stared at her a moment longer before he nodded. "I accept your terms."

"What is your name?" Lili asked.

"That wasn't part of the deal," the prisoner said.

Lili inclined her head. "As agreed then." The smell of magic filled the air.

"Dione." The prisoner's answer brought silence. He looked at each of them. "What happened to setting me free?"

Trinity turned to Kinnon. "Why are you staring at him like that?"

"He tricked us," Darak said.

"I didn't. That's who hates him most. He killed two of her knights."

"Who is Dione?" Trinity asked.

Before anyone could answer, Emery appeared beside the double bed wearing a shirt and having changed out of his blood stained trousers, the scent of his magic lingering in the room. He dumped an armful of blankets on the bed. "What is going on?" He strode forward.

"You're the one who tricked me." The prisoner tried to draw back from Emery.

"He's under our protection." Lili put out a hand to stop Emery from coming any closer.

Emery took a step back, nodding. "That doesn't answer what is going on."

"I gave you a name. You said you'd set me free."

Trinity wanted to assure their prisoner that he was safe, but she wasn't sure of that. How many people had she tried to kill recently? If the prisoner attacked one of them, what would she do in an effort to protect those she cared about? "Can someone untie him?"

Emery drew a dagger, stepping forward.

"Not him. Anyone but him." Again the prisoner tried to draw away, pressed against the back of the chair.

Trinity took the dagger from Emery, surprised when Troy took it from her and stepped forward. "I can cut-" She broke off abruptly when her gaze settled on what he'd been bound with. "Vines?"

The moment the prisoner was free, he grabbed his bow and quiver and ran from the cottage. Silence was left in his wake, all of them looking through the doorway.

"Do we need to go after him?" Emery asked.

"No." Lili turned to Emery. "Thank you for bringing bedding."

"I wasn't able to collect bedrolls."

"What happened?" Troy handed the dagger back to Emery.

"Tarrant visited my lands earlier today, demanding to know if I'd been there. I took Roland and Naida somewhere safe."

"He didn't hurt them?" The last thing Trinity wanted was to have the elderly couple hurt over all of this. They didn't deserve that.

Emery shook his head. "They managed to fool him into believing I never visit. That I don't care for my lands."

"They can lie?" She'd thought they had magic.

"No." Emery glanced around the room. "What happened while I was gone?"

"If someone can explain it, I'll start dinner," Lili said.

Emery gestured towards the bed. "There's a parcel of meat I'd planned to cook on the fire. A handful of vegetables too. It isn't much, but they can be eaten by humans."

"It will be enough." Lili drew a dagger. "I'll dice up these ones if someone else wants to get the rest of the food."

Trinity watched as Troy and Kinnon helped Lili, Darak heading outside to scout around and make sure there was no one else who wanted to shoot them. She wanted to ask Lili how she could be so calm, smiling and laughing with Troy and Kinnon.

"Trinity?"

She turned to Emery, surprised at the uncertainty she could hear in his voice. "You weren't hurt, were you?" She reached for him.

He captured her hand. "Walk with me?"

She nodded, continuing to hold his hand as they headed outside. "Is something wrong?"

"What did the one you captured say?"

She almost censored what had happened, deciding at the last minute that he deserved to hear it all. Even the accusations. They ambled over the field, Trinity occasionally stumbling in the limited light from the moon. Silence followed her words. She stopped, turning to face him, wishing the moonlight was brighter so she could see his expression. "Say something."

"I could have told you Dione is his greatest enemy. She's the one who keeps sending her knights after him."

"What did Tarrant tell you? How did he convince you he was innocent?"

"He asked me what he was expected to do when someone attacked him. Let them kill him?" His hand momentarily tightened on hers. "How could I have been such a fool?"

"You trusted him." She placed her other hand on his chest, keeping hold of his hand. "You weren't the only one he fooled."

"That doesn't make it any easier. Not after all I've done."

"What did you do?"

"I never tortured anyone on his behalf. Not even when he told me to use whatever means necessary to gain information from his enemies."

"But what did you do?"

"Nor did I kill anyone on his behalf, but I'm beginning to think it might have been kinder if I had done so."

"Emery." The word was soft and she slid her hand up his chest to brush her fingers across his cheek. "Tell me."

"I gave them to him. Left him alone with them so he could supposedly ask them why they came against him." Emery paused. "After seeing what he did to Lili, I doubt he would have been gentle."

"I'm sorry."

"What have you to be sorry for?"

"That Tarrant took advantage of your loyalty like that. He didn't deserve it. And he will pay for it." Anger twisted through her and she had to fight against the overwhelming feeling of wanting to kill. She took a deep breath, trying to regain herself. "What will killing someone do to me?" The words came out through clenched teeth, her voice sounding like it belonged to another.

Emery drew his hand from hers, clasping her face with both his hands. "Let it go. The anger. Release it. Find peace before it consumes you."

She tried, but fear tried to rush in to take its place, which made the anger rush in again. "Tell me."

"You'll lose yourself. Become one filled with hate and anger." His thumb brushed back and forth across her cheekbone. "I'd hate to see that happen to you."

Her hand curled into a fist, clutching at the cloth

of his shirt as she struggled with her anger. "How long?" If it was a year she wouldn't last that long without killing anyone. The urge to do so continued to increase, worse every time it swamped her.

"A full cycle of the moon."

"A month?" Surely she could manage that amount of time. At least it wasn't as bad as a year. "We need to do something about Tarrant before then." Before her anger became too great to contain.

"We will. We'll find others to help us."

"What about Dione?"

"No one would ask the queen of the arachnid people for help."

"Arachnid? As in a spider?"

"Yes."

Chapter Thirty

Trinity shuddered, not wanting to know how it was possible for a spider to be a person. "Surely if-"

"No. It'd be more dangerous than facing Tarrant and his people without help."

"We can't face him alone."

"We'll let Tomas' uncle know what happened to him. Surely he'll go after his nephew."

She shook her head. "You can't go anywhere near his uncle. He's your enemy."

"He'll hear me out."

"That doesn't mean you're safe."

"If you were looking for safe, you shouldn't have come to this realm."

She glared at him when she heard humour in his voice. "Be serious."

"Haven't you been listening? I'm frequently accused of being too serious."

Both hands clutched at the material of his shirt. "Are you trying to get yourself killed?"

"Lili has her sons. She wouldn't miss me as much as you think."

"I'd miss you." She hit against his chest, still clutching at the material of his shirt, her words fierce.

"There are others who-"

"I would miss you." She emphasised the first word. "Why can't you understand that?" She hit against his chest again.

"Because I'm as good as landless. I saw your expression when you looked upon my land."

"I wanted to fix it." She breathed out heavily. "I guess I'm more interested in the land than I thought. But I don't want to be a landscaper like my dad. Making people's yards pretty for them has never interested me." She slid one of her hands up his chest to slide her fingers into his hair and tug his head towards hers. "I never have problems recognising what I'm interested in."

"What are you interested in?" His lips were centimetres from hers.

"What do you th-"

"Trinity!"

She nearly groaned at Troy calling out her name, interrupting the moment. When Emery started to draw away, she slid an arm around his waist, tugging his head back to hers. Troy could wait. Her lips met Emery's and she sank against him, his arms encircling her.

"Trinity."

Sighing, she drew back from Emery, remaining in his arms. Troy's voice had sounded closer. "We better see what's wrong." She kept hold of Emery's hand, walking back to the cottage, calling out to Troy as they came closer.

"Dinner's ready." He remained outside until she started to follow Emery inside. He took hold of her arm, tugging her to him so that her hand was drawn from Emery's. "Are you okay?"

She looked up at him, unable to say yes. Annoyance arrowed through her. Being forced to always tell the truth was more of a problem than she thought it would be.

"Trinity?"

"I'm still figuring this out."

"Are you hurt?"

She glanced down at her body, holding up her hands as she met his gaze. "Does it look like it?"

Troy sighed. "Why can't you answer me?"

"I don't want to worry you."

"Have you considered you're worrying me more by avoiding the question?"

"I don't know how to answer you. Every word I try to speak feels like a lie. Words have too many meanings. One meaning suits, but another doesn't and I know that. How do I convince myself that I'm speaking the truth when I want to use only one meaning of a word?"

"I don't know."

She smiled up at him, feeling the sadness in it. "I guess I'll figure it out somehow."

Troy wrapped his arms around her. "Of course you will."

She remained in the security of his arms for a moment before pulling away. "Didn't you say dinner was ready?"

Troy nodded. "Kinnon collected some bowls and spoons from somewhere. I think he went a little overboard in his choices though."

Stepping inside she faced the table, grinning when she spotted the gold bowls and spoons. "Have you been raiding your treasury?"

Kinnon returned her grin. "I didn't think anyone was likely to be in there at this hour. They're probably having their own meal."

"Taking foolish risks as usual," Darak muttered.

Trinity took the bowl Emery held out, smiling her thanks. The meal was silent and afterwards, Emery cleaned the dishes at the stream, shaking his head at Trinity's offer to help. Her and Troy were given the double bed to share while Lili had the single bed. The rest had blankets they lay before the fire.

Emery stood by the blankets he'd placed on the floor. "I'll take first watch."

"Why does anyone need to watch?" Trinity demanded. "We need sleep."

"I'll take second watch," Darak said.

Trinity sighed heavily. She supposed they knew their world better than she did. "I can help."

"We wouldn't want to interrupt your sleep," Darak said.

Trinity glared at him even though he likely couldn't see her. "I will help." No one answered her and she was tempted to repeat her words.

Emery walked across the cottage to the doorway, looking outside. "I'll wake you in a couple of hours, Darak."

She stared at Emery, smiling when he turned his head to look in her direction, as if he could feel her gaze on him. When he smiled before returning to gazing outside, she thought he might well have felt her watching him. She drifted off to sleep watching

Emery by the light of the fire, not waking until the sun had risen.

Turning on her side, she glanced around the cottage. Seeing no one, she sat up. She was alone. Her heart raced. What had happened to everyone? Before she could rise, the smell of old campfires filled the cottage.

Emery placed two large pies on the table, turning to face Trinity. His smile faded. "What is wrong?" He was across the room in seconds, clasping her hands as he sat on the edge of the bed.

"Where is everyone?"

"Lili's visiting the lord of these lands. Darak refused to let her go alone. She doesn't think he'll be able to help, but she wanted to ask anyway. Troy and Kinnon went to fetch water, thinking it best no one wander about alone after yesterday's incident."

"But you left me alone?" She couldn't believe they'd done that, but obviously they had.

"Naida called for me. I was only gone a couple of minutes." Emery glanced towards the table. "Long enough for her to give me the pies she baked this morning for us."

"Oh." She felt like an idiot.

"She told me to make sure you had plenty to eat

before I worried about feeding the rest." He met her gaze. "Did you think I'd desert you?"

She couldn't say no. Obviously she had. "I woke alone."

Letting go of one of her hands, he brushed her hair back from her face. "I'm sorry for that. I didn't think you'd wake so soon. You were sleeping deeply."

"One of you were meant to wake me so I could take a turn at keeping watch."

"No one agreed to that." He rose to his feet, drawing her up with him. "Do you want a slice of pie?"

She glanced around. "I don't suppose there's a bathroom around here."

"No, but I can take you to one."

She'd barely nodded when the world shimmered and reformed around her, the scent of Emery's magic fading. She looked around the area. "Where are we?"

"That is the tavern I took you to previously." He nodded towards the back of the nearby building before turning away from it. "The bathroom." He gestured to a small, timber building. "It's not much I'm afraid."

She didn't mind. "Thank you." It had to be better than going behind a tree. It didn't take her long to use the bathroom, washing her face after she'd washed her hands, the sink having a hand pump. She looked into the timber framed mirror that hung above the basin. The dim interior did nothing to hide how terrible she looked. Running her fingers through her dark brown hair, she grimaced, fingers snagging on numerous knots. It was going to take a lot more than that to make her look less rumpled.

When Trinity stepped outside, Emery held out a hand. "Ready to return to the cottage?"

She took his hand, now awake enough to realise no one knew where they were. "We didn't leave a note or anything."

Emery crushed a piece of bark in his hand, taking them back to the cottage in time to see Kinnon and Troy walk inside. He let go of Trinity's hand, gesturing towards the pies. "Compliments of Naida."

Seeing that Troy was about to say something, and expecting it would be something about her having left from the look of his expression, she grinned. "Naida said I was to have plenty to eat before worrying about feeding the rest of you."

Kinnon chuckled. "That doesn't surprise me. Every time I've seen her she's berated me about leading Emery into trouble."

Emery cut a piece of pie, placing it in one of the

gold bowls that were stacked on the table. "Do you think she has no reason to worry?"

Kinnon chuckled, helping himself to a large slice of pie once Emery had finished serving Trinity. "I never said that."

Trinity took a bite of the pie, waiting until her mouth was empty before she spoke. "Naida is an amazing cook."

Emery handed Troy a piece of pie in a bowl. "She said she cooked it so the human could eat it too."

"Thank her for me next time you see her." Troy took the bowl, glancing at it before grinning at Kinnon. "You couldn't have brought back something a little less fancy to serve our meals on?"

Kinnon shook his head. "They were convenient. Who keeps ordinary bowls in a treasury?"

Lili and Darak returned and it didn't take long for both pies to be eaten and arguments to start.

Chapter Thirty-One

Trinity glared at Darak. "We're not getting anywhere against Tarrant. We need more help." She looked at each of them. "He has enemies. Not just Dione. I can't see why we don't ask them for help."

"They would expect something in return," Darak said. "Are you willing to owe them a favour?"

"We're doing them a favour by letting them have their revenge against Tarrant," Trinity argued.

"It doesn't work like that," Kinnon said.

"Why not?" Trinity demanded.

"If we find more doses of the antidote we will have more help," Lili said.

"We can split into two groups. One can go after the antidote, the other can seek help," Darak said.

"I'll ask Tomas' uncle for help on his behalf," Emery said.

"I'm going with you," Trinity said.

"No." Emery, Troy and Kinnon spoke at the same time.

Trinity glared at them. "I'm not sitting around waiting." She glanced at Darak. "He didn't say no."

"That doesn't mean much," Troy muttered.

"Would you leave her here alone?" Darak demanded. "Or do we break into three groups. One to keep her safe while the rest of us go into danger?"

Trinity stepped closer to Darak. "Where are you going?"

"With Emery. If I have to go with the human I'm as likely to shoot him as to shoot an enemy. And Kinnon can't go with Emery as he upset Tomas' uncle a few years back."

"I forgot about that," Kinnon said.

Lili formed a flower, handing it to Darak. "Call if you should have need of us."

Darak formed a clove bud and held it out to his mother. "You call if you have any problems."

She pocketed the clove bud before holding a hand out to Kinnon. "Take the human's hand. We'll see if we can find a few doses of the antidote."

Troy met Emery's gaze, taking hold of Kinnon's hand. "You better not let anything happen to her."

"We need nine doses." Trinity barely managed to

speak the words before the three of them disappeared. She turned to Emery. "Will they get nine?"

"I'm sure they'll bring back as many as they possibly can."

That didn't reassure her. Before she could say anything else, Darak spoke.

"Are we going to convince Tomas' uncle to help or are we going to stand around here all morning?"

Emery held out his hand to Trinity, forming a piece of bark in the other hand. "Shall I meet you there?"

Darak inclined his head. He vanished, leaving behind the scent of cloves. Emery took her to Tomas' uncle's place, hurriedly speaking when they were greeted by weapons. Trinity looked around her in awe. She doubted she'd ever become accustomed to the magnificent castles some of the Fae lived in. Her awe quickly turned to annoyance when Tomas' uncle refused to believe them.

"Are you going to let Tomas spend the rest of his life as a garden ornament?" Trinity demanded.

"I have only your word that he's under a Troll enchantment." The Fae's expression showed how little he thought of her. "You think I should believe a human?"

"A human with magic. Which means I'm telling the truth."

"Or the truth as you see it." He gestured towards Emery and Darak. "Did they tell you to tell me these untruths? What are you really planning? Are you helping him gain revenge for his family?"

"I'm trying to help Tomas." She didn't bother hiding her exasperation.

"What do you get out of helping Tomas?"

"Nothing." She nearly yelled the word at him, shrugging Emery's hand off when he rested it on her shoulder.

"No one does anything for nothing. Leave before I decide to do the realm a favour and call for your deaths."

"I'll tell your nephew how little care you have for him." Darak turned away.

The Fae grabbed hold of Darak's arm before he could leave. "You'll do no such thing. This will not make me fall for your trick."

"Have you considered we might not be trying to trick you?" Emery asked.

"Why would you want to help either of us? What do you owe Tomas?"

"We owe him no debt," Emery said.

The Fae gave a single nod. "Which is why I refuse to believe you."

Trinity took a step closer to the Fae, trying to remain calm. "Are you willing to take that chance? Why not send others to check our claim? You don't have to go yourself."

The Fae released Darak to face Trinity. After a moment he gestured to a servant. "Bring my writing desk."

Trinity had expected something large, surprised that it was a timber box with a flat lid that the Fae used to write on, having first taken paper, ink and a pen from inside it. He dipped the nib of the pen into the ink before writing three separate letters and folding them. "These Fae owe me unspecified favours." He held the letters out to Darak. "Assure them that this will cancel their favours."

Darak tucked the letters away. "What have they done to earn your animosity?"

The Fae smiled, no humour in it. "They tried to trick me. They were the ones that ended up losing." His smile faded. "You will tell Tomas I offered help even when I didn't believe he was in need of it."

Darak inclined his head before walking to the exit.

Trinity started after Darak, stopping to face the

Fae. "I did ask a favour of Tomas, but I told him I wouldn't hold him to it."

"What was the favour?"

"To make barren land fertile."

The Fae stilled. "This was to repay me for what I did to Emery's lands?"

"No. This is about stopping Tarrant and rescuing those he's harmed." Her words caused a shiver to go through her. Not one of fear. One of anticipation. Her lips curved into a smile. Maybe all those years of rescuing things and people were about to come in handy.

"How can you expect me to believe you when you give me a look like that?" The Fae gestured towards Trinity.

Her smile widened into a grin. "Oh I've given up trying to get you to believe me. Doesn't mean we're going to let Tarrant get away with everything." She had no idea how they'd stop him, but she wasn't about to let him win. "Don't worry. We'll tell Tomas about the limited help you offered." She strode towards the exit, not bothering to look over her shoulder.

Darak had waited at the door to the room, falling into step with them. "He didn't offer any more help?"

"No."

"Guards patrol the gardens. Day and night."

She glanced at Darak, wondering what he was trying to do. "Are you being helpful or arguing against helping Tomas?"

"Neither."

She glanced at him again, unable to figure him out. But she supposed at least he wasn't glaring at her for a change. Outside, she looked at each of them. "Now what?"

Darak withdrew one of the letters. "We visit the first one." He frowned. "I've never been to his residence before."

Emery took the letter, his jaw tightening. "I have." He tucked the letter away, taking hold of Trinity's hand and forming a piece of bark.

She was about to ask him why he seemed bothered by the fact he'd visited the location before, when Darak took hold of her hand. Before she could say anything, the world reformed around her, a mansion now in front of them. "I was beginning to think most Fae live in castles."

Darak let go of her hand. "You think we are common?"

She frowned, trying to make sense of what he was saying. She shook her head, still confused. "What?"

"If all lived in castles that would make them the residence of the common people."

She glanced at Emery when he made a sound and her eyes narrowed. Had he been trying not to laugh? His expression remained neutral so she returned her attention to Darak. "I know very little about this realm."

"I don't need you to tell me that." Darak paused. "When are you going to tell me what you want? Or will it be an open ended debt like this Fae owes?" He gestured towards the mansion.

Again she struggled to work out what Darak meant.

"He's talking about when you saved his life," Emery said.

"Oh."

Emery nodded towards the approaching Fae, all of them armed. "You'll have to talk about it later. We have other things to focus on for now."

She rested her hand on Darak's arm. "You're already returning the favour."

Darak frowned. "How can I possibly be doing that when I'm working on getting my family's home back?"

"Stopping Tarrant." She glanced at the approaching Fae, close enough to hear what they might say. "Sometimes helping yourself also helps someone else." She nearly grinned when she saw the argumentative look in his eyes. It was more familiar than the neutral one and surprisingly comforting. Like everything in the world was right again.

"What are you doing here?" the Fae, who was in the lead, demanded.

"We request an audience with the lord of this manor," Emery said.

The Fae looked them over before nodding. "This way."

Trinity followed, Emery and Darak on either side. She glanced over her shoulder to see some of the Fae fall into place behind her. The swords hanging at their sides caught her attention. It felt uncomfortable to have weapons at her back. Especially weapons owned by those she had no reason to trust.

Inside the entrance, the Fae turned to them. "Wait here and I will see if my lord is available."

Emery held out the letter. "I am certain he will be available."

The Fae took the letter, nodding his head once before walking off.

Trinity watched him go, wishing he'd taken the rest of his companions. Conscious of the listening strangers, she remained silent, but was unable to remain still. Her gaze was drawn around the entrance room. Stairs headed upwards and doors led further into the dwelling. She shifted to her other foot, fed up with waiting. Was the Fae at home?

A different Fae joined them, holding the letter. "He sends me to fulfil his obligation?"

Emery nodded.

"Then I can send some of my knights to fulfil mine."

"How many?" Darak asked.

The Fae shrugged "A handful."

"Five isn't many," Emery said.

"He didn't specify how I was to help, only that I was to give you some help. Five knights is a great deal of help. Especially since you are likely to get them killed."

Chapter Thirty-Two

Trinity shook her head. "I don't want to get anyone killed."

The Fae shrugged again. "You might not want to, but these things happen. Do you think Tarrant is going to give up and let you win?"

"Of course not," Trinity said. "Do you think I'm an idiot?"

Once more the Fae shrugged. "I do not know you, do I?"

One of the Fae, who had remained to guard them, stepped forward. "My lord, are they going against Tarrant?"

"From what I've been told it would appear that way," the Fae said.

"Are you looking for volunteers?"

"Did you miss the part where I said you're likely to be killed, Cai?"

"No, my lord." The Fae paused. "Are you looking for volunteers?"

The Fae slowly shook his head. "I never would have thought you lacking in wit." He gestured towards Trinity and her companions. "Join them if you wish and find four knights to go with you."

"I know four who would gladly volunteer. I know three or four times that figure who'd be willing to help."

The Fae shook his head. "Five is all I need to send." He turned to Emery. "You may wait outside while my knight gathers another four to fight at his side." The Fae didn't wait for a reply before striding away.

Trinity stared after him, reeling from his attitude. He was sending knights to help them even though he thought they'd die. Somehow that seemed wrong. She waited until they were outside and alone before she voiced her concerns.

"What did you expect?" Darak demanded.

"I don't know. But not this. It feels wrong."

Emery took her hand. "We're not planning on getting them killed. We need them to create a diversion so we can sneak in and take the statues before Tarrant realises what we're up to. We'll ask Tomas to help us against Tarrant."

"You won't tell him he owes his help." She pointed a warning finger at Emery.

"He won't need to ask. Tomas will volunteer," Darak said.

"How do you know?" Trinity asked.

"You think any knight would willingly allow someone to get away with capturing them and forcing an enchantment on them? Would you?"

She was relieved when five knights strode towards them, allowing her to avoid answering the question. Once she'd have known exactly how to answer and it was a different one than what she feared she would have given Darak. She tried to push away the anger that rose in her. A darkness accompanied it and she took a deep breath, refusing to think about Tarrant. That made her feel like killing. A thoroughly alien feeling.

"What would you have us do?" Cai asked.

Emery drew the remaining two letters from his pocket. "We need to request more help."

Cai shook his head, pointing at the name scrawled on the letter facing him. "He is Tarrant's friend."

"Are you certain?" Emery asked.

"I know his every friend and enemy. I've gathered information in the hope of finding a weak point." Cai met Emery's gaze. "I even know who you are and what you have been to him. What I don't know is why you're currently searching out those to go against him."

"Yet you agreed to come with us," Darak said.

Cai turned his attention to Darak. "As I said, I know who Emery is. I knew one day he'd learn the truth of who he served. I'm hoping this is that day. His honour would never allow him to ignore what he's done through misguided loyalty."

"I've never had any dealings with you on behalf of Tarrant. Only your lord."

"My sister was caught up in that mess. You protected her."

Emery inclined his head. "She was innocent."

"So was my lord," Cai said.

Worried what the news would do to Emery, Trinity interrupted. "What are we going to do about the other two letters?"

Emery showed the second letter to Cai. "What does this lord think of Tarrant?"

"He's not above being on Tarrant's side when it suits him, but has gone against him previously as well. Not openly though."

Emery tucked the letters away. "We'll make do with what we have." He turned to Darak. "The cottage?"

Darak nodded. "I can take two. If you take Trinity and Cai I can come back for the rest."

"I could help." Trinity formed a seed.

Darak looked at the seed on the palm of her hand. "Are you certain?"

"I've travelled using this method before." It had been one location, but she was certain she could find her way to the cottage. It was clear in her mind.

Cai held out a hand. "I'm willing to chance your abilities." He grinned, pale blue eyes lighting with mischief. "Becoming lost with a beautiful human wouldn't be the worst experience."

"She is under my protection," Emery said.

Darak spoke at the same time. "If any harm befalls her while she's in your company you'll wish for death."

Trinity stared at Darak, startled by his words and the menace in his tone.

Cai continued to hold out his hand. "My offer still stands. I wouldn't harm someone with a connection to Emery. Without him my sister would have lost her life."

Unsettled by Darak's words, Trinity took Cai's hand, bringing the cottage to mind. The last thing she needed was yet one more who thought they needed to look out for her. Next time Troy, Kinnon and Emery told her 'no' would Darak echo them? "Are you ready?"

Cai nodded.

She crushed the seed, the rich smell of Christmas cake filling the air, the image of the cottage replaced by the bent and twisted tree at the last second. She swore when the world reformed, drawing her hand from Cai's. "Why can't I travel anywhere else?" Frustration filled her words.

"You might need more practice," Cai suggested. "I'm willing to help you."

She recognised the look in his eyes. "I have more than enough help in my life already." She stressed the word 'help'.

"That is disappointing." He held out his hand. "But I'm willing to help anyway."

Before she had the chance to take his hand, Emery appeared at her side, the scent of his magic fading away. She faced Emery. "I tried. But it became this place at the last second."

"I'm surprised you can travel anywhere since you've had no training." Emery took her hand with a smile.

"Fascinating." Cai took her other hand. "That must be some powerful magic you wield."

Trinity opened her mouth to tell him it came from

Arwyn, but Emery interrupted before she could speak.

"As powerful and dangerous as her allies."

"I meant my earlier words." Cai held Emery's gaze. "She's safe in my company. That will not change. My debt to you is great."

"Yet you never came forward to repay it," Emery said.

"I was waiting for the time when it wouldn't be twisted into a debt to Tarrant."

Emery inclined his head before forming a piece of bark, taking them to the cottage. He drew Trinity outside once Cai let go of her hand, bending his head close to hers. "You're unharmed?"

"I'm annoyed. Why can't I do this? I can obviously travel to that one location, so why can't I go to other places?"

Emery's expression relaxed, a smile momentarily forming. "It's not something easily learned. Some take weeks to learn the ability."

"Then what's wrong with me that I could do it the first time I tried?"

"I was serious when I said your magic is powerful and dangerous. Going to that location could possibly have something to do with taking Tarrant there the first time you used it."

She sighed heavily. Of course it would somehow be related to Tarrant. Wasn't everything these days? "How do I fix it?"

"Practice."

She growled in frustration. "I want to know how to do it now."

Troy came outside. "What's wrong?"

"Nothing new," Trinity muttered. Problems with Tarrant. She started to walk towards the cottage, freezing when she realised what she'd done. There were new developments, but she'd been so focused on how they were related to Tarrant who wasn't a new problem. A smile slowly formed. "I think I figured something out."

"Are you going to share it?" Troy asked.

Her smile widened into a grin that made her cheeks ache. "Nope." She strode inside the cottage, brushing past Troy, stopping when she realised how crowded the building was. "We need bigger headquarters."

Troy laughed softly. "I think the problem is that someone stole the bigger headquarters."

"Then how about we work on getting them back." Trinity looked to Lili. "Did you get the antidote?"

Lili inclined her head. "Five doses."

"She wanted to take them to Arwyn and Braeden, but we don't know how long that will take. Even if it only takes her a few minutes, and she leaves Rod to deal with it, she could be gone from the realms of the Fae for hours," Troy said.

"They need to be freed of the enchantment," Darak stated.

"We have to help Tomas and his knights." Trinity looked at those crowding the cottage. "Although I don't know where we'll put them."

"What about Tarrant?" Cai demanded. "That's why we're here."

"I won't have anyone else destroyed by Tarrant's lies. We rescue Tomas first," Emery said.

"Since when do we answer to the landless or almost landless?" one of Cai's knights demanded. "We volunteered because we're going after Tarrant. No other reason." There were murmurs of agreement from his companions, Cai remaining silent.

Darak took a step towards the knight who had spoken. "We will not go after Tarrant until we can be assured he won't escape." He took one more step towards the knight, eyes narrowed. "I am not a landless knight."

The knight took a step back, glancing away, clearing his throat. "It's why we're here." His words were low, his gaze on the floor.

Darak turned to Troy. "You will go with my

mother to the human realm and wait with her for the twelve hours." He lowered his voice. "If she's harmed while in your care you will not appreciate what happens."

"I came to look out for Trinity. I'm not going home until she does." Troy met Darak's gaze, holding it steadily.

"You think she will be going home?" Darak demanded.

Troy held Darak's gaze a moment before turning to Trinity. "Are you staying here? In this realm?"

Chapter Thirty-Three

Trinity shrugged, unable to say the word 'no'. The human world was too painful for her to remain in for long periods of time. She glanced at Emery before returning her gaze to Troy. She didn't regret anything. "Would you visit me if I stayed here?"

"You know I would."

Kinnon formed a flower, the scent of his magic filling the cottage. "Looks like everything is sorted. I'm going to visit one of the kitchen maids who's rather fond of me and see if she knows where the new statues are."

"Fond of you?" Troy asked.

Kinnon chuckled. "She gave me treats when I was younger and I was sent to bed without dessert." He glanced at his mother. "Apparently I was too charming to refuse."

"Then why did you make such a production over missing dessert?" Lili asked.

"You would have come up with another punishment if I hadn't." Still grinning, Kinnon crushed the flower and vanished.

Lili sighed, turning to Troy. "Are you ready to go?"

"What about the other three doses of the antidote you brought back?" Trinity asked before Troy could speak.

"I have them," Darak said.

Troy crossed the distance between him and Trinity, crushing her to him. "Any messages for Rod?"

"Tell him I'm alive." She returned his hug. "But don't tell him what I plan on doing."

"What do I tell him?"

"That we have others we need to wait for so we can give them the antidote."

Troy let her go, stepping back. "If you think he'll focus on the word 'wait' you don't know your father."

She shrugged. "It's worth a try." She paused. "Be careful when you return here."

Darak looked to his mother. "We'll leave a message

under the mattress of the double bed if we need to relocate."

Lili nodded, taking Troy's hand. The scent of her magic filled the cottage a moment before her and Troy vanished.

Trinity stared at the spot where they'd been. How long would it be before they returned? She looked to Darak, surprised when he moved to her side. "What now?"

"We wait for Kinnon to return so we can make our plans."

"I'll bring back lunch." Emery gave a nod to Darak, leaving when Darak returned the nod.

"What was that about?" Trinity asked Darak.

It was Cai who answered. "He left him in charge." He turned to the knights with him. "You two scout the area." He nodded to another one. "You're on watch at the rear of the cottage." He turned to the last one. "You watch the front." He glanced at each of his companions. "All of you remain out of sight."

Trinity waited until they'd left. "Why are you in charge of them?"

"The same reason why most people are in charge in this realm."

Trinity turned to Darak, about to ask him what Cai meant.

Darak spoke without needing to be asked. "Those with the most power do the best in our realm. Land, gold, magic. If you have all three you do even better."

She slowly shook her head. "Guess there isn't much difference between your realm and my world."

Cai chuckled. "I've been to your world. There's a great deal of difference."

"Not when it comes down to it." She glanced at the doorway. "I'm going for a walk." She stopped at the front door, turning to Darak who followed her. "Alone."

"That will not be happening."

She glared at Darak, walking away, frowning when he walked at her side. "Why have you suddenly become my shadow?"

"I would have thought that was clear."

"No." Her annoyance lifted and she held back a smile. "Unless I was right and I really do own you and your brothers."

"You'll have to do better than that if you wish to chase me away."

Her annoyance returned and she went back to glaring at her surroundings. A sigh escaped and she pushed away the annoyance, worried it might lead to anger. "What do you know about the old blood magic?"

Darak stopped abruptly, grabbing her arms and turning her towards him. He kept his voice low, standing close. "Is that what happened?"

"Let me go." She spoke through gritted teeth, anger instantly rising.

Darak kept hold of her, loosening his grip, but remaining close. "Why would you meddle in that?"

"I didn't know. I was trying to save Emery."

"Keep your voice down." Darak glanced around. "Tell no one."

"Why not?" She kept her voice low, not wanting to share her problems with the other Fae.

"Because in your modern terms, one who gives into that kind of magic would be considered a serial killer."

Shock raced through her at his words. Twice she opened her mouth to question him. She didn't bother a third time. What answers would he give her? Ones she'd be afraid to hear? "I didn't know it was that bad."

"You will fight it and your magic will become what it should be," Darak stated.

"That's easy for you to say," Trinity muttered.

"I never said it would be easy." He looked past her. "Emery has returned." He released her arms.

Trinity turned to see Emery stride towards her,

concern visible in his eyes when he drew near. She wanted to demand why he hadn't explained things as clearly as Darak. "What did you bring for lunch?"

Emery looked from one to the other a couple of times before he spoke. "Bread and cold roast beef. Naida sent biscuits for you too."

She slipped her hand in Emery's watching as Darak strode away before turning to Emery and smiling up at him, trying not to think about what Darak had told her. "Stop worrying."

"Are you telling me I have nothing to worry about?"

A smile escaped. "Not unless I can learn how to lie in the next few minutes."

"Then how can I not worry?"

"Because it won't change anything." She took a step towards the cottage, not looking forward to returning to the too small building. "I want my biscuits."

Emery drew her back to him. "What were you and Darak discussing?"

"Serial killers and magic." She was looking into his sky blue eyes so it was impossible to miss the flicker of anger that briefly appeared in them.

"He had no right."

"He had every right. Why didn't you tell me?"

"Sometimes knowing what might happen can cause it to happen. It can prey on your mind until it becomes a reality."

A shiver ran through her and she drew in an unsteady breath. "I can't sit around waiting for the next month to pass." Even if being in the thick of things was dangerous. "I don't do well sitting around doing nothing." The slightest thing would probably have her losing her temper. Worse than what she'd done so far.

Emery held her close. "We'll help you through this."

She sank against him, feeling his warmth and the strength of his arms surrounding her. "I know." But she didn't know if it'd be enough. Taking a deep breath, she drew back, smiling up at him. "Now where are my biscuits?"

Holding her hand, Emery walked back to the cottage with her. They were nearly finished lunch when Kinnon returned with news of where the statues were. They were lined up along one of the paths behind the castle, swords raised to create an archway. Tarrant had obviously used the minute the potion took to take effect to pose his victims. Trinity stared at Kinnon when he said the maid had told him there were ten statues. More than what they were expecting.

It took over an hour for them to settle on a plan everyone was happy with and they waited for the sun to set, Emery taking Trinity for a walk along the stream when she became frustrated with pacing the confines of the cottage.

She peppered him with questions about his childhood, grinning when Kinnon joined them, telling her of some of the escapades he and Braeden had dragged Emery and Darak into. When the sun drew close to the horizon, Emery left Trinity with Kinnon so he could collect their dinner.

Kinnon stepped close to her, keeping his voice low. "Darak told me."

She didn't bother acting like she didn't know what he was talking about. "Is he planning to tell the entire world?"

"Only those of us who'll protect and help you. There are some who might use it to their advantage."

She was about to demand who would do something like that when an image of Tarrant came to mind. No doubt he'd find a serial killer useful to have around. "We should go back to the cottage." She didn't want to think about the problems that loomed over them.

By the time night fell, she was rethinking her insistence on joining them, but it would have been worse to sit around the cottage waiting and wondering what was happening to all of them. She held Emery's hand, taking Cai's when he reached for her, the world shimmering and reforming around them. The night was broken by lanterns placed throughout the surrounding gardens. The shadowy rose arbour they stood in kept them hidden.

Emery let go of her hand. "Stay out of sight until I return to let you know everyone is in place." He vanished, the smell of old campfires lingering.

Trinity peered around the edge of the arbour, her gaze drawn to the statues lining the path several metres from them. "I wonder who else Tarrant forced to drink the Petrification enchantment."

Cai drew her back from the edge as a guard came closer. "You were the one who agreed to this plan. If we're discovered I will go with my plan."

"You didn't have a plan. You had a suicide mission."

"He must be stopped. No matter what it takes."

Before Trinity could continue the argument, Emery returned.

"Your knights have attacked out the front, led by Darak. Give it a minute and we'll start transporting the statues to the cottage." Emery took hold of Trinity's hand. "Stand guard. Warn us if anything changes between our journeys."

She nodded, wishing she could help transport the statues. Leaving them under the tree where Tarrant's father had died probably wouldn't be a good idea. "I know what to do."

Emery drew her close, his lips briefly meeting hers before pulling back, staring at her for a few seconds. "Be careful."

She watched him hurry after Cai, noticing that Kinnon was already standing by one of the statues. He disappeared, taking the statue with him, the other two doing the same. She took a deep breath, trying to keep the fear at bay. That tended to be quickly replaced by anger and a desire to kill. Which was the last thing she needed. Relief rushed through her when the three Fae returned, taking another three statues with them. Her gaze was drawn to Tomas, the closest statue. He'd be collected last, along with her.

The three Fae appeared once more taking statues with them. Trinity waited a couple of minutes before creeping out of her hiding place, heading towards Tomas. Before she reached him, Tarrant appeared by the statue.

He drew his sword. "I knew it. There were too few

attacking for it to be anything other than a diversion." He swung his sword at Tomas.

Chapter Thirty-Four

"No!" Trinity flung a gust of air at Tarrant, preventing his sword from impacting with the stone, driving him back a few metres.

Cai appeared beside Tomas, drawing his sword to attack. The clash of metal rang out in the garden, a constant sound as Cai was driven towards Tomas.

Trinity rushed forward, drawing the air from around the fighters, anger rushing through her. It seemed to make no difference to Tarrant, only Cai stumbled, his hand going for his throat. She drew more air from around them.

Tarrant remained on his feet, his sword coming for Cai. The knight had no chance of escaping the blow.

Shock raced through Trinity as it hit her that she was about to get Cai killed. Releasing the air, she caused the ground to erupt beneath their feet. Both knights were thrown backwards, Tarrant's blade missing Cai by centimetres. Trinity grabbed Cai's hand, wrapping her arm around the statue of Tomas, crushing the seed she'd formed, taking them to the twisted tree.

"What did you think you were doing?" Cai dragged his hand from hers. "I have to go after him."

She grabbed his hand again. "No. He'll kill you."

"I've waited two years for this chance and you stole it from me." He tugged his hand from her again.

This time she threw herself at him, her arms wrapping around him. "He won't go free."

Cai stilled. "Release me, Trinity."

"Not until you promise to forget about going after Tarrant tonight."

The scent of old campfires filled the air. "I thought I might find you here."

Trinity kept hold of Cai, looking over her shoulder. "Help me convince him not to go after Tarrant alone."

"Tell her to release me," Cai ordered.

"I'm surprised you didn't take her back to the gardens," Emery said. "I thank you for not putting her in danger."

"I wish I could accept your thanks. It wasn't from lack of trying. You were right when you said her magic is powerful. I wasn't able to leave here."

Trinity let go of him, stumbling back. "I didn't–" She shook her head. "I wasn't doing anything."

"Willing him to stay?" Emery asked.

Her mouth opened, but no words escaped. A plan began to form and her lips curved into a smile. "Can I do that to anyone?"

Emery shrugged.

"Who is more powerful than Tarrant?" Trinity demanded.

"Arwyn," Emery said.

"I need to test this."

Cai sheathed his sword. "Tell me your plan. Will we be able to bring Tarrant down?"

Trinity held his gaze a moment, seeing the hope in his eyes. "We can set a trap for him. Away from his knights. With no one to protect him we can easily take him down."

"You have my help," Cai said. "I promise not to go after him tonight."

She turned to Emery, a question in her eyes.

"We don't know if it will work."

"Only one way to figure that out." She grinned. "Well?"

Emery nodded. "I'll always protect you."

She threw herself into his arms, holding him tight,

hearing a sound of surprise from Cai. She grinned up at Emery. "That goes both ways." Her lips met his.

Cai spoke when they broke apart. "I thought you were Darak's pet."

Trinity met Cai's gaze, her chin rising. "I am no one's pet." A grin formed. "Actually, they belong to me."

Emery chuckled. "Not from what I've noticed."

"They were given to me. So that makes them mine."

Emery looked past her to Cai. "I'll meet you at the cottage." A piece of bark formed in his hand.

Trinity wrapped an arm around Tomas, her gaze drawn to Cai. "We'll get Tarrant. He won't get away with all he's done."

Cai nodded. "Thank you."

The world shimmered around her and reformed. She was standing out the front of the cottage, surrounded by statues, their swords raised. Letting go of Tomas, she stepped through the maze of statues, Emery at her side. "We have to get them out of the starlight."

"We only have three doses," Emery reminded her.

"How do we choose who receives them?" Stepping inside the cottage, Trinity turned to face the statues. "Other than Tomas."

"We bring him in out of the starlight. He can decide tomorrow morning."

She slowly shook her head. "More waiting." A chuckle behind her had her turning to face Kinnon. "What do you find so amusing?"

"I'd only finished saying something similar to Darak minutes before you arrived."

Darak pushed his brother aside. "If you're not going to help bring Tomas in then get out of the way."

Trinity stepped out of the doorway and watched as Tomas was brought inside. She helped wrap blankets around him.

Cai stopped in the doorway. "My companions and I will be back in twelve hours."

Trinity hurried over to him. "I'm sorry about earlier."

"Which in particular?"

"Taking the air from around you. I can't understand why it didn't work on Tarrant again."

"I thought that was Tarrant." Cai inclined his head. "Your apology is accepted. As long as you remember that a trick you've used before is likely to be anticipated and planned for a second time. Tarrant was probably drawing air towards himself before you started taking it away from him."

"Oh."

Cai smiled, a crooked one that lingered. "It takes time to learn how to fight with magic." He nodded towards the other occupants of the cottage. "I'll see you in the morning. There isn't the space for all of us and there's no point in getting no rest when we still need to face Tarrant."

"See you in the morning." She watched him return to his companions, seeing them standing amongst the statues. Seconds later they were gone, only the statues remaining. "Is it safe to leave the statues outside?"

Kinnon shrugged. "It isn't like we have anywhere else to leave them."

"We could take them to my place," Trinity said.

"No," Darak stated. "We can't risk the time differences." He paused. "We'll take turns at keeping watch."

Trinity met his gaze. "You will wake me so I can take a turn."

"You can have first watch."

She nodded at Darak's words. "Thank you."

Once Emery had brought them dinner and the meal was eaten, they argued over who had which bed. Emery took the single bed since he had second watch and then Trinity would use it. The others would take turns at sharing the double bed. Emery gave her his pocket watch so she could keep track of the time.

The quiet settled around her and she began to wish she hadn't insisted on taking a turn. It left her with too much time to think about everything. She couldn't stop thinking about serial killers, starting with Jack the Ripper all the way through to more current ones. That wasn't her. Yet several times now she'd wanted to take a life. More than one life.

The time passed slowly and her thoughts raced through too many unpleasant topics. She was relieved when it was time to wake Emery, giving him his pocket watch before lying down on the single bed. It didn't help. Sleep was a long time coming and when it arrived her dreams were filled with knives dripping blood, dead bodies piled high and Tarrant encouraging her to kill.

She woke to find two pies on the table, Emery standing nearby. "Is something wrong?"

He shook his head. "I was about to wake you. Tomas will be ready for the antidote shortly. We've covered the windows and door so no light can get in and we'll unwrap him soon."

She staggered out of bed, feeling like she'd barely slept.

Emery held out a hand. "Did you want me to take you to the tavern again?"

For a second she was confused. "Yes. I don't suppose there's somewhere I can wash."

"We've been using the stream." Kinnon grinned, sitting at the table, his legs stretched out. "Want someone to keep an eye out for intruders?"

She rolled her eyes. "If I did it certainly wouldn't be you." She was startled when Darak chuckled. She was accustomed to his anger. Her gaze remained on him, finding it easy to see why Troy had initially been drawn to him.

Darak sobered. "Is something wrong?"

She shook her head, turning to Emery and holding out her hand. "I'm ready to go now."

They weren't gone long, but returned to find Cai had arrived and Tomas had been unwrapped. Cai joined them for breakfast, explaining that his lord had said their obligation was done. Tomas had been rescued.

"Does that mean you won't be able to help us anymore?" Trinity licked the crumbs from her fingers, eyeing the empty pie dishes. Naida certainly could cook.

"It would if I continued to serve him. The knights

that were with us yesterday are currently regretting their oaths."

She frowned, trying to figure out what was going on. "What do you mean? Don't you still serve him?"

"I told him that my oath to him is finished. I only served him for as long as our goals coincided. They no longer do."

"What will you do once this is over?" Emery asked.

Cai shrugged. "I'm sure I'll find another knight to serve. One who'll help me earn enough gold so I can buy my own land."

"Doesn't your family have land?" Trinity asked.

Cai's crooked smile appeared. "They also have many children."

Movement caught Trinity's attention and she saw Tomas lower his sword. Rising to her feet, she collected the potion bottle from the table, taking it to him.

He held her gaze, not taking the potion. "What are your terms?"

"You already know them." She continued to hold out the bottle.

"They were not terms. You might as well have told me to do what I want."

Trinity grinned. "I thought I did."

"What are your terms?" Tomas demanded.

Chapter Thirty-Five

Trinity lowered her hand. "That you take your dose and choose two people to take the other two doses and the three of you find enough of the antidote for the rest of the statues out there."

Tomas stared at her for a moment. "You are serious."

She nodded.

"I'd be crazy not to accept your terms."

"Are you crazy?" Darak asked.

Tomas looked from Trinity to Darak and back again. "I think I must be."

She sighed heavily. The morning wasn't going as planned. "What terms do you want?"

"I want Tarrant."

"Don't we all," Cai said.

Tomas glanced around the cottage. "I want to be a part of your plans. I want to see him taken down."

"That's it?" Trinity asked.

Tomas met her gaze again. "I'll help you make barren land fertile. But it'll take more than those of us here. Likely two or three times." He glanced towards the covered doorway. "How many statues are outside?"

"Nine."

"Even they wouldn't be enough."

She smiled. "It's a start. We don't have to do it straight away. We can wait until we have enough."

Emery came to stand beside Trinity, taking the potion from her and holding it out to Tomas. "We have a deal?"

Tomas nodded, taking the potion bottle, the scent of magic mingling in the room. "We do." He took a sip of the potion before holding the bottle out to Emery.

"It's for you to administer to another two." Emery drew two letters out. "Your uncle gave us some help in rescuing you. Only one of the lords he directed us to were of any use."

Trinity took the letters from Emery. "What do we do with the ones we didn't use?"

Tomas started to reach for them, then sighed. "Return them."

"You were going to say something else?" Trinity studied his expression, but it gave nothing away.

"I was tempted to trick you out of them, but that would have been poor payment for what you've done for me." He grinned, amusement in his eyes. "Although I doubt your knight would have allowed it." He nodded towards Emery.

She grinned. "My knight." She glanced at Emery. "I much prefer that to being called someone's pet."

"I bet you do," Darak muttered from where he stood behind Trinity.

Still grinning, she faced him. "Can you blame me?"

Darak gave a half shrug before turning to Kinnon. "Help Tomas take the statues somewhere secure. Surely he has somewhere they can be kept."

"What will you be doing?" Kinnon asked.

"Scouting the area." Darak strode outside.

"What can I do?" Trinity asked.

"I'll remain with you," Emery said.

"I can help."

"Not until you've had more practice at travelling with magic," Emery said.

She started to argue, then realised it wasn't her that wanted to do the arguing. Her anger faded as quickly as it had come and she tried to hold back the fear. She glanced at Emery, unable to meet his gaze for more than a second, worried at what he might see. "I'll help Darak. You help Kinnon and Tomas." She hurried outside, scanning the area for Darak. Spotting the Fae, she strode after him.

He glanced at her when she reached his side, but remained silent. They did a circuit of the area, including wandering along the stream. Darak stopped by a deeper section, gesturing towards it. "This is where we bathe." He turned his back on the stream, taking several steps away, crossing his arms over his chest as he kept his back to the stream.

She hesitated. When he remained where he was, she stripped off and plunged into the water, drawing in a sharp breath from the cold. "A warning about how cold the water is would have been good."

Darak chuckled. "Where did you get the idea that I was that kind?"

She grinned. "I don't think you're as bad as you would have me believe." After a quick wash she returned to the bank, struggling to drag her clothes on over wet limbs.

"I'm worse than you think if you're a threat to my family."

She pulled her t-shirt over her head, tugging it down. "I'm dressed."

He faced her. "I'd hate to see you become a threat to my family."

"Why would I ever become one?"

"The potential is there." He paused. "Until a cycle of the moon has ended."

She couldn't stop the shiver that ran through her. "Did you have to remind me?"

"Yes. You are not to ever forget the danger you're in. That those around you are in."

Images of Cai came to mind, his hand at his throat. They were quickly followed by ones of Emery also struggling to breathe. "I don't want to end up killing anyone."

Darak came closer. "I visited someone early this morning while Kinnon was on watch."

"Who?"

"Someone who accidentally ended up in your situation."

"Did they survive the month?"

"Think of someone you'd never harm. One person it would hurt you to harm. Do you have someone like that?"

A smile formed, relief filling her. "It's that easy?"

"No. It won't be easy. But if we have a name we can tell you it can help you return from the brink."

"I can do better than that. I can give you lots

of names. My baby brother, Sebastian. My parents. Rod and Christine. My best friends Troy and Yvette. There's also Emery, you and your brothers. Even your parents. I wouldn't want anything to happen to any of you."

"I don't think you understand how serious this is. Who would you risk your life for? Who is someone you couldn't imagine not having in your life?"

"Nearly every name I mentioned."

"If each person you named stood in front of archers, bows drawn, an arrow pointed at each, who would you save? Who would you fling yourself in front of to keep them from being shot?"

She glared at him, refusing to make such an impossible decision. "I would cause the ground to erupt beneath the feet of the archers." Her words were fierce.

Darak smiled. "Emery is very fortunate."

"I hope you weren't expecting me to disagree."

"Not at all." He gestured in the direction of the cottage. "Shall we see if they're finished?"

She hesitated.

"What bothers you?"

"Who else has magic as strong as your father's?"

"This is about the trap you want to set for Tarrant?"

She nodded.

"Emery was talking to me about it this morning while you slept. There's no one else we can ask to help test your abilities. No one we could trust."

"Oh."

"They'll return to the cottage as soon as possible. Then we'll see what happens and make plans accordingly."

Anticipation raced through her at the thought of facing Tarrant again. It was immediately followed by shock. She couldn't kill him. Her breath froze in her throat, fear clawing at her. She couldn't.

Darak rested a hand on her shoulder. "Focus on the names. On the faces that go with the names. Picture them."

She focused on his soft words, her gaze roaming his face, none of the other faces able to come into focus over the sensations swamping her. Darak might not be her favourite person, but she wouldn't want him to die. His family would be devastated. Family. Images of her family finally began to form. All of them, including Troy.

Darak relaxed his grip on her shoulder. "Who was it?"

"You."

He drew his hand away as if bitten, taking a step back. "How could it have been me?"

"I couldn't bring a single face to mind. But staring at yours helped. It made me think of how your family would feel to lose you. Which made me think of my family. All of my family." She stepped forward. "I have more than one person I'd be devastated to lose." She met his gaze. "How about you? Who would you choose to save?"

"All of them." His words were as fierce as hers had been.

She laughed. "And you expected me to be able to choose?"

"Maybe you're more Fae than you think."

"Or maybe the one you talked to had a lack of people worth loving in their life."

Darak shrugged. "It's always possible." He turned sideways, gesturing in the direction of the cottage again. "Shall we?"

She nodded, walking beside him to the cottage, wondering if it was possible she'd get through the month without killing someone.

The day dragged on and Trinity began to rethink her earlier optimism, alternating between boredom, anger, fear and murderous thoughts. When Lili arrived late afternoon, bringing with her Troy, shortly followed by returning with Arwyn and Braeden, Trinity initially felt relief. It was followed by the other emotions. She focused on Troy's face, taking his hands as she looked him over.

"You're unharmed?" Troy asked.

She nodded, unable to speak while she fought to gain control over her emotions.

"Rod asked when you were coming home."

She shrugged.

Troy frowned. "Are you sure you're okay?"

Kinnon, Cai and Tomas arrived back, Kinnon coming forward to greet his family, a grin firmly in place. He turned to Troy, thanking him for helping, interrupting Troy and Trinity.

Chapter Thirty-Six

Trinity was relieved, stepping away to compose herself, surprised to find Darak at her side. He momentarily rested his hand on her shoulder and she met his gaze, giving him a brief nod of thanks for watching over her to make sure she didn't hurt anyone she cared about.

Everyone seemed to talk at once. Tomas said they had enough doses of the antidote, and a few spare. Troy talked about Rod being worried Trinity wouldn't be back in time for the next school semester the following week. And Trinity could hardly believe it had been Wednesday when Troy had left their world.

Eventually the conversation got around to Arwyn helping Trinity with something. Darak took him aside, Cai and Tomas still with them. Trinity was glad he didn't tell everyone what was wrong with her. While they were outside, Lili asked Tomas if he could take Braeden to his place since he was too weak after letting his magic become so low.

Arwyn entered the cottage, holding a hand out to Trinity. "Shall we see if you have the strength to trap Tarrant?"

"You're going after him now?" Troy demanded. "On your own?"

She shook her head. "We're checking what I'm capable of first."

"How do you do that?" Troy asked.

She glanced at Cai and Tomas. "I'll tell you later." And she would, when they were alone. She didn't trust Cai and Tomas with her problems. Not after everything Darak had said. She didn't know them well enough. Forming a seed, her gaze remained on Troy.

He nodded. "I'll see you soon."

Even though he hadn't made it a question, she nodded before crushing the seed and taking Arwyn to the bent and twisted tree. The only place she was capable of travelling to with magic. She held onto Arwyn's hand, meeting his gaze, willing him to remain with her.

"What will you do if Tarrant tries to pull away from you?" Arwyn asked.

She grinned, reaching for the roots beneath the soil. They fought her and her grin faded as she focused on keeping them around Arwyn's legs. When he tried to draw from her grip, she sent one of the roots through the soil to bind their hands together. Then everything changed and she narrowed her eyes, determined to win. To keep him bound, to never let him escape. The scent of magic filled the air and the ground heaved beneath her feet. The roots of the tree kept her anchored.

"Trinity. You can stop," Arwyn said.

But she couldn't. The roots tightened, climbing higher up his body.

"Trinity." Emery wrapped his arms around her.

The shock of finding Emery with her when she hadn't noticed him arrive brought her back to her senses. "Sorry." The word was a whisper and she was unable to meet Arwyn's gaze as she released his hand, the tree roots returning to the ground. The soil smoothed out beneath her feet and she wondered if it was Arwyn who'd done that. It certainly hadn't been her.

"Did you have something to tell me, Emery?" Arwyn asked.

Trinity raised her chin, looking directly at Arwyn. "He didn't do anything wrong."

"I never claimed he did." Arwyn looked past her. "A warning that she isn't in control of her magic would have been appreciated."

"That's why we followed you," Emery said.

"We?" Trinity turned in his arms to see Kinnon and Darak were nearby. She glared at them. "I don't need three babysitters." She was surprised they hadn't brought Troy.

Kinnon came forward. "Don't you keep telling us you own us?" He grinned. "If that's the case then would it not make sense we'd follow you to attend to your every need?"

Her glare didn't falter. "As if you believe that."

"You won't face Tarrant alone." Emery released her, taking hold of her hand. "Shall we return to the cottage and discuss with everyone what sort of trap we'll set for Tarrant?"

She wanted to argue, but there was no reason to. Realising it was the magic messing with her mood, she breathed out slowly. It didn't help. She wanted a fight. "Let's get this over and done with." Before she ended up killing someone.

Emery nodded, forming a piece of bark and taking them to the cottage, the rest of their companions coming with them. He glanced around. "Where's Tomas?"

Cai leaned against the wall near the door, his arms crossed over his chest. "Went to talk to his uncle. He's not happy with his uncle's limited help."

Before Trinity could say that if he wasn't here then he'd miss out on being a part of the discussion, Tomas appeared in the doorway, stepping inside. "We were about to begin planning."

"My uncle learned some news that will change what we might want to do," Tomas said.

"What has happened now?" Irritation arrowed through her and she realised it was the magic once again. A month was starting to look like it was going to be a very long time.

"Dione has put out the word that Tarrant is hers. Anyone else takes his life and her knights will hunt them down and hold them responsible for all that Tarrant has done against her."

She started to protest that she didn't want to take Tarrant's life, but the words wouldn't come. Closing her eyes, she tried to find a sense of calm. There was none. Opening her eyes she found that Emery, Troy and Kinnon had moved closer. Only Darak had remained where he was, but his gaze was focused on her. She felt like a wild animal that had escaped and they were waiting for her to attack something. Or someone. "We don't need any more problems."

"He's ours," Cai protested.

"Does it matter who is the one to punish him?" Lili asked softly.

"My lady-" Cai began.

Darak interrupted him. "What have you lost to Tarrant?"

"Nothing." Cai glanced at Emery. "But I almost lost my sister. I promised her I'd see to it that he could never harm her again."

"Did you tell her you'd see to it personally?" Arwyn asked.

Cai stared at Arwyn for a moment before shaking his head. "No."

"Who's going to visit Dione to let her know we're setting a trap if she'd like to take what we catch off our hands?" Kinnon asked.

"I will," Tomas said. "She has no issue with any of my family. At least not at the moment." He grinned. "There was an incident with a distant relative a couple of decades ago, but I believe it was sorted. Not to my relative's satisfaction though."

"Thank you for your offer," Lili said.

With a nod, Tomas left, the scent of his magic fading.

Arwyn glanced around the crowded interior of the cottage. "Someone will need to wait at the cottage with Trinity while the rest of us seek Tarrant out. In pairs. We need to make sure someone is capable of coming back here to fetch Trinity so she can take Tarrant to the trap."

"Why is she more powerful than you?" Cai looked directly at Arwyn. "I've heard stories about how powerful you are."

Arwyn smiled. "There's always someone more powerful. It's the way of things." He shrugged. "I'm sure there'll be someone more powerful than Trinity, but it won't be Tarrant."

Cai nodded. "I'll go with one of your sons."

By the time Tomas returned they'd sorted out the groups. Troy was to remain behind with Emery and Trinity. Tomas stayed in the doorway, gesturing outside. "One of Dione's knights returned with me to discuss things. Then I'll take him to the location so he can organise the trap."

"I'll talk to him." Arwyn followed Tomas outside.

Trinity moved to the doorway, barely managing not to gasp when she saw the creature outside. The dark skin of his torso blended with spider legs, his head turning in her direction. Their gazes clashed. Her magic rose, recognising a kindred soul. She fought not to shrink back from the arachnid, struggling not to give into the magic.

The arachnid smiled, a menacing one. "This one will keep Tarrant from escaping?" His voice was filled with disbelief.

"Looks can be deceiving," Arwyn said.

Emery tugged Trinity back into the cottage, an arm around her waist. His lips lowered until they were close to hers. "Don't catch their attention." His words were a whisper.

"Why?" She spoke equally quietly.

"They are the type who'd love to teach you how to use your magic."

She wished he hadn't confirmed her fears. "I know. It recognised them."

Emery breathed in sharply. "It shouldn't be separate from you."

"It isn't me. I can tell that."

"I don't know if that's a good or bad thing."

"What about when I can't tell it's not me?" Those were the times she feared she might kill someone.

Darak moved close. "You can stop pretending you want time alone. Everyone has gone outside."

Trinity drew back to look around, surprised she hadn't noticed. "When did they leave?"

"What is wrong?" Darak asked.

Emery looked towards the doorway, before he

briefly explained what they'd discussed, keeping his voice low.

"Can't I get rid of it and get other magic?" Trinity asked.

"Once this is over, we'll drain off as much magic as we can. Less power should mean less risk," Emery said.

Darak shook his head. "We can't do that. What if someone else gets a hold of the dark magic? And if she takes it back, she'll have to go through this again."

Trinity groaned. "Don't you have anything good to tell me?"

"Return to your world and the iron sickness will help make it hard to use your magic. As long as you don't let the iron sickness go too far and end up insane instead," Darak said.

"I'll go with you," Emery promised.

Kinnon entered the cottage in time to hear Emery's words. "Where are you going?"

"Once this is done we're returning to the human world with Trinity until the month is up," Darak said.

Trinity turned in Emery's arms so she could face Darak. "You don't need to come."

"We'll go." Kinnon grinned. "I haven't had much to do with the human world. It should be interesting. We'll go with you wherever you go."

"I have school every weekday," Trinity said.

"I've never been to school before," Kinnon said. "Guess it's past time I did."

Trinity didn't know what to think when each of them nodded. "It's not that simple. You can't just decide to go to school and turn up."

Emery drew her back against him. "We have magic. There are a lot of things we're capable of doing. We'll find a way to remain at your side."

Chapter Thirty-Seven

Trinity looked from Kinnon to Darak, trying to relax against Emery. Her magic kept her on edge. "School won't know what hit it. There are going to be a lot of broken hearts."

Kinnon chuckled. "Sounds like fun. As long as it isn't my heart that's broken."

Everyone crowded back into the cottage, only Tomas and the arachnid missing. Arwyn looked at his sons before speaking. "We should prepare for this evening."

Trinity didn't want to think about the coming evening let alone prepare for it. A burst of anticipation raced through her, reminding her that part of her was looking forward to the coming fight. The dark part. Emery's arms tightened around her and she tried to focus on him rather than the magic that wanted to burst free.

The time passed far too quickly as they prepared for the evening ahead. They discussed their plans, in greater detail, over the food Emery brought back from Naida, along with a handful of biscuits for Trinity.

When night fell only Trinity, Troy and Emery remained behind. After telling Troy the information she'd promised him earlier, she paced the cramped cottage, a fire flickering in the fireplace. Emery captured her as she paced past him again. She glared at him, pulling out of his arms.

Emery let her go. "You need to find a way to be calm. Your agitation will make it difficult to focus on what must be done tonight."

She tried to tell him she was calm, her eyes narrowing when the words wouldn't come. Anger twisted through her and she tried to ignore it, focusing on her breathing. It didn't help. Her hands tightened into fists. She wanted Tarrant to pay for everything he'd done. Before she could voice her thoughts, Darak appeared in the cottage.

"We found him."

Emery grabbed hold of Trinity's hand, reaching for Darak's. "You left Lili with him?"

"She's hidden." The scent of Darak's magic filled the cottage as he took them to the gardens behind the castle, further away from the castle than they were the previous time.

Tarrant spun to face them, the Fae with him drawing a sword. He gestured to his companion. "Fetch my knights."

Before the Fae could leave, Darak and Emery threw themselves at him, pinning him to the ground.

Trinity faced Tarrant, her magic twisting inside her, wanting to take over. Before she could draw on the nearby plants to help hold Tarrant in place, he hurled lightning at her. For a split second she nearly threw herself to the ground. Then her magic exploded through her and she took control of the lightning, throwing it back at him.

"No!" Lili threw a gust of air at Tarrant, knocking him from his feet.

Trinity stalked forward, air swirling around her, cocooning her and Tarrant in the gusts that were forming.

"You think I won't try and attack you if you're going to attack me?" Tarrant rose to his feet, drawing his sword.

"You can't harm me." Lightning formed in her hand, crackling across her palm. A small part of her shrank back in fear. She ignored that part.

"But I can harm those you've sided with." Tarrant

spun, swinging his sword at Emery who had his back to him, wrestling with the Fae he and Darak tried to overpower.

"Leave him be." Forgetting the lightning, she threw herself at Tarrant. It crackled around them.

Tarrant yelped, dropping his sword, the lightning striking the ground next to them. "I don't have to kill you to stop you from being a problem." He transported them to the dungeon.

She formed a seed, continuing to hold him tightly. "I don't have the same problem you have. I can kill you." Her words were low. "You will not drag me to places and leave me there." She crushed the seed, taking him to the one place she was capable of going. Anywhere had to be better than a dungeon.

"You can't hold on forever." Tarrant caused the ground to buckle beneath their feet.

She held on tighter, drawing the roots up from the ground, entwining them around him as she smoothed the ground. "You won't manage to live forever."

"Release him!"

Trinity didn't bother checking to see who called out the order. She kept the tree roots tightening around Tarrant. They rose higher, at his chest now, his breathing laboured.

"Others will avenge me," Tarrant promised.

"Who? It won't be Emery." The vines faltered when she spoke his name. She forced them higher and tighter, ignoring the voices around her ordering her to give them Tarrant.

"There are others who owe a debt to me. They'll come after you."

"Will they owe you a debt if you're no longer alive to collect it?" Triumph raced through her at the fear she saw in Tarrant's eyes. "That's what I thought." Triumph was replaced with fear when she tried to breathe, unable to. Her eyes narrowed as she focused on making the tree roots rise higher. "Stop it."

"He isn't stealing your air."

Shocked at hearing Darak's voice, Trinity loosened her grip on Tarrant. Before she could tighten it again, Darak dragged her away from Tarrant. She fought to escape him. "He's mine. I caught him." She took in a deep breath, Darak no longer stealing the air from around her.

Darak glanced past her. "Take him. Now." He met her gaze. "Remember the plan."

"I don't care about the plan." She lifted a hand, filling it with lightning.

"Sebastian. Troy. Emery. Kinnon."

"Stop talking." Hate and anger swamped her.

Darak's hands tightened on her. "You told me you

could give me lots of names. Even mine. Has that changed?"

Her hand lowered a fraction. "He was mine. I caught him."

"We caught him. We had a plan."

"Mine." The word wasn't as fierce as it had been.

"What about your best friends? Troy and Yvette. Your parents. Rod and Christine. Your family. Would you hurt them?"

A shaky breath escaped and the lightning dissipated. "No."

"Trinity?"

She turned her head to see Emery nearby. The last of the anger faded and she launched herself into his arms, holding him tight. "I don't want to hurt any of you."

"You won't." Emery held her equally tight, his lips meeting hers.

She kissed him back, eventually drawing away to stare up at him. "What happened when Tarrant took me from the gardens and I brought him here?"

"We took the castle back. The arachnids have Tarrant and his knights are in the dungeon awaiting Arwyn and Lili's decision as to what will happen to them."

"Everyone is safe?" She looked around, seeing Kinnon was with them too. "Where's Troy?"

"With my parents," Kinnon said. "I didn't think you'd want him left at the cottage on his own."

"Thank you." She drew away from Emery, her hand slipping into his. Her gaze was drawn to Darak. "You were wrong."

"About what?"

"My best friends. You missed a couple of names." She smiled, looking from Darak to Kinnon and back again.

Darak inclined his head. "Are you ready to go to the castle? There'll be a lot to deal with."

She chuckled. She should have known better than to expect anything else from him. "Okay. Let's go to the castle."

Emery formed a piece of bark, the scent of old campfires filling the night air. "How about we work on teaching you how to travel to different places?"

Trinity nodded, trying to hang onto her relief rather than think about how close she'd come to killing Tarrant. But it was going to be a long time before that moment stopped preying on her mind.

It took hours to sort things out at the castle and Trinity was exhausted by the time Lili noticed how tired she was and had one of the servants show her to a room. She stared at the spacious bedroom, about to head to the inviting four poster bed. A noise had her spinning to see Emery enter. She smiled at the sight of him. "I missed you. Where did you go?" She went into his arms, resting her head against him, stifling a yawn.

"I took Roland and Naida home now it's safe for them to be there."

His words made her think of Tarrant. "I wanted to kill him."

"But you didn't."

"I nearly did." Exhaustion dragged at her. She couldn't have used her magic if she'd wanted to.

"We'll figure something out. Between all of us we'll make sure you last the month without killing someone."

She drew back from him, a plan already forming.

"You've figured something out." He smiled down at her.

"Exhaustion. If I keep using my magic there won't be enough power left to do anything terrible with it. Darak's idea of returning to my world should help."

Emery gave a single nod. "Then that's what we'll do. We'll be there for you. Every minute of the day and night."

She giggled. "I'm not sure what my dad is going to

say about all of you being there. Our house isn't that big." She couldn't help thinking about how crowded her bedroom had been with three stone statues in it. Alive they seemed to take up more space. She yawned again.

Emery pressed his lips against her forehead. "Sleep. We'll sort it out in the morning."

"That's not much of a kiss. Is that the best you can do?"

"I can do much better, but you look like you're about to collapse."

"Then I guess I'll have to do better than what you've managed." She drew his head down to kiss him, eventually letting go and taking a step back. "I'll see you in the morning."

He captured her hand, raising it to his lips, pressing a lingering kiss against it. Letting go, he nodded before disappearing. The scent of old campfires faded away.

Trinity stumbled to bed. Her lips curved into a smile. She felt like herself, the magic too drained to be a problem. Now if only her dreams would cooperate. She dreaded to think what nightmares might form after her night. Collapsing on the bed she fell instantly asleep, no dreams disturbing her.

Chapter Thirty-Eight

Trinity slowed for Yvette to catch up with her, glancing at Kinnon to let him know to make space for her friend. Emery was on the other side of her, Darak beside his brother.

Yvette came alongside Trinity. "Are you sure you have to leave this evening? Can't you stay a couple more days?"

She linked her arm through her friend's. They'd managed to return from the realms of the Fae the morning school had started back, after the September holidays, with barely enough time to get ready for school. "We had our going away dinner last week. Before exams started." She'd promised her father to remain in the human world until she'd finished year twelve. It had been difficult until her magic had settled, becoming less powerful. Then she'd drained most of it off like her companions had done, making it possible to remain in Brisbane for so many months.

"We should celebrate the end of high school," Yvette said.

"I'll visit."

Yvette glanced at Kinnon. "Alone or are you bringing company?"

Trinity chuckled. Yvette had given up on Troy in favour of first Darak and then Kinnon.

"Only you would come back to school with three guys following you around. Or is that five?"

She could only smile. There was no way her magic would allow her to comment. Yvette didn't know they were Fae. They used a glamour to hide their ears. Cai and Tomas had joined them during some of the weekends, interested in learning more about what the human world offered.

Yvette let go to slide her arm around Trinity's waist. "I'm going to miss you. Why couldn't Emery live in a less remote area?"

Trinity leaned her head against Yvette for a second. "I'll miss you too." But she missed the realms of the Fae more. Her father had been trying to convince her to stay in this world since she'd told him her decision last month. She'd had to promise to come back next month for Christmas. Her mother wasn't impressed that she was moving away, particularly since she was going with Emery.

"Then stay." Reaching the school gate, Yvette stopped and faced her.

"I can't."

"Can't or won't?"

She shrugged. They'd decided not to tell Yvette about the realms of the Fae. Her friend wasn't good at keeping secrets. "I have to go." She nodded towards the vehicle parked further along the road, Braeden in the driver's seat.

Yvette sighed heavily. "Don't forget me."

"How could I?" She glanced at Kinnon who was surrounded by students saying goodbye to him. When she noticed Darak stood alone, she grinned. He'd gone out of his way to discourage friendships, pointing out they wouldn't be here long.

Yvette threw her arms around Trinity, causing her hand to be dragged from Emery's. "Keep in touch."

Trinity hugged her friend. "We better not keep Braeden waiting." She tightened her arms once more before letting Yvette go and hurrying towards the car.

Emery caught up with her, taking hold of her hand. "You'll see her again."

"I know, but it's difficult. There's so much I want to tell her."

Before Trinity could open the car door, Darak opened it for her. "People drift apart. You'll only miss her for a little time."

She held his gaze before speaking. "If you're trying to be reassuring I think you need to work on that skill a bit."

Braeden chuckled, looking over his shoulder, a hand resting on the steering wheel. "Only a bit?"

She grinned at the teasing look on Braeden's face. "Measurements are all relative." She got in the car, moving over so Emery could sit next to her.

Once they were in the vehicle, Braeden pulled out into the traffic. "Rod said to remind you that you promised not to leave until after he was home."

"I haven't forgotten." She looked out the back window, surprised she felt a moment of sorrow at saying goodbye to high school. But it was only a moment and she faced forward. "He made me promise with magic so it's not like I can leave before he gets home."

Kinnon chuckled. "I think that's his favourite part about you having magic."

"Tell me about it," she muttered.

Kinnon, who sat in the front next to Braeden,

asked his brother, "You sure you want to stay? Why not convince Troy to come to our realm?"

"We'll stay here for now." Braeden glanced at Trinity in the rear view mirror. "Rod will need Troy for a while." He grinned. "Besides, Troy said he has other things to teach me that I'll enjoy more than driving a car. He was talking about extreme sports last night. He asked me not to look it up, that he wanted it to be a surprise."

Laughter escaped and Trinity struggled not to grin. She failed. "It's certainly going to be a surprise."

"He didn't make me promise not to ask anyone," Braeden said.

"Maybe I should point out his failing." Trinity was relieved her father would have Troy and Braeden to help him through her leaving. He liked Braeden who'd helped the plants settle into the gardens they'd landscaped since his arrival.

They pulled up at the house minutes before Rod and Troy arrived. No one spoke until they were inside. Rod pointed a finger at Trinity. "At least give us the chance to get cleaned up before you leave."

Trinity nodded.

"I want your promise with magic," Rod said.

"Of course you do." She smiled at her father. "I promise to wait until you've had a shower before I leave." The rich scent of Christmas cake filled the room, mingling with another scent. For a second she thought there was something wrong, then realised someone else had used magic. Turning she spotted Tomas and Cai. "What are you doing here?"

Tomas nodded towards Darak. "We asked him to call us when you were home for the last time."

"Why?" Trinity's phone rang before Tomas could answer her and she checked who it was. "I have to take this." She glanced at the corner of the screen to see how much charge was left before answering. "Mum. My phone's nearly flat."

"That's okay. I only wanted to say goodbye before you leave."

"You said that last night." Trinity listened as her mother gave her yet more advice, including repeating some from last night. She was almost relieved when her phone beeped to warn of low charge. "I have to go. My phone is about to shut down."

"Be careful."

"Mum, you've told me that already." She couldn't exactly say she would. The realms of the Fae wasn't the safest place. It took her a minute to finish saying goodbye, her phone shutting down as she hung up.

"Did I miss anything?" Troy came into the living

area, his hair damp from showering, stopping beside Braeden.

"I should hope you missed me." Braeden slipped an arm around Troy's waist.

Troy chuckled. "Of course I did."

Rod's door opened and he paused, catching sight of Tomas and Cai. "Why are you both here?"

"That's what I'm waiting to find out," Trinity said.

Rod came into the living area. "Well?" He looked from Tomas to Cai. "What's going on?"

Cai nodded to Tomas. "He was the one to organise it. I'll let him tell you."

Tomas grinned when everyone looked towards him. "I've found enough people to turn barren land fertile.

"You have?" Trinity could barely believe she'd heard him correctly.

"Now that's something I wouldn't mind seeing," Rod said.

"We can arrange that," Tomas said. "No day was settled on with the differences between the realms."

"My lands will be healed?" Emery sounded dazed.

"I guess you'll have to find some other burden then," Trinity teased him.

"I already have," Emery said.

She was speechless for a moment. "You have?"

Emery nodded. "I'll repair what Tarrant did. What I helped him do."

"It's not your job." She wanted to tell him that he should think of himself for a change. He'd spent enough of his life looking after Tarrant.

Emery took her hand. "Someone needs to rescue his victims."

"Rescue." A smile slowly formed. Now that was something she could understand.

Troy groaned. "Did you have to use that word?"

"Emery is right. If there are people in need of rescuing..." Her voice trailed off as her smile momentarily returned, her gaze travelling around the room. "Someone needs to do it." After all, look what her last rescue had brought into her life.

"Doesn't mean it needs to be you," Troy said.

She grinned at Troy, tightening her grip on Emery's hand. "Doesn't it?" She couldn't wait. She looked into Emery's sky blue eyes, seeing the same anticipation she felt. "I'm willing to share the fun." Again her gaze travelled around the room.

Darak inclined his head, Kinnon grinned, Cai looked startled and Tomas chuckled.

Emery drew Trinity to his side. "First my land and then the rescues. After that, who knows."

"I know what to expect." She grinned. "There are

always rescues to be made." It was something she loved to do. Again her gaze was drawn around the room. And obviously it was something she had a talent for. Her grin remained in place as she met Emery's gaze. "I can't wait to see what the next rescue brings."

Free Ebook

Subscribe to Avril's newsletter and receive a free ebook. This ebook is exclusive to those on her mailing list. To find out more about this offer visit: www.avrilsabine.com/free-ebook

*

We value your privacy and will not sell, rent, exchange or loan your email address to third parties. Your information is confidential and you are under no obligation to remain on the mailing list and can unsubscribe at any time.

Acknowledgements

As always, many thanks to all those who helped make this book what it is.

To The Reader

If you enjoyed this book, why not consider leaving a review to help other readers discover it too? Reader engagement is one of the few ways that lets an author know readers want more books in a particular series or genre. So leave a review and tell friends, not only about this book but also about other ones you've enjoyed, so you can continue to enjoy books by your favourite authors for years to come.

Dreams are meant to be lived,

Avril.

About The Author

Avril is an Australian author who lives with her family on acreage in South East Queensland. She writes mostly young adult and children's speculative fiction, but has been known to dabble in other genres. You can find more information about her at www.avrilsabine.com where you can also subscribe to her newsletter to be kept informed about new releases, current projects, blog posts and exclusive news.

Titles By Avril Sabine

Stories about strong characters and characters who discover their strengths.

SERIES

Assassins Of The Dead- Young Adult Fantasy/ Paranormal

Book 1: Dark Blade

Book 2: Dragon Touched

Book 3: Society Against Vampires

Book 4: King's Request

Dragon Blood- Young Adult Urban Fantasy (with elements of romance)

(5 book series)

Book 1: Pliethin

Book 2: Wyvern

Book 3: Surety

Book 4: Knight

Book 5: Mage

Dragon Mage- Young Adult Urban Fantasy (with elements of romance)

(Series two of Dragon Blood series)

Book 1: Promise

Dragon Blood Chronicles- Young Adult Urban Fantasy (with elements of romance)

(Companion stand alone series to Dragon Blood)

Book 1: Oath

Book 2: Betrayed

Guardians Of The Round Table- Young Adult Fantasy LitRPG

(Co-written with Storm and Rhys Petersen)

Book 1: Dexterity Fail

Book 2: Goblin Boots

Book 3: Singed Feathers

Book 4: Frog Mage

Book 5: Crystal Mine

Book 6: Cursed Harp

Rosie's Rangers- Young Adult Western Steampunk

(6 book series)

Book 1: Justice

Book 2: Vengeance

Book 3: Treachery

Book 4: Accused

Book 5: Wanted

Book 6: Corruption

Mark Of Kings- Children's Fantasy

(Upper middle grade/preteen)

(4 book series)

Book 1: The Arena

Book 2: The Island

Book 3: The Assassin

Book 4: The King

STAND ALONE SERIES

Demon Hunters- Young Adult Urban Fantasy/ Horror (with elements of romance)

Book 1: Blood Sacrifice

Book 2: Retribution

Book 3: Tainted

Book 4: Premonition

Book 5: Cursed

Book 6: Feud

Book 7: Extrication

Plea Of The Damned- Young Adult Urban Fantasy/Paranormal

(6 book series)

Book 1: Forgive Me Lucy

Book 2: Forgive Me Aiden

Book 3: Forgive Me Jena

Book 4: Forgive Me Kobe

Book 5: Forgive Me Marti

Book 6: Forgive Me Dawson

***Realms Of The Fae- Young Adult Urban Fantasy
(with elements of romance)***

The Sword (short story in Like A Girl Anthology)

Heart Of Stone

Book 1: A Debt Owed

Book 2: Marked By The Hunt

Book 3: The Magic Collector

Book 4: An Unexpected Betrayal

Book 5: Imprisoned By Iron

Fairytales Retold (Short Stories)

Snow-White And Rose-Red

The Twelve Brothers

The Light Princess

Beauty And The Beast

Sleeping Beauty

Aschenputtel

The Golden Bird

The Frog Prince

The Death Of Koshchei The Deathless

Myths And Legends Retold (Short Stories)

Ion, Son Of Apollo

Sir Gawain And The Maid With The Narrow Sleeves

Princess Ilse, The Giant's Daughter

YOUNG ADULT NOVELS

Young Adult Fantasy (with elements of romance)

Elf Sight

Earth Bound

Young Adult Urban Fantasy

Stone Warrior (with elements of romance)

The Jungle Inside

Young Adult Contemporary (with elements of romance)

Through Your Eyes

The Ugly Stepsister

Perfect Little Princess

Young Adult Contemporary/Paranormal

Whispers In The Dark (with elements of romance and same sex relationships)

Over Too Soon (with elements of romance)

Young Adult Sci-Fi

Experiment X-One-Six (Urban Sci-Fi/Superheroes)

An Endless Dawn (Post Apocalyptic Sci-Fi)

CHILDREN'S BOOKS

Dragon Lord (Preteen/early teens) (Fantasy)

The Irish Wizard (Upper middle grade) (Urban Fantasy)

SHORT STORIES

Urban Fantasy

Eternally Late

Dealings With Joe

Glimpses (short story in That Moment When Anthology)

Contemporary

The Brat Next Door

Fantasy LitRPG

(Set in the same world as Guardians Of The Round Table Series)

Tales Of Inadon 1: The Disc (Co-written with Storm and Rhys Petersen) (short story in Game On! Anthology)

Post Apocalyptic Sci-Fi

Compulsive Directive

NONFICTION

A Year Of Weekly Writing Exercises (Creative Writing)

Cooking For Families With Allergies (Cooking) (Co-written with Storm Petersen)

Tell Me A Story, Grandma (Memoir)

For the most up to date details on available titles visit:

www.avrilsabine.com/books/bibliography

Realms Of The Fae Series

To learn more about this series visit:

www.avrilsabine.com/series/rotf

BOOKS AVAILABLE IN THE REALMS OF THE FAE SERIES

The Sword (short story in Like A Girl Anthology)

Heart Of Stone

Book 1: A Debt Owed

Book 2: Marked By The Hunt

Book 3: The Magic Collector

Book 4: An Unexpected Betrayal

Book 5: Imprisoned By Iron

Disclaimer

This is a work of fiction. Names, characters, businesses, places, events and incidents are either the products of the author's imagination or used in a fictitious manner. Any resemblance to actual persons, living or dead, or actual events is purely coincidental. The opinions expressed or beliefs held are those of the characters and should not be assumed to be the opinions or beliefs of the author.